THE BURNING PAGES

THE
BURNING
PAGES

A SCOTTISH BOOKSHOP MYSTERY

Paige Shelton

MINOTAUR
BOOKS
New York

First published in the United States by Minotaur Books, an imprint of St. Martin's Publishing Group

THE BURNING PAGES. Copyright © 2022 by Paige Shelton-Ferrell. All rights reserved. Printed in the United States of America. For information, address St. Martin's Publishing Group, 120 Broadway, New York, NY 10271.

www.minotaurbooks.com

Library of Congress Cataloging-in-Publication Data

Names: Shelton, Paige, author.
Title: The burning pages : a Scottish bookshop mystery / Paige Shelton.
Description: First Edition. | New York : Minotaur Books, 2022. | Series: A Scottish bookshop mystery ; 7
Identifiers: LCCN 2021054831 | ISBN 9781250789488 (hardcover) | ISBN 9781250789495 (ebook)
Subjects: GSAFD: Mystery fiction.
Classification: LCC PS3619.H45345 B86 2022 | DDC 813/.6—dc23
LC record available at https://lccn.loc.gov/2021054831

Our books may be purchased in bulk for promotional, educational, or business use. Please contact your local bookseller or the Macmillan Corporate and Premium Sales Department at 1-800-221-7945, extension 5442, or by email at MacmillanSpecialMarkets@macmillan.com.

First Edition: 2022

10 9 8 7 6 5 4 3 2 1

For Tyler and Lauren
and their wonderful adventure ahead

THE BURNING PAGES

ONE

"I love the hat," I said, trying to ease my way into this unexpected conversation.

"Aye, it's a tam o'shanter." Clarinda repositioned it on her head full of dark curls.

It was like a beret, only poofier.

"It suits you." I smiled.

"Have you read the poem?" she asked, her voice airy and almost whimsical. Or maybe that was just the way it reverberated off the walls of the small old building we sat in, facing each other over a messy desk.

She was asking if I'd read the poem for which the hat had been named, "Tam o'Shanter" by Scotland's Robert Burns. It's the story of a hat-wearing farmer named Tam who comes upon a coven of witches and is then pursued by one of them. Though it was written in 1790, it's still a Scottish favorite. All of Burns's works were almost as beloved as he himself.

"I have," I said. "Well, I've read through it a few times now, but I can't say it's an easy read for me. There's so much of the Scots language, and I'm still . . . well, I'm getting better at understanding, but it's slow going."

"Aye. You'll get it eventually."

Given long enough, I might fully understand it without needing translation. Maybe I would someday finally comprehend all the Scots I heard spoken in my everyday life, had heard for some time now. But certainly not yet.

That was only one of the reasons I didn't feel worthy of the invitation that had led me to this meeting with Clarinda. The building, the House of Burns, named for the esteemed poet, was ancient, with chipped paint and weary furniture. It was also chock-full of interesting things—well, just papers, really, but probably fascinating ones if I could take the time to look closely at any of them. How could a bunch of pieces of paper inside a place called House of Burns not be?

"Can you imagine being so popular or writing something so beloved that they name a hat for it?" She readjusted hers again.

"I can't." I folded my hands on my lap, more to try to warm them than to strike any sort of ladylike pose. Despite all the interesting things on the shelves around us, I didn't sense any heat coming from anywhere, and there was no fire in the oddly large fireplace along one wall. I could still see my breath.

The House of Burns had been difficult to find. Tucked next to the entrance of a deep-set close, similar to an alley but usually much more interesting in Scotland, in a part of Cowgate I had yet to explore, sat this tiny stone building. It was maybe only five hundred square feet inside, with a peaked roof and a carved wood sign hanging outside above the front door. I had been both happy to find it and a little scared to enter.

It wasn't until I'd moved to Edinburgh that I became aware of Robert Burns societies, clubs formed to honor the Scottish bard. In fact, they were everywhere, including some long-standing ones in the United States. Hearing about them, along with so many other people who simply celebrated Burns with a yearly dinner, made me feel like I'd missed something good for the first few decades of my life. How had I not paid better attention?

The society headquartered in this paper-filled building wasn't the first one formed in Edinburgh. The Edinburgh Burns Supper Club was originally founded in 1848 by the author's friend and publisher George Thomson. It had been suspended in 1986 but reintroduced in 2007. The one I'd been invited to, however, the Cowgate edition, named for the area of Edinburgh it was located in, had only begun in the late 1990s. I wondered why it had formed in the first place—though the bigger mystery was why I'd been invited to be a part of the group at all. I couldn't imagine how the members of this group (only one of whom I'd now met in person a few minutes ago) even knew who I was or thought I would fit in with the rest of them.

I didn't have the answers yet, but maybe Clarinda would tell me, hopefully today, or at least before the annual dinner that was being held tomorrow night. I wasn't going to just show up to the dinner without understanding a little more.

I rubbed my hands together and blew on them.

"Oh, the heat. I always forget to turn it on." Clarinda stood and went to a machine attached to the wall.

It was a similar setup to the electrical unit I'd had in the cottage I'd lived in when I first arrived in Scotland. Coins had to be inserted for it to work. I smiled as I watched her gather some change from her sweater—or, as I'd come to know it in its Scottish form, jumper—pocket and plug the change into the meter before she turned the dial.

Quite a bit had happened since the days I'd done the same, but I was still just as close with Elias and Aggie, the owners of the old cottage, as I'd been since practically the day I'd landed in Scotland and Elias had been at the airport with his taxi. In fact, they were joining me and my husband, Tom, for dinner at our house this evening. Though also old, our place was at least updated enough to have a modern furnace.

Almost as soon as Clarinda turned the dial, I could feel heat cut through the chill. I squelched the urge to rub my hands together again. Clarinda sat back behind the desk and switched on a lamp that was perched on its corner. The light from the small fixture didn't illuminate so much as cast a few small shadows on the desktop and at the edge of Clarinda's face.

"You'll be surprised tomorrow night. This place will be transformed into a dining hall."

"About that . . . ," I began.

"Oh no," she rushed in, "you're going to tell me you won't be able to attend? It's the biggest night of the year! Please say you'll be here."

"It's not that, exactly." Actually, it *was* exactly that, but she seemed nice enough, so I thought I'd ease into declining, if that's what I ended up doing. "I guess I just don't understand why I was invited to be a part of the group."

It hadn't been a handwritten invitation. Clarinda had called me at the bookshop where I work, the Cracked Spine, yesterday morning.

"Delaney, hello! This is Clarinda Creston, and I'm a local solicitor, but I'm also part of a fun group that's been together for a while. We celebrate Robert Burns. You've heard of him, aye?" she said, her voice ramped up to extra-cheery.

"Of course."

"Anyway, twenty-five January is his birthday, and we have a dinner every year. That's two nights from now. Please join us."

"I . . ."

"Here's the address. Everyone else will be in costume but you won't be required to this year. Next year, of course, but this year, just come eat and meet our small but lively family."

She proceeded to give me the address. I jotted it on my hand, using a pen that had been in my pocket. "I . . ."

"Oh dear, I must go. So much to do. I'll see you on the twenty-fifth, though I'll be at the house tomorrow if you'd like to stop by. Farewell for now."

At my current admission, genuine surprise widened Clarinda's eyes. "Oh aye, well, I'm not sure why you were invited. Let me think a wee bit." She tapped her finger on her chin. "It was a vote from last month's meeting, that much I know. It was my duty to call you, but I forgot all about it until yesterday. Apologies. I've been very busy in court lately. Anyway, someone mentioned you in that meeting, though I can't remember who. You work at the Cracked Spine, aye?"

"I do."

"That must be where or how someone, though again I have no idea who, heard about or met you. We are a bookish group, though that's of no surprise."

"I suppose not. And you can't remember who recommended me?"

"I can't think of who it was, and I don't have the minutes of the meeting here with me." She lifted her hands.

I bit my lip and felt my eyebrows come together. This place was packed with pieces of paper. Wood shelves overflowed with it. There were stacks on the desk, piles on the floor next to it.

"This is the . . . place where you meet, right?"

"It is."

"And in all these pieces of paper, there are no minutes from the meetings?"

Clarinda laughed. "Gracious, no." She reached for the top piece of paper on the stack nearest her, turned it over, and showed it to me. "These are just my doodlings. Someone else keeps the minutes."

I looked at the paper. "Calligraphy?"

Clarinda smiled proudly. "Aye. Look closely."

I took the piece of paper and held it under the weak light from the lamp, reading the words at the top of the page.

THE BANKS O' DOON
Ye banks and braes o' bonnie Doon,
How can ye bloom sae fresh and fair?

"A Burns poem," I said.

"Aye, one of my favorites. Well, they're all my favorites." She took the paper from my hand and read the words aloud, her normal light accent now thick and reminding me again of Elias and Aggie's accents.

I smiled. "I can tell you love it."

"Don't you?"

I almost said that I didn't, not as much as she did, at least, but that seemed rude, and as she'd spoken the lines aloud I'd been reminded that, yes, if I cared for anything other than the people I loved so deeply, it was words, and Mr. Burns certainly had a way with them.

"I guess maybe I do, some," I said.

Clarinda smiled big. "See, whoever nominated you, and I really wish I could remember who that was, knew that about you. You are perfect for our group." She folded the paper and handed it to me. "Take it. I have others."

A moment later, I took the paper and opened it, again reading silently the words she'd just said aloud. There was more on the page, but I didn't take the time to decipher all the scribbles. I refolded it. "You said these were your doodlings. Are all of the pieces of paper covered in your calligraphy of Burns's words?"

"Aye. All of them." She looked around proudly. "I'm a wee bit obsessive-compulsive, and I like to spend some of my days off here. I just like the atmosphere, aye? Anyway, I knew I would have to do something with myself. I can't just sit here. I can always read, but I don't always want to read. This"—she tapped her finger on the stack from which she'd taken the single page— "felt right. I started, and I haven't been able to stop."

"I see."

She laughed again, and I noticed ink-stained fingers on her right hand. "Delaney, I know I'm odd, and I simply don't care. I work very hard as a solicitor, but my days here, covering and filling my soul all the way up with Burns's words, are the days I most adore. I'm normally here on Saturdays, but this week is special, of course, and I have some people coming to help me prepare. Now, please don't tell me you are going to decline our invitation. You will love the group. Give us at least the dinner to prove it to you."

I wasn't afraid, really, but I still didn't quite understand what was going on, why I'd been invited. If Clarinda had been able to give me at least a little more, a name of who'd recommended me or even a story that someone had, indeed, come into the bookshop one day and thought I'd make a good addition, then maybe my hesitation would wane.

"May I bring a guest?" I said.

Clarinda's happy features transformed immediately, falling into a frown. "Well, we are very particular about who we invite.

If we'd wanted you to bring a guest, we would have mentioned a plus-one."

I scooted to the front of the chair and opened my mouth to thank her for thinking of me but that I wouldn't be joining them, when she smiled again.

"But I guess this one time it would be all right. I can't promise you they will be invited to the group, but for this one time, this dinner, aye, please bring a guest," she said.

I was still hesitant. I hadn't liked her tone and, yes, she was odd. This was all very odd, but then again, I had come to Scotland for an adventure, and so far it hadn't disappointed.

"Wonderful. Thank you, and I promise, we won't eat too much," I said.

Clarinda clapped once. "I'm so happy to hear that you'll be there."

"Thank you," I said again as I stood and made my way to the door.

Before I could reach for the knob, the door opened, bringing in a cold, wet wind along with two young men.

Suddenly it was crowded inside, with the four of us.

"You're here!" Clarinda stood. "Wonderful! Delaney, these are the strong boys who will be doing all the hard work to get this place in shape for tomorrow night."

I nodded at the teenagers, neither of them as bundled up as I would be when I redonned my hat and scarf. They nodded at me as I made my way outside. Clarinda quickly moved her focus to supervising them and didn't even tell me goodbye. To be fair, I only sent her another nod as I left.

I stuck the paper she'd given me into my coat pocket and met the cloudy January afternoon with a sense of relief. Though it was colder outside than in that frigid building, and while I usually enjoyed the scents that came with old paper and ink, the fresh air gave a welcome sense of freedom.

I crossed to the other side of the street and turned around to watch the goings-on. A truck was parked there. I saw one of the teenagers climb into the back of it and retrieve a chair, carrying it inside.

I heard Clarinda's voice in my head again.

Ye banks and braes o' bonnie Doon.

The words weren't speaking to me in the way my intuition sometimes did. They weren't trying to tell me something. These simply soothed and left me feeling curious.

If nothing else, it would be interesting to see how the space was transformed into some sort of dining hall.

I wished I'd asked more questions: How many people would be there? Should I bring anything?

But I'd been too distracted by the mystery to worry about logistics.

It was *probably* an honor and I was *probably* overthinking. I should just enjoy the ride, which was something I usually did well.

But the phone call, along with the visit with Clarinda, still felt strange, suspicious even. Originally I wasn't even planning to show up, but when Clarinda told me that she'd be at the House of Burns today, and since it wasn't a far walk from the bookshop, I decided it was worth a little exploration.

And now there wasn't much more to see. I hurried on my way, back to work. The only real question now was, who was I going to take with me?

TWO

You'd think I'd take my husband, Tom, but he was also a pub owner and he had plans. A wedding reception had been booked at the pub for the next evening, for an elderly couple, both of whom had separately been going to Tom's pub for years. They finally met a month ago. Since they liked each other so much and "time is a-tickin'," they planned a quick wedding, with the reception at the only place they could see fit—the pub, of course, and, coincidentally, the same place Tom and I had not only met, but had our reception too. His pub. Our pub, actually—but I still couldn't quite make that leap in my mind.

That still left a myriad of possible invitees. Everyone I knew enjoyed books, and Robert Burns was probably high on their list of favorite writers; I couldn't come up with any other imme- diate eliminations. My boss, and the owner of the bookshop, Edwin MacAlister, was always a fun time. My coworkers, Rosie and Hamlet, were also great company. Then there were my previous landlords, of course, Elias and Aggie.

I'd made other friends too, but Brigid, a newspaper reporter and one of my husband's former girlfriends, didn't sound like a good fit, though Brigid and I got along very well.

I pulled open the door to the bookshop, always glad to hear the familiar ringing of the bell secured above.

Hector, the miniature Yorkie, whom Rosie took care of but whom we all loved, trotted from the back of the store to greet me. He seemed particularly happy that I had returned. I heard voices, but I couldn't immediately see anyone.

I picked up Hector and held him to my cheek. "Hello, best dog in the world."

Though he kissed my cheek quickly, he was more squiggly than usual. I sensed he wanted me to put him back on the floor.

"Okay, okay," I said as I lowered him down again.

His tiny feet slipping a little on the old marble floor, he took off toward the voices. I figured I was supposed to follow.

I could distinguish Rosie and Hamlet's laughs, but I couldn't quite place the third person I heard, though he certainly seemed familiar.

I gasped when I came around the wall. I even put my hands up to my mouth as tears immediately filled my eyes.

"Hey, Sis," my brother said. "Before you get all worried on me, Mom and Dad are fine. Everyone is okay."

I was frozen in place, but Wyatt stood from the table and came to me. He pulled me into one of his bear hugs and held tight. Tears were now doing a free flow down my cheeks.

They were the happiest of tears. I missed my family terribly. Though I loved my new life in Scotland, I hadn't seen my Kansas family since my wedding, which had been almost a year ago. Tom and I had planned a summer trip to Kansas, but seeing my big farm-boy brother—though he looked slightly more sophisticated than what I was used to—sent all my emotions into a spin.

"Why didn't you tell me you were coming?" I said as I looked up at him between sniffs.

"I wasn't sure until last week, and then I thought the plans still might change. I'm here for work."

"I want to hear all about it," I said. "But first, another hug." He obliged.

Rosie and Hamlet were in charge of refreshments, and we all sat around the table in the back where Hamlet did most of his work. Rosie gathered stuff for coffee and tea from the kitchenette on the other side of the building, the dark side—named such because of the lack of lighting, not anything sinister. And Hamlet ran next door to the pastry shop for more goodies.

My coworkers helped customers who came in, but there weren't many on this cold morning. The afternoon would pick up, but for now Rosie and Hamlet seemed glad to have the opportunity to visit with Wyatt some.

My brother, three years older than me, had grown up well, even more so since I'd seen him at the wedding. He'd always been a big farm boy, but also incredibly smart. After obtaining an engineering degree, he'd risen in the ranks at different manufacturing facilities. Now he was a manager with an operation out of Detroit, Michigan. His haircut was shipshape, and his clothes, while still casual, were actually now without the wrinkles that had been his signature style growing up.

I was very proud of him.

"Your company is looking to set up an operation here, in our fair city?" Rosie asked as Wyatt grabbed the carafe of coffee she'd brought over and poured some into her cup.

"Well, kind of. We are looking at working with a shipping port. We get some raw materials from France and Germany. I'm here to look at the port possibilities."

"Och, verra interesting," Rosie said, saluting him with her steaming full mug.

"I think so too, and usually my world is more about numbers and computer plans than shipping possibilities in Scotland. It's a welcome change of pace." Wyatt poured me a cup too.

"How long will you be here?" I asked.

"A week or so."

"Need a place to stay? We have a spare room," I offered.

"In fact, I don't need a place to stay, but I would love to move from the hotel and stay with you and Tom if that isn't an imposition."

"We would love it."

I didn't have to think twice. Yes, both Tom and I would enjoy having Wyatt stay with us. Elias and Aggie had spent some time in our spare room when their cottages were being worked on, and though Wyatt wouldn't cook and bake like Aggie had, we loved having company.

"Thank you," Wyatt said.

"I'm glad Mom and Dad are well, but tell me details," I said.

"They are very well, excited to see you and Tom this summer. Dad broke another finger, but it's healing just fine."

My dad, a farmer, had broken his fingers several times.

"But they're all still attached?" It was a question that we'd all asked a time or two.

Wyatt nodded. "All still attached. And Mom is incredible. She's started lifting weights."

"What?"

"Nothing overly weird, but, yes, she read somewhere that weight training is the best way to keep your muscle mass, and she's all over it now."

"I love that."

Pangs of missing my family were slightly muted because Wyatt was sitting across the table from me, but they were there, mostly in my throat and behind my eyes. I smiled but had to blink a little too enthusiastically to keep the new swell of emotions at bay.

Hamlet came around the corner after helping a customer. "How was the House of Burns?" he asked me as he sat down again.

Wyatt's eyebrows lifted. "House of Burns?"

I nodded. "Robert Burns, the poet?"

"Ah. Well, little sister, I can tell you honestly that I *have* heard of the man, even though I couldn't tell you one thing he wrote."

"Well, for one, the words to 'Auld Lang Syne,'" I prompted.

"Really?" Wyatt said.

"Aye," Rosie added. "The lyrics were set to an old folk tune, but, aye, he's the writer."

"Well, the words did change some from the original poem," Hamlet said. "But his were the inspiration. In Scots, even. 'Auld lang Syne' is the Scots language."

"I admit, that's interesting." Wyatt shrugged.

With that one gesture, I saw the brother I most knew, the one I'd grown up with, and my heart squeezed a little as I smiled even more at the "big lug."

"These are his words: 'The best laid plans of mice and men often go awry,'" Hamlet said.

"From the book?" Wyatt asked.

"No," I said. "*Of Mice and Men* was written by John Steinbeck, the title surely inspired by Burns's words that were originally part of a poem. . . ." I looked at Rosie and Hamlet.

"Aye," Rosie said. "The poem is titled 'To a Mouse.'"

"Of course!" I said. "There's also the poem 'Tam o'Shanter,' which is about a man and some witches, but from which a hat was named. I saw one just today."

"So, how was it today? Full of Burns's books?" Hamlet asked again.

I shared with Wyatt the phone call I'd received the previous morning from Clarinda, and then told everyone about my time at the small old building.

"Sounds interesting," Rosie said, though doubt lined her words. She would always lean more to suspicion.

"It sounds wonderful!" Hamlet said.

"Yeah," Wyatt added less than enthusiastically as he sipped his coffee.

Still, though, I was about to ask him to come with me to the dinner. It seemed like the right thing to do. But then a voice spoke in my head.

To be or not to be? That is the question: Whether 'tis nobler in the mind to suffer the slings and arrows of outrageous fortune, or take arms against a sea of troubles and by opposing end them. To die—to sleep, no more . . .

It was Hamlet, of course. Not my Hamlet, but Shakespeare's. I'd heard him a number of times over the years and had come to recognize the voice my imagination had made for him. It shouldn't have taken my intuition for me to notice how intrigued my coworker Hamlet sounded by the idea of the Burns House, but it must have needed a Shakespearean nudge that I simply couldn't deny. Usually when the bookish voices speak to me, I can't pinpoint exactly what they're trying to say—what my intuition is trying to tell me. But I understood this voice with certainty. I was to invite Hamlet and only Hamlet.

"I'm going to the annual dinner tomorrow night," I said as

I looked at Wyatt, noticing exactly what I expected to see—a widening of his eyes, telling me he hoped I wouldn't make him go. I turned to Hamlet. "Want to go with me?"

"I would love to!"

I'd invited the right person. "They can't promise that you will be invited to be a part of the group, but Clarinda thought it was a grand idea if I brought someone to my first event." It was just a small lie.

At any rate, I was pretty sure that once the group met Hamlet, they'd think he was a perfect fit, much more so than me, even.

Hamlet resembled a young Shakespeare, even the facial hair. It took only a few moments of knowing him to sense he was a creative type, as well as gentle and kind.

"A Burns dinner, though," Hamlet said with awe. "I would be very excited to go."

"It's a date!" I looked over at Wyatt, who now appeared relieved. "Tom has a wedding party tomorrow night. You can join him or look around the city on your own."

Wyatt nodded and then looked at Rosie. "Dinner tomorrow night, Rosie?"

"Och," she said with real surprise. "Sounds wunnersome!"

Hamlet translated, "Wonderful."

"It's a date!" Wyatt echoed my words.

We were such Midwesterners. He'd keyed in on someone who might like to have something to do the next night and just taken care of it. I would tell him later that Mom and Dad would be proud of him.

I'd consider telling him I felt the same. Wouldn't want him to think his sister was going easier on him, though.

Rosie, Hamlet, and I had work to do for the rest of the day, so we sent Wyatt up to Tom's pub to say hello before he headed to some shipping offices for a round of meetings.

As I held Hector again, I looked out the front window and watched Wyatt make his way up to the pub. Once he was inside, I reluctantly set down the dog and headed over to my warehouse to get some work done.

Another day, I might have invited Wyatt to see the warehouse again. He'd seen it when he was in town for the wedding. For years, it had been a secret place, and very few people had known about it. We still didn't advertise the room, which held Edwin's treasures, things he'd found and collected over the years. One of my jobs was to organize the room, which I'd been doing without much of a hitch.

Until recently.

For the past few days, I'd not only not invited anyone over to join me in my room, but I'd double-checked locking the door behind me.

I'd come upon a mystery of sorts, and before I shared it with someone, I wanted to make sure that what I'd uncovered wouldn't cause irreparable harm to the people I'd become so fond of—Rosie, Hamlet, and Edwin were my family too.

I'd come face-to-face with something that could potentially be cause for some very hurt feelings. I would do just about anything to prevent that.

THREE

The warehouse was located in the building next door. It was attached to the retail side of the bookshop via a walkway that Edwin had retrofitted decades earlier. Though the windows of the retail portion of the shop were always clean and clear, the windows in the other building were blacked out, painted over. Someone had filled in the front window space with bricks, but the back glass was grungy, somehow left unattended, though Edwin and Rosie were both usually very particular. The outsides of both buildings were in the best shape they could be after sitting in those spots for a few centuries.

Offices took up the top level of the dark side, but they were rarely used. The loo, a kitchenette, and the warehouse took up the bottom level. The stairway was illuminated by one bare light bulb hanging on the high ceiling.

The door to the warehouse was ornate and oversized, carved wood that had been painted red. A large blue skeleton key was used to turn the lock—which somehow required three revolutions to undo the mechanism.

Once through the walkway door, I flipped the switch to the bare bulb, giving everything a familiar eerie glow.

I made my way down the stairs on this side and hurried to the blue door. I looked all around. I knew no one had followed me over, but I wanted to be certain. I inserted the key, turned it three times, entered, closed the door behind me, and triple-checked the lock.

High windows above the shelves made it so I could always see a little during the day even without lighting and even when it was cloudy like today. The gloom wasn't bad. I flipped the switch on the wall, bringing a warm but vivid brightness to the space.

I loved this room. I loved my job. But I was still bothered by what I'd found.

The room was full of shelves, packed all the way up to underneath the windows. There were some books, but mostly other items—things Edwin enjoyed enough to purchase, thinking maybe he'd create a collection. However, he simply had too much money and not enough patience to cultivate any specific collection beyond an initial interest.

After one more check of the door—yes, it was locked, for goodness' sake—I made my way to my desk and sat.

The desk had been mentioned in the ad I'd answered regarding my job. It had "seen the likes of kings and queens," and come to find out, that hadn't been false advertising. My desk had literally been used by royalty, inside at least one castle.

I used to be terrified to work at it, afraid I'd mar the historical treasure, but I'd become less so. I still covered its top with paper that I unfurled and then cut from a roll I kept to the side of it.

I hadn't found the thing that had bothered me on a shelf, nor in the desk.

The surprise I'd uncovered had been inside one of the two

short file drawers set up against a wall, in between two tall shelves. The drawers were chock-full of files, pieces of paper—much less organized even than all the paperwork inside the Burns House where I'd just been. I'd looked through the papers a number of times, but a couple weeks ago I'd been inspired to search for secret cubbyholes in the drawers.

It might not occur to most people to do such a thing, but it wasn't very long ago that priceless items had been found inside my desk, tucked away in secret spaces. Since it was my job to organize the warehouse, it crossed my mind that I should make sure I wasn't missing something.

If I'd learned anything about Edwin, it was that he liked secret spaces, and he often forgot where he'd discovered them, and even more frequently, what he might have hidden inside them.

I hadn't found any secret hiding places in the file drawers; however, I had come upon something I hadn't noticed during my previous explorations. I'd placed the piece of paper into a file folder and then hidden it in my desk.

I retrieved the file from a drawer—which I'd also locked. I opened the file as I fired up my laptop, hoping for an email response to one of my recent inquiries.

Inside the manila folder were some of my handwritten notes and the item—a birth certificate. At first, the only intriguing part about it seemed to be that I hadn't noticed it before—but that could have been just an oversight, right?

I wasn't pleased with myself if that was the case.

However, as far as I knew, Edwin had been the only one to look through the file cabinets until I'd arrived. Now it was just me—he very rarely even came into the bookshop anymore.

Birth certificates were important documents, and they

shouldn't be left to be found by just anyone, and if they are, they would be something that needed further attention. When I first came upon it, I glanced at it, realized what it was, and then just put it on my desk, thinking I would give it to Edwin the next time I saw him, ask if he wanted me to do anything specific with it.

Then I fell into more explorations of the file cabinet, coming upon all manner of things, things I'd seen before: land deeds, handwritten letters, poems, so many pieces of paper. Though some of them were valuable and even historically significant, the birth certificate remained on my mind.

I'd decided I needed to take a closer look at the document and at least be prepared to talk to Edwin with more details.

But then suddenly other questions that should have been at the forefront of my mind finally made it through all the other distractions. Had I really missed it before, or had someone hidden it recently? If so, who and why? This unquestionably needed a closer investigation.

The baby boy named on the certificate had been born on August 16—twenty-four years earlier. The birth parents' names had been listed as Dora Strangelove—a wonderful name that made me smile—and M(something) Edison—this was a photocopy and the rest of the father's first name was indistinguishable. The baby was named Edwin H. Edison.

I wouldn't have thought much more about any of this, would have simply continued to be entertained by the woman's wonderful last name, if it weren't for the fact that I thought I'd heard something about Hamlet's name actually being Edwin too. Someone had said that his middle name suited him much more, so "Hamlet" had been what everyone called him. His last name was McIntyre, not Edison.

It all made for a sketchy memory, something from when I'd first met all my new friends and Scottish family, and I might be creating a mystery where there really was none.

I knew that he was twenty-four years old, though we celebrated his birthday in October, not August.

But there was more.

When I'd first come to the Cracked Spine, my boss Edwin told me that Hamlet had been a vagrant living on the streets before he'd started spending some of his days inside the Cracked Spine.

Rosie had taken a quick liking to the boy and started talking to him, feeding him, welcoming him in. He'd gotten in some legal trouble—stealing, mostly food. Then, one day, Edwin took him under his wing, made sure he had a place to stay, food to eat, clothes, and now he was at the university, about to graduate, and was considering continuing with his education. He could be anything he wanted to be if he was willing to put in the work. Edwin and Rosie's kindness had changed his life, at least according to the story I knew.

This birth certificate certainly made me wonder if Hamlet's lucky fate had truly been random or if there had been more to it.

On the other hand, if the certificate *had* been hidden, what right did I have to find it? Okay, that was easy. It was my job to organize the things inside the warehouse.

But then, what right did I have to research it, delve deeper? I could put it away and never think about it again. I could give it to Edwin without comment and let it go, forget about it. I could continue to keep the discovery to myself.

In fact, leaving it all alone was probably what everyone wanted. At least anyone who knew the truth behind the certificate, whatever and whoever that was.

But I had a little history of my own that kept me hanging on. After my maternal grandmother died, I learned that my maternal grandfather hadn't been who I'd been told he was. I'd been told that my mom's dad had died young, before my mother was even ten years old.

My biological grandfather in fact had lived the next town over. I'd never met him, and he died right before my grandmother had, when I was twenty-five.

For twenty-five years I could have gotten to know my biological grandfather, if he'd been inclined to know me too, but no one had told me the secret. There was no one left who could tell me if he knew it. He and I would never meet. It was too late—and too late is a horrible feeling.

I loved my family, but I had resented the secret for a long time. I still resented it, wished for that lost time again, sometimes daydreamed about how it would have been to have a grandfather until I was twenty-five. My paternal grandfather had died when I was eleven.

It was dicey stuff, though, messing with family histories. It could get ugly, and, frankly, this one *was* none of my business.

Or it wouldn't have been before I moved here, before these people became my other family, before I would have even considered asking Hamlet to attend a Burns dinner with me. He was like a little brother, and I knew this with one hundred percent certainty: If I were him, I'd want to know the truth of everything, no matter what it was. I would have wanted to know my biological grandfather, even if, for some reason, he hadn't wanted to know me.

I also had to consider that maybe none of this was a secret. Maybe Hamlet did know. Or maybe this birth certificate wasn't even his; my imagination could just be on overdrive, again.

I'd done some preliminary research, of course, looking up Dora and the last name Edison, finding mention of a family of women named Strangelove in Edinburgh and many Edisons, lots with first names beginning with *M*. I hadn't found Dora specifically, but I felt like I could narrow it down. I'd ordered another copy of the certificate from the National Records of Scotland website, hoping that one would have a complete father's name.

I turned to my laptop to check my email.

I refreshed, and a thrill zipped through me when I saw a message from the National Records.

I couldn't open it fast enough.

Thank you for your recent inquiry and purchase. We have attached the requested birth certificate. Please let us know if we can be of further service. I opened the attachment.

"Matthew Edison," I said aloud when I read the clearly printed name. It seemed like this new information should give me more satisfaction than it did, but it still didn't solve the other mysteries.

I had everything I could get without asking some questions of my coworkers, letting them in on my discovery.

So what was I going to do now?

I sat back in my chair. I just wasn't sure.

FOUR

I ended up saving the certificate on the laptop and then moving the email to another folder. I re-hid the paper file back inside the locked drawer and sat at my desk a long few moments, contemplating the possible ramifications.

Though I didn't make a move to do anything else with the certificate at that moment, I still came back to the fact that if it were me, I really would want to know everything. But knowing everything can come with serious ramifications. I had to find a good middle ground.

I decided to put off making any other decisions until the next day. When in doubt, procrastinate a little, see what the universe sends your way; maybe that check-engine light will actually turn off by itself—at least that's what Wyatt always used to say to me, usually with a roll of his eyes.

I attended to other work and even helped out on the light side of the bookshop when they got busy in the late afternoon.

When it was time to go home, I realized I hadn't talked to Tom or my brother since earlier in the day. I hoped everyone, including Elias and Aggie, would show up for dinner at about the same time.

Tom and I had already decided that I'd take the bus home.

Supposedly he had left the pub early and was already working on dinner preparations. As I hurried through the cold to the bus stop, I wished I'd left with him, in his warm car. Tom and I had discussed me purchasing a car of my own, but I really didn't want one. I'd become accustomed to Edinburgh's public transportation, and I mostly enjoyed it. If the desire hit me, I could hop on a train to another city. Or I could call Elias at any moment, and he would pick me up in his taxi and take me where I wanted to go. I could figure out how to get anywhere without needing my own car. It wasn't like getting from place to place in Kansas, where your own vehicle was almost a necessity.

I texted Tom once I got on the bus, but there was no immediate response. That wasn't unusual.

On the way home, I thought about the next evening's event. I was glad Hamlet was excited to go, but I was also having commitment regret, particularly now that Wyatt was in town. Nevertheless, Hamlet and I would have a good time, even if we had to make our own fun.

I was glad to see that not only was Tom home, but Elias's cab was there too. I disembarked the bus only one house away from my and Tom's blue house by the sea. My phone buzzed just as I tipped my head down against the wind coming off the ocean. This was a very different cold than the Kansas winters I grew up in. Kansas winters had seeped into my bones in a deeper, colder way—usually. Tonight, though, the wind coming off the water was almost as sharp as a winter wind back home.

I grabbed my phone from my pocket.

"Hi, Edwin," I said as I answered.

"Lass, how are you this evening?"

"I am well. You? It sounds like there's something wrong." I stopped walking, even as the cold pelted my face.

"All is well, but I have received a message. . . ."

Guilt bloomed inside me. Because of his wide and vast connections, someone from the Scotland National Records had put everything together, and they knew Edwin, so they'd called him and told on me.

It was a ridiculous notion, but it was the first thing that came to my mind.

"Go on." I swallowed hard.

"You've been invited to a Burns dinner tomorrow evening?"

"Yes!" I was relieved this wasn't about the birth certificate. I did not have the constitution for sneaky. "Why do you ask?"

"Are you going?"

"I was planning on it. I'm taking Hamlet with me."

"Aye? That's a welcome relief."

"Why?" He had my full attention.

"I think there's an ulterior motive to you being invited. I have a history with . . . well, with at least one of the members of the group, and I suspect they might be trying to get at me through you."

"Oh. Well, we won't go."

"No, no, I think you're safe. I just wanted you to be aware. There will be a man at the dinner who will probably attempt to ask you questions about me."

"What kind of questions?" I started walking again. It was really cold.

"My address, how often I come into the bookshop, my mobile number, et cetera."

"Okay." Didn't everyone know where Edwin lived—in a stately manor just outside of town?

"Just don't offer any answers."

"I never would."

"I know. I just . . . well, I'm glad you're taking Hamlet. It will be a lively event. There will be enjoyable people there, but just . . . always be careful."

There was no way I was going to that dinner now. "I will be. I promise. But I'd like to know more about who you know there."

Edwin hesitated. "I'll stop by the bookshop tomorrow morning and we'll discuss this further."

"That sounds great." Maybe I could kill two birds with one stone and have a conversation about the birth certificate too.

"I look forward to it," he said cheerily.

"Me too."

"Good night, lass."

He disconnected the call before I could tell him the same.

This had shaped up to be such a strange and surprising day, I thought as I put my phone back into my pocket and made my way inside the house.

Everyone was there, including Artair, Tom's father. I hadn't seen him or talked to him for a few weeks, and his joining us was another wonderful surprise. I was lucky to not only adore my husband, but also his father, a good man and a librarian at the University of Edinburgh library.

We ate dinner immediately, all of us wanting updates from one another. Artair, Aggie, and Elias wanted details of my brother's visit. I determined that all was well—in fact, everyone around the table seemed to be in good health as well as good humor. After the meal, and to Wyatt's delight (well, mostly his—he had quite the sweet tooth), dessert was served. We dug into some of Aggie's carrot cake, and I finally shared the details of my time with Clarinda.

"I think you should go!" Wyatt said as he sliced himself another piece of the cake.

"Hamlet will be with ye," Aggie said.

Of everyone around the dinner table, I'd been certain that both Elias and Aggie would adamantly express that I shouldn't go to the Burns dinner, but as I'd told everyone about my time in the small Burns building and then the call from Edwin, it was Aggie's eyes that had been the most curious.

Robert Burns was her favorite poet of all time. In fact, had I given it just a few more minutes' thought, I would have invited her instead of Hamlet, though I'm sure I would have then felt guilty about not inviting him.

I made an executive decision. "If we go, come with us, Aggie. Please."

"As much as I would love tae, lass, I've other things tae do at the church."

Aggie rarely missed her services.

"I understand, but missing one night might not hurt," I said.

She shook her head. "I've missed too many lately. But, ta, lass, for inveetin me."

I would have gone if she'd said she would come along, but now I was back to not going, though I kept that to myself. I looked at Tom. "What do you think?"

He smiled crookedly. It was an extremely endearing look on him. "Trick question, but I think you should do exactly what you want to do."

"Artair?" I said.

My father-in-law's eyes got big as he reached for his cup of water, taking a drink instead of answering.

"I think ye should stay home," Elias interjected.

His vote was not a surprise. He would always err on the side of extreme caution and his first impressions of anything would be met with doubt.

I smiled at him. "I hear you. I will continue to think about it."

He nodded and sent me a stern frown.

I turned to Wyatt. "How did your meetings go?"

"Amazing. I'm learning so much about . . . well, a bunch of nerdy stuff, but it was great. My bosses back home were incredibly pleased when I spoke to them earlier."

"Congratulations," I said.

"Thank you, baby sister."

"I have an idea," Elias interjected again. "If you go tomorrow, I'll drive ye and the lad Hamlet. I'll sit outside in the cab while ye enjoy the festivities."

"Good idea," Aggie said.

"I like that," Artair added.

I smiled at him too.

"I do love Burns," Artair continued. "I've been to more Burns dinners than I can count." He looked at Tom. "I can't believe we haven't hosted one specifically for your bride."

"Is he one of your favorites too?" I asked Artair.

"Aye." Artair's eyebrows came together. "In fact, lately I've been trying to remember from which work was one of his characters. Something like 'Weatherby.' Does anyone know a character with that name?"

We all shook our heads.

Aggie's eyebrows came together. "Doesnae sound familiar."

Artair smiled. "I wish I could place it. Maybe it will come to me."

"I'll think about it too," Aggie said, clearly bothered by the fact that she might not perfectly remember something Burns had written.

We ate more dessert, but even with my brother there, and though Artair, Elias, and Aggie were all a part of my Scottish family, I was distracted for the whole evening. I tried to hide it, and probably did okay, except that Tom could see right through me.

After we told our guests good night and showed a very tired Wyatt—suddenly overwhelmed with jet lag and too much carrot cake—his room, we went to bed too.

"Lass, of course you should do whatever you want to do, but I think you'll regret it if you don't go to the dinner tomorrow. You love that kind of stuff, and it's just a dinner, no matter what Edwin wants to warn you about," Tom said as we turned out the lights.

The wind blew outside the small house, but we were tucked inside, cozy and warm.

He wasn't wrong, but the one thing I hadn't relayed to anyone else was that it all just *felt* off somehow, like a premonition. I hadn't had many of those without bookish voices, but something seemed wonky, though the voices were silent.

I rolled over and put my head on his shoulder. "I hear you. Thank you."

"For what?"

"For lots of things, but, tonight, for two reasons specifically—first, for that half-smile thing you do, and second, just for being the best."

"You like my half smile?" he asked. In the dark I could hear it was there again.

"I like all your smiles," I said.

"Aye?"

"Oh yes. Aye." Every single one of them.

FIVE

"The sun is out!" I proclaimed as I entered the book-shop, the bell above the door sounding even happier because of the bright morning.

"Aye, it's cold but lovely oot there," Rosie said as Hector trotted toward me.

It was rare that the sun was ever out in Scotland, let alone on January 25.

"Maybe it's in celebration of Mr. Burns's birthday," Rosie said, worry belying her positive words and crinkling her fore-head.

I unwound my scarf as I picked up Hector, who was wear-ing a red sweater Rosie had put on him this morning. "You talked to Edwin?" Hector wasn't as wiggly today, so we were able to say hello for a good long minute.

"I did, lass, and he's on his way in tae talk tae ye."

"Do you know what he's going to tell me?"

"I ken some of it, but dinnae ask me aboot it. I want him tae tell ye."

"I'm anxious to hear. It sounds intriguing."

"That's one word for it, I suppose."

"You're truly worried?"

Rosie's mouth pinched tight. "I've ken Edwin a long time, lass. He's been up to lots of things over the years."

I nodded. I knew about some of the worst things he'd done, but I'd never tell.

Suspicion is a heavy armor and with its weight it impedes more than it protects.

I paused. It was Mr. Burns himself speaking to me with words he'd written. I could hear the voice my mind had conjured for him: deep, and heavily accented. I wondered if he was trying to tell me to rein in any suspicion Edwin might try to share, maybe keep an open mind.

"Delaney?" Rosie said.

I refocused on her. "Sorry, my mind wandered."

"Aye," she said.

She'd seen it happen plenty of times before.

We didn't have to wait much longer. By the time I had my hat and scarf off and over a hook next to the door, Edwin came through, bringing in crisp cold air and looking even more dapper than usual.

Though even his casual clothes were pressed and fit him perfectly, today he wore a suit.

"Ye have a meetin'?" Rosie asked him as he took off his coat and then folded it over his arm.

Edwin never used the hooks. He left his coat draped over one of the chairs—he'd always had the habit, according to Rosie.

"I do. Nothing about the bookshop, though." He smiled at Rosie and then picked up Hector for the same greeting I'd received.

Hector loved us all equally, even though he didn't see Edwin nearly as much as he did the rest of us. In fact, I was pretty sure the dog gave the man a look that was meant to inquire where he'd been and what he'd been up to.

Edwin glanced around. "Anyone else here?"

"No," Rosie said. "Hamlet will be in, in aboot an hour, and there are no customers yet. Shall I gather some coffee or tea?"

"I'll do it," I offered as I turned toward the stairs. I hurried over to the other side and to the kitchen. I was anxious to hear what Edwin had to say, but coffee would make the morning story easier for all of us, and Rosie's knees didn't relish the trip.

However, when I made it over there, I saw that a pot had been brewed—Rosie had been over and back already. A tray had been set out. After I poured the coffee into a carafe, I carried everything back over to the other side, wondering, as I had a few times now, if maybe we should consider putting a coffee station closer to Rosie and her knees.

She and Edwin were sitting around the back table, in the middle of a friendly discussion, but I couldn't distinguish what it was about. I thought about the birth certificate again and how convenient it might end up being to ask both of them about it when Hamlet wasn't around.

One thing at a time.

When mugs were filled, I sat down and looked at Edwin. The echoes of Burns's words were still in my mind. I wanted to make sure not to jump to any immediate conclusions or suspicions, which was probably always good advice. "I'm ready to hear what's going on."

Hector was curled up on Rosie's lap, but he sent Edwin a quick look, pushing him to proceed.

"Aye." Edwin nodded. "Delaney, I was one of the original members of the Burns group you've been invited to."

"Oh? What happened?"

"Have you met any of the members? I don't know if it's all the same people or not," he said.

"Just Clarinda Creston."

"I see. A lovely woman, and, aye, one of the original members."

"A local solicitor, right?"

"Aye. A good one, at that. She's now a defense attorney. She's represented a few of our more famous criminals."

"Really? I didn't ask her specialty. A defense attorney . . . I mean solicitor?"

"Aye. She recently won a case for an alleged murderer. He was found not guilty, though he admitted to the crime. He's a free man."

"What's his name?" I asked as I reached for a pen and some scratch paper from some stacks that Hamlet had stored on a shelf.

Edwin looked at Rosie. "The man who killed two fishermen. Do you remember his name?"

"Och, aye. Donald Rigalee, or something like that. Maybe Regaly." Rosie spelled them both, and I wrote them down for later research.

"Did everyone know he was guilty?" I asked.

"Oh, aye, he did the deed. Clarinda was able to save him from the consequences because of bad police work. The evidence that would have convicted him was deemed inadmissible in court." Edwin waved a hand. "But that has nothing to do with what I need to tell you, I don't think. She's very good at her job, and I do want you to know that part."

I put down the pen and nodded.

"I purchased the building that houses the club," Edwin continued.

"The small place in Cowgate?"

"Aye."

"It's . . . charming," I said.

Though his expression had been serious since he'd come inside the bookshop, he laughed once now. "No, it's old and was falling down when I purchased it. I had it . . . reinforced the best I could. It's probably not in the best of shape, but I haven't been there in many years."

Rosie added, "You said it was haunted."

"It seemed that way, many years ago," Edwin agreed. "But, again, that probably doesn't have anything to do with what I need to share with you." He looked at me. "It's imperative that you know what happened, that you go into this fully informed."

But I had to interrupt "Wait. Haunted? By Robert Burns?"

Edwin paused and then nodded. "Aye, the man himself."

"He thought that before he bought it," Rosie said. She turned to Edwin again: "And ye thought it would be perfect for a club."

"Why did you think it was haunted?" I asked.

Edwin could tell his story had been diverted. He must not have been in a hurry, though, because there wasn't a tense set to his shoulders. His legs were comfortably crossed, his hands folded on his lap.

"Let me tell you a little about Rabbie Burns first," he said, using Burns's common nickname.

I nodded eagerly. Even Rosie, who'd probably heard every story there was about Burns, was fully attentive.

"Though he was a great poet, a talented writer, he probably wasn't a great man, I am sad to say. We Scots will always hold him with the highest of regard, but he was rowdy, had affairs and children with women other than his lovely wife, Jean Armour. He thought very highly of himself." Edwin fell into thought a moment. "He wasn't ever successful when he was alive, but after he died, it seemed his words took on a new and important life. I came upon the wee house when I was at a point when perhaps I wasn't the best man I could be. Though I've never married and never fathered a child, I can tell you with complete shame that I didn't always behave as I should have."

I nodded. This was not new, though I sensed I was getting a few more pieces of his story, vague though they may be. I wouldn't ever hold any of that against him. He was a good man now, and even if it hadn't shown back then, I couldn't imagine him ever being anything other than good.

"I came upon the building in Cowgate at a time in my life when I was studying the metaphysical and wishing for a better version of myself. It was close to the turn of the century, Y2K approaching. I was middle-aged, healthy, and felt . . . at loose ends. I was searching." Edwin sighed. "It was over twenty years ago now, but it seems like yesterday. Anyway . . ."

"You studied the metaphysical?"

Edwin nodded as he frowned. "I did, but then I had a dream, lass. It was transformative, I must say."

"Okay." While I'd been in Scotland, I'd had my own moments, interactions I couldn't quite explain. I wasn't one to doubt, but I always did anyway.

"I dreamed specifically about Mr. Burns showing me the building. I must have come across it over the years, but I didn't remember doing so. I've lived here all my life, though, and it's not far from here. I woke from the dream. It was early in the morning, the sun not up, though it was twenty-five January, just like it is today, but cloudier. It rained and even snowed some later that day. I dressed and set out to find the place I'd seen so vividly in the dream, to search for the ghost of Rabbie Burns. And I drove directly to it. Again, I didn't remember ever seeing it before, but I seemed to know exactly where it was."

"Was the ghost there?" I asked.

"No, I'm afraid not. When he'd shown it to me in my dreams, I'd also seen him sitting at a desk inside it. That desk was there, though."

"It was?" I said.

"Aye, and in the dream, he wrote something for me as he sat behind it, handed it to me just as I awakened."

"Oh my. So you never read the words he wrote for you in the dream?"

"No. I thought if I spent some time in the building I would find that answer, lass, but there was no going in it as it was. I peeked in the one window that hadn't been boarded up, and it was a garbage heap inside, along with the desk."

"Papers?" I interjected.

"Some, but mostly rubbish. It had been used to store things that had been forgotten, as well as shelter for those down on their luck. I purchased the place and got to work cleaning it out and then fixing it up some. There *were* some papers inside, but I assure you, I had every single item in there looked over from top to bottom, inside to out, and there was nothing there written by Robert Burns."

"Edwin wasnae just a member, Delaney. He was the one to begin the club."

"I was." He looked at me.

"Was the building there back when Burns could have been inside it, maybe left something he'd written?"

"Aye. It was old enough, but there is no proof, no indication at all that he was there," Edwin said. "Back then, though, I was guided by that dream. I knew I couldn't let it go. I asked one of the local established Burns clubs if they wanted to use it, but they didn't. Their membership was too big, they had proper locations they were accustomed to, et cetera. I then asked if they would mind if I attempted to create another club, something smaller, with just a few friends. They gave me their blessing and even invited me to join them. I declined." Edwin frowned. "Sometimes I bite off a wee bit more than I can chew, Delaney."

"Suithfest," Rosie said.

I looked at her with raised eyebrows.

"The truth," she translated.

I smiled.

Edwin continued, "Anyway, I wanted to handle this new club myself. I didn't want someone telling me what to do or how to run it. I sensed I was on to something." His mouth made a straight line. "The warehouse is proof that I've had that inspiration more than once in my life and then later became distracted."

Rosie cleared her throat. "Though Edwin does more good than bad with his money, ye ken that sometimes he spends it a wee bit frivolously."

"Well, it's given me a job I love, so I'm good with it," I said.

"Aye. I got to work, setting up the club. I invited friends. Neither Rosie nor my friend Burk were interested."

"Though I appreciated the inveet," Rosie assured us.

I'd also become friends with Burk, and I was surprised he hadn't been intrigued by the group. I knew that though Burk and Edwin had been friends for decades, some of that time wasn't without contention, mostly having to do with misunderstandings.

Edwin continued, "Burk and I already spent enough time together, or so he thought. But, believe it or not, I do have other friends. Clarinda was one. She was kind enough to help me with legal questions I've had over the years. Nothing overly serious, but it was lovely to be able to ask an expert when I needed one. He paused. "And I invited three others too. They were all men, but Clarinda didn't seem to mind. Charles Lexon, a businessman who founded an import/export company, is a Burns fanatic. He used to come into the bookshop all the time."

Rosie nodded as she frowned, but she didn't interject with the reason he might not have been in for a while.

"And Neil Watterton was a librarian at the time, though I'm not sure he still is. He was a young lad then, now probably close to the age I was back then, I'm guessing. Good men, both of them."

"What about the third man?" I asked.

"The third one used to own another bookshop in town. It's no longer open, but that's how Malcolm Campbell and I met. We were very close friends for a long time."

"Malcolm." Rosie said his name with an airy breath as if trying it out after not speaking it for a while.

"Oh dear. What happened?" I said.

"Bottom line, Mr. Campbell thought I burned down his shop."

"What? With fire?" I said stupidly.

"Aye."

"Oh no."

"I didn't, of course." Edwin shook his head.

"I would never think you did!"

"There was no proof that he had," Rosie said. "None at all."

"Why did Campbell think that?"

"The fire occurred on twenty-six January 2000, two years into forming the club. We'd had our second annual dinner the night before, and Campbell and I had argued. It was ridiculous, frankly. I'd purchased a valuable book from a seller, a couple of weeks before the dinner," Edwin said.

"That's a daily occurrence around here—almost at least."

"Aye, but this one was being sold by Campbell's ex-wife, Maria. He thought it was all a ploy, done by the two of us to get back at him. He eventually claimed it was his book and Maria had no right to sell it."

"Oh. Not good."

"No, but I had the provenance, Delaney. It was all very legitimate. Maria brought the book to me, saying she needed the funds because of the financial disaster that had befallen her after their divorce, which was finalized six months earlier. She claimed to me that Malcolm didn't have the money to buy it from her, or she would have sold it to him."

"But he did have the money?"

"He did." Edwin nodded. "Aye, it was a valuable book, but not outrageous. She came to me, and she asked me—no, she stipulated that she would only sell it to me if I agreed to never sell it to Malcolm. At the time, I wasn't aware of the layers of conflict the book had caused between them. I just wanted the book, and she needed the money. I thought she just didn't want me to deal with the man she was no longer married to. I gave her a little more than it was worth. I thought it was a positive transaction."

"What was the book?" I asked.

"*The Poetical Works of Robert Burns.*"

"Of course it was."

"Aye."

"So she thought selling it to you would get back at him?"

"Aye," Edwin said doubtfully. "But I didn't see that until later."

"It sounds like there's more to the story."

"Isnae there always?" Rosie said.

Shame pulled on Edwin's features. "By that time, and this was six months after the divorce, remember, Maria and I had become . . . friends. Truly, there wasn't a romance to our friendship, but I'm afraid I might have led her on in some way. . . ."

"You didnae," Rosie said. "She was just . . . she was confused and trying to find her way."

Edwin frowned. "Anyway, we kept it casual. I never let it get far because she was the ex-wife of someone who, at the time, was a good friend. It probably wasn't appropriate that she and I were friends, but she seemed like she needed someone."

"It was fine," Rosie said. "Maria was very upset and did need a friend. She . . . struggled. And Malcolm wouldnae have even noticed were it not for the book."

"How did he find out about the transaction?" I asked.

"He came into the bookshop the day of the dinner, and I had the book out on my desk," Rosie said as she threw her hands into the air. "I hadn't taken it out of the drawer I'd put it in when Edwin gave it to me until only a few minutes before Malcolm came in. The book was sitting right there and he saw it. It was uncanny, as if the secret was not meant to be kept." She fell into thought. "My husband, Paul, was alive at the time. He was here. Malcolm was so angry that Paul put himself between Malcolm and me. Paul got him to leave without calling the police, but it was a wee bit frightening."

"I'm sorry," I said, wishing, as I had a number of times now, that I'd met Paul.

Rosie shook her head and smiled sadly. "'Twas a long time ago. 'Twas the timing that was so uncanny."

"Those things happen, I suppose. Did you suspect he knew about the book?"

"No, not at all," Rosie said. "It all seemed very random."

"A wee bit of karma, maybe," Edwin said.

"Then you two argued at the Burns dinner?" I asked him.

"Aye. That night. It was quite ugly, if I remember correctly. I was in my fifties; Malcolm was in his late forties. Both of our tempers flared much more easily back then."

"And the fire occurred the next day?" I said.

"Aye. Malcolm's anger exploded. He was sure I'd done the deed," Edwin said.

"Did the police or the fire department figure it out?"

"Not to my knowledge."

"Where is Maria now? She was probably a suspect in the arson, right?"

Edwin shook his head. "Not even by Malcolm. Rosie and I concluded that she left quickly for America right after selling me the book. No sign of her. I've long lost track of her, but I think she must have gone directly to San Francisco, California."

"You think Malcolm's anger has . . . what's the word you used? *Exploded* again, for some reason? And he wants to get at you through me?"

"I think it's a real possibility."

"I don't understand, Edwin. You live here. You've lived in your house for years. If Malcolm wanted to find you, you're right here and he knows your address."

"Aye, but I had an order of protection in place."

"Oh. That bad?"

"He was showing up wherever I was, threatening me. It was not good. I felt I had no choice. I don't know what's behind Malcolm's motives, Delaney, but if you go tonight, I'm glad you're taking Hamlet."

"Do you think he's dangerous?" I asked.

"To you? I don't know. Long ago, there were moments I thought he could be tipped over the edge, but I haven't seen him in years. I have no idea what's behind this. In fact, maybe nothing. Malcolm might not even be a member any longer. Maybe you were invited by someone else and Malcolm doesn't know our connection, but I thought it important that you go into this with your eyes open. I don't know if the rest of the original members are still there, but if they are, they all know what happened."

"And no one ever figured out what happened to the bookshop?"

"Not to my knowledge."

"Did you? I mean, did you suspect anyone?" I asked.

"No one. To this day, I think it might have been something in the old electrical system."

"What's Malcolm doing now? What's he been doing for all these years?"

"I have no idea. I haven't investigated. I haven't kept up. I went on with my life, hoping he'd go on with his and we wouldn't run into each other. The years have flown by, as all of them do. As far as I know, we haven't ever crossed paths once the order of protection was put into place."

I looked at Edwin. "You gave them the building, didn't you?"

"The dream, Delaney. It was real. I couldn't let go of the

idea that Robert Burns had written something inside there. It seemed only right to let them continue to meet there. I excused myself."

"You don't own the building, though?"

"No."

"Who does?"

"I signed it over to Clarinda."

"Okay."

"It seemed like the right thing to do." Edwin smiled sadly.

I was going to this dinner. I couldn't deny my curiosity, but I was glad to be taking someone with me.

As if on cue, the bell above the front door jingled and Hamlet joined us in the back before any of us could stand up to see who'd come in.

"Hello. What'd I miss?" he said as Hector jumped off Rosie's lap and trotted to greet him.

SIX

I did not ask anyone about the birth certificate. I didn't even think about it for the rest of the day. Edwin left the bookshop for his appointment, and Rosie, Hamlet, and I got to work. Burns's birthday, along with the sunshine, brought in more customers than I'd seen since before Christmas and Hogmanay, the celebration of the new year that Scottish people took very seriously and the one when "Auld Lang Syne" is always sung. I was beginning to see Robert Burns at every turn.

I overheard a few customers talking about their dinners planned at home this evening. I knew he was an important Scottish figure, but my awareness of him was taking on a whole new light.

Though I helped on the retail side, I did make it over to the dark side a few times for some work in the warehouse, but I didn't even unlock the drawer with the certificate inside it.

When we could finally take a breath, it was time for Hamlet and me to leave for the dinner. Neither of us changed out of our casual work clothes, but I didn't think the occasion called for dressing up, and Clarinda had already said we wouldn't need to don costumes like the others would be wearing.

I had forgotten all about Elias's offer to drive us, but he showed up at five anyway. He came into the shop, sent me a look that told me he was glad we hadn't left without him, and then took a seat in the back, waiting until Hamlet and I were ready to go. Hector had grown fond of my former landlords, and the dog, sans sweater by then, kept Elias company.

Wyatt had swung by about an hour earlier, telling Rosie he'd pick her up at her flat in a couple of hours. When he left again, Rosie smiled at me.

"Yer brother doesnae need tae take me tae dinner, but I'm not going tae tell him that. I'd appreciate if it ye didnae either. He's being so polite."

I laughed. "It's our secret, but I do think you'll both have a great time."

Tom was so busy with the wedding reception that his return texts to me weren't profuse. *Have fun* and *love you* were his only real messages. I glanced out the bookshop's front window up to the pub once or twice. There were no people gathering outside, but I could tell it was going to be a busy evening; shadows danced on the walkway outside the front window.

It was highly unusual for the bookshop to actually close when its posted hours of operation said it did, but we were punctual this evening and all piled into Elias's cab. He dropped Rosie and Hector at their flat and then took Hamlet and me over to the Burns House.

"Come in with us, Elias," I said, again not caring if they had enough food. I didn't mind sharing.

"No, lass, not my style," Elias said. "I'll be close by, though. You'll see me no matter when ye step out of that wee building. If ye need tae make an escape, I'll be ready."

I tried to convince him again, but he wasn't budging out of that taxi.

Hamlet, however, was another story. Though he wasn't giddy, I could sense his excitement as we exited the cab that Elias had parked across the narrow cobblestone street from the building. He'd parked under a short streetlamp and was able to angle a book just right on his steering wheel so he could read while we were inside.

"I've been to the cottage he was born in—now attached to a museum. It's in Alloway, on the other side of the country," Hamlet said as we set out toward the building.

"Did you enjoy it?"

"Very much. It's a wee home. It was a rough beginning for him. The house gives a sense of where he and his words were born. He never lived a luxurious life, but it did get somewhat easier and better, I believe."

"Did you sense any ghosts?" I asked.

It wasn't necessarily a literal question, but Hamlet and I had talked enough about the importance of history to Scottish people for him to know what I meant. Ghosts were at every turn in Edinburgh, but sometimes they were made of only memories or the blood of fallen warriors. There were many rich layers.

"Aye, but not like Edwin's dream."

"Had you heard about that before today?" Rosie and I had shared with Hamlet everything we'd discussed with Edwin.

"No, I wasn't even part of their lives twenty years ago. I was born in 1998."

I bit back some questions. Now wasn't the time, but maybe I could find a way to ask Hamlet what he might know about the details on the birth certificate without sharing any secrets. I'd work on it.

"What do you love so much about Scotland's national poet?" I asked as we approached the front door.

"His way with the Scots language. I don't speak it much, but I know it and I love it. I don't want it to ever go away. It's beautiful to me."

I looked at him as he peered into the building through the small window next to the front door. If there was such a thing as reincarnation, and after my time with my friend Mary, who was convinced she was Mary, Queen of Scots, reincarnated, I might be persuaded that Hamlet could very well have been someone like Burns in a previous life, someone artistically gifted.

"Edwin said he wasn't the best of men," I said.

Hamlet moved his attention back to me as he sighed and folded his hands in front of himself.

"He was poor, very poor. Because of his austere beginnings, he lived a rough life, a sickly one. He was liked, adored by some, but though he was married, he did have children with other women. I don't know that any Scot could reasonably call him a bad man, though. It was a different time. He was extraordinarily gifted."

"Ah, I see. Well, who's to say what life dictates?" I swallowed, now wondering very much about Dora Strangelove and Matthew Edison. "Life is never as linear or uncomplicated as we would like."

"Very true."

"How does it look in there?" I nodded at the building. "Crowded?"

"It's hard to tell. The glass isn't clear, but I hear voices."

"I do too. No time like the present." I reached for the knob.

"I'm ready!" Hamlet said with a smile.

Clarinda had underplayed it. The place *was* truly transformed. There weren't any stray pieces of paper visible anywhere.

"Delaney! Welcome," she said as she wove her way around a dining table and two men.

Though the dining table, overflowing with food, and its chairs took up most of the middle space, it was the perimeter spaces that were so different.

The fireplace along the back wall was now fully exposed, and enthusiastic flames burned inside it, warming the building thoroughly. Two wood chairs framed the fireplace, but I suspected they were more for show than to sit upon.

A cabinet ran along one wall, a dish shelf with dishes in racks on the wall above it. A large grandfather clock ticked away against another wall.

"It's very much like the real cottage, Burns's home," Hamlet said quietly to me as Clarinda approached.

"It didn't look a thing like this yesterday," I said with no tiny bit of awe.

"Welcome!" Clarinda pulled me into a hug.

"Thank you. This is my friend Hamlet," I said.

"Hamlet? Is that your real name?" she asked with a welcoming handshake.

"Well, it's my middle name, but it's what people call me," he said as he returned the shake. "I'm so glad to be here this evening. Thank you for allowing Delaney to bring a friend."

"My pleasure!"

I could sense the wheels turning behind her eyes. They might not invite many new members aboard, but even she could quickly see how Hamlet would be a wonderful addition to any club that celebrated art in any form.

"Come, meet everyone else." She gestured with her hand.

The space was small enough that the three men behind Clarinda took only a couple of steps toward us as we did the same toward them.

"Charles Lexon is acting as Mr. Burns's father this evening, Mr. William Burnes, with an *e,* which is how he spelled it back then." Clarinda smiled.

Charles Lexon was dressed in a costume from that time, similar to what the other two men wore: a jacket, knickers, socks, and pointed-toe shoes with a buckle over the top. The blouse he wore underneath the jacket included an ornate tied collar that probably served the same decorative and functional purposes a necktie does these days. Something had to keep the collars closed. Probably close to Edwin's age, with dark hair and lively green eyes, he was a handsome man who spoke with such a deep Scottish accent that I wondered if it was an act put on just for this evening.

"And this is Mr. Malcolm Campbell. He is also dressed as the bard's father." Clarinda laughed. "When it comes to choosing characters, we don't have that many."

Malcolm Campbell greeted us with just as much warmth as Charles had. If he knew we were employees of the man he thought had burned down his bookshop, he didn't show it.

Malcolm was a tall man with wide shoulders. He was striking—his hair was very dark, wavy, and longish like Hamlet's, but on his bigger frame it reminded me more of a lumberjack than an artist. His friendly blue eyes sparkled in the light from the fireplace.

We were also introduced to Neil Watterton, who was the youngest of the three men, in his fifties as Edwin had mentioned he'd be by now. He was dressed as the poet, at least on his bottom half—he was slipping on a shirt and jacket over an old T-shirt. We'd caught him mid-dress, but he only smiled and shook our hands once he was put together.

The membership seemed to be the same as when Edwin had founded the group.

"You even put on a wig," I said to Neil.

"I did," Neil touched the wig. "The pictures of Burns are very distinctive. I feel the wig helps me pull it off."

"It does," I said.

Burns had a handsome face, with pale skin, big brown eyes, and noticeable thick eyebrows. So did Neil Watterton. Burns had more hair than Neil, which he proved to us by lifting up the edge of the wig to show us his bald pate underneath.

I caught a moment of hesitation when Hamlet and Neil shook hands. I didn't understand it, but they moved past it quickly, and there was too much to soak in for me to dwell. I filed it to the back of my mind.

"And I am either Mr. Burns's mother, Agnes Broun, or his wife, Jean Armour, whichever one you'd like for me to be," Clarinda said.

Her brown curls were not topped by the tam o'shanter this evening, but a bonnet instead. She wore a long dress, tied at the waist with an apron over the top.

"Thank you for the invitation," I said. "We're glad to be here."

Hamlet nodded and smiled.

"Let's all have a seat, then. We have a number of traditions we must get started on," Clarinda said.

We took seats around the table. Hamlet and I were asked to head to the far side because the others would need to get up and down a few times. We took our seats, and the entertainment began immediately. The table had been set with primitive plates, bowls, and silverware. Covered platters and serving dishes filled the space, the scents of the delicious food permeating the air. We'd been so busy at the bookshop today that neither Hamlet nor I had eaten lunch. I hoped my stomach wouldn't growl too loudly as I changed my mind about wanting to eat only a little. However, judging by the amount of food on the table, Elias could have joined us easily—if only there'd been space for another chair.

Malcolm stood and said, "I will recite the Selkirk Grace."

I watched for hands clasped in prayer or bowed heads, but no one did any of that. Instead, everyone looked at Malcolm as he spoke.

"I'll begin in Scots. This blessing has been attributed to Mr. Burns." He looked at Hamlet and me as he spoke, then paused and seemed to fall into character. "Some hae meat and cannae eat / And some wad eat that want it / But we hae meat and we can eat / And sae the Lord be thankit." He cleared his throat. "Not too difficult to translate, but I will now give my best English version: some have meat and cannot eat, and some would eat that want it, but we have meat and we can eat, so let the Lord be thanked."

"That's lovely," I said.

I looked at Hamlet. I thought maybe he'd teared up some, but I didn't want to bring attention to it, so I turned back to Malcolm.

"Thank you," he said as he sat down.

Charles and Neil stood, and Charles reached to a small tape recorder on the counter. He pushed a button, and bagpipe music began to play.

"Tradition is that the haggis is now brought in by a piper.

We don't quite go that far, but Neil will grab the tray of haggis from the cupboard while the music plays," Charles said.

Neil grabbed the covered tray. He carried it the short distance to the table and set it in the middle. I wasn't a fan of haggis, but I knew its importance to this particular meal and would not be impolite.

Homes all over Scotland, perhaps the world, were partaking in some similar version of this meal this night. The universality of that made the dish seem somewhat more appealing to me. But only somewhat.

Neil sat down, but after Charles turned off the music, he uncovered the haggis platter and took hold of some carving tools.

"As I carve open the haggis, I will recite the 'Address to a Haggis.' I'll recite only in Scots, because it's long and we need to eat while the food is still warm," Charles said with a smile.

Again, I enjoyed the tradition of the long poem, another one attributed to Burns, of course. And, again, it wasn't too difficult to understand, but we all shared smiles at some of the sillier parts. It was, after all, a poem written to honor a food made of sheep's heart, liver, and lungs, stuffed into a sausage made of sheep's stomach.

"Mr. Burns must have really loved haggis," I said when the poem was finished.

Everyone laughed.

"Clearly," Clarinda said as she stood and opened a soup tureen. "Though the haggis has been carved, we begin the meal with cullen skink, which is much tastier than its name. It's a smoked haddock chowder."

When the soup was served, we were finally able to begin

eating. It was a savory delight, chock-full of herbs. I wondered if it had been as delicious back in the day or if the recipe had been modified over the years.

We made some small talk as we ate, but it seemed everyone was hungry enough to focus on their food for a while. The first moment of contention of the evening came when Charles asked Clarinda about Donald Rigalee, her "murderin' client" who had been found not guilty.

Though I didn't think he'd really meant to sound so angry, something vile came through in his tone, sending a cloud of discomfort through the air.

"My clients trust me not to spread gossip or rumors, Charles, you know that," Clarinda said easily, though *her* tone left no doubt that she was not going to remain friendly if he pushed further.

"I'm just asking his whereabouts, Clare," Charles said with a smile. "Should we be watching our backs this evening?"

Clarinda smiled too. "I would think the fact you're all with me might make you safer than normal. I was, in fact, the solicitor who made sure he was a free man."

"Excellent point," Charles said, his accent still thick.

I was glad when they didn't continue to bicker.

After the soup, the haggis was served, along with the traditional neeps and tatties—turnips and potatoes. I had enjoyed every serving of neeps and tatties I'd eaten, and these were no exception. They were delicious, and the haggis was . . . haggis.

To be fair, it probably didn't taste as bad as I thought. It was just me and my notions of the ingredients.

However, again, those neeps and tatties were absolutely perfect.

"Delaney, as you probably know, this dinner is a tradition for many Scottish people, not just those of us who are lucky enough to be a part of a Burns group," Clarinda said.

"Mr. Burns is very important to the country's history," I said.

"Aye, and we're not the only group in Edinburgh," Malcolm said. "In fact, we're a wee small contribution to the whole, but we enjoy our cozy gatherings."

I nodded, wondering if I should interject that Hamlet and I knew their founder. Charles helped by suddenly moving the conversation in that direction.

"This group was founded by a local bookseller. He no longer participates, though," Charles said.

"He's s bit of a scoundrel," Malcolm said with a laugh.

Clarinda leaned over to me and spoke quietly. "I knew who you were, and Charles knew, but you working with Edwin is going to be a surprise to Malcolm and Neil."

"I wouldn't say he was a scoundrel," Charles said as he winked at me.

I put my fork down. Hamlet did the same. Suddenly I wasn't hungry, and a sense of dread washed over me. Was I being played? And for what reason? Hamlet picked up on the same vibes.

I looked at Clarinda. She blanched when she saw the expression on my face. "Oh no, it's not that, really," she said to the accusations she saw in my eyes.

I cleared my throat. "Excuse me, everyone, but I think it's imperative I make something very clear."

Everyone turned their attention in my direction.

"Now?" Clarinda asked.

"Now," I said to her.

"Is something wrong?" Neil asked.

We hadn't even finished our haggis.

"I don't know which of you invited me to be a part of the group. Who was it?" I asked.

Everyone seemed to fall into thought a moment, and a beat later Charles raised his hand. "It was me."

"Why did you invite me?"

"I thought you'd be a fine addition."

"How did you know me?"

Charles frowned and then had the good graces to appear somewhat ashamed, but he didn't answer my question.

"Charles?" Malcolm asked him. Malcolm looked at me. "It was at our last meeting. He said he met a lovely lass who was all about books, thought you'd be a fine addition, thought it would be good to have another lass in the group, to help even it out some. It's been a long time coming. It was unanimous that you come aboard."

"I didn't know you worked where you work until I rang you," Clarinda said, though she was speaking to everyone.

I looked at Malcolm and Neil. "Do you know where I work?"

Both sets of their eyes were on me, eyebrows furrowed, and they shook their heads.

"I . . . we didn't ask," Neil said.

"I work for Edwin MacAlister at the Cracked Spine."

"What?" Neil said.

Malcolm, on the other hand, remained silent. He sighed heavily and then put down his own utensils. He frowned at his plate.

"Why did you do that?" Neil asked Charles. He turned to Clarinda. "And why didn't you tell us? This is all quite rotten; you know that as well as you know anything."

Hamlet put his hand over mine on the table. We needed to leave but not quite yet. I wanted some answers first.

Neil looked at me. "Oh, I apologize. I didn't mean . . . gracious, this is all very impolite, and I apologize from the bottom of my heart, for all of us." He glanced at Hamlet, and again they seemed to share a moment of something that seemed like a question, but Hamlet looked away from his glance before it could be further explored.

Neil was genuinely distraught.

"I thought it was time," Charles finally said, his words slow and deeply toned. "We needed to forgive and move on. I thought this would be the best way."

Malcolm finally looked up from his plate and at Charles. "You had no right. No right at all." Malcolm turned to Hamlet and me. "I apologize too. I should have recognized the lad—Hamlet, aye? Ye're related . . . or something. I now remember seeing you with Edwin a time or two over the years, from a distance. I've never seen you before, Delaney. If I knew . . . what this was, I would have intervened sooner. Please forgive us." He looked at Clarinda, who had her eyes tilted down in shame too, and then at Charles again, whose eyes were now more pleading than shamed. "This was a terrible way to handle a situation that should have been forgotten, not forgiven."

Without further ado, Malcolm stood from the table and left the building, an icy cold blowing in as he slammed the door behind him.

For a long moment, everyone was silent. I didn't know I'd grasped Hamlet's hand, but I suddenly felt him grasping back. I still didn't understand what was truly going on, but suddenly I didn't care. I just wanted to be away from these people.

"Delaney . . . ," Clarinda said.

I wouldn't look at her.

"Let's go," I said to Hamlet.

The door opened, and Elias stood there in silhouette, the wind stirring his scarf. "Lass, lad, yer ride is ready."

We made our way out of the building, Elias shutting the door firmly behind us.

"How did you know?" I asked him as we hurried across the cobblestone road.

"I watched an angry man hurry away. I couldnae wait a moment longer," Elias said. "I hoped I judged it right."

"You judged it perfectly," I said as we got into the taxi and Elias started the engine.

As we sped away, I glanced behind at the building. Clarinda stood in the doorway, and with her costume and the old architecture in the background, she looked like Burns's mother or wife might have truly looked a long time ago, perhaps as they were bidding an adieu to the beloved bard.

SEVEN

"I'm so sorry, love," Tom said.

Tom and I were the last revelers in the pub, though we weren't doing much reveling. The celebration had been a fine one, though. Most of the paper confetti pieces that had covered the floor had been swept up and thrown away. The glasses were all clean, the liquor bottles restored—those that hadn't been emptied and tossed in the recycle bin at least. I'd never seen the shelves so bare, but Tom informed me that a delivery was scheduled for the next morning.

The pub always closed at nine on Tuesdays, and tonight was no exception. In fact, the reception had, though lively, been finished by eight, the elderly couple having had more than enough celebration.

With the doors locked and all but the security light behind the bar doused, we sat on stools and faced each other as I told him about the events of the evening at the Burns House.

"It was mighty uncomfortable." I laughed. "But I must admit, I will never forget the image of Elias in that doorway, there to save the day. He was the vision of a Scottish superhero."

"I'm glad he was there."

"Me too, though I don't think Hamlet and I were in any danger. We were just . . . being used, I guess. I can't quite understand what was behind it, but I decided that I didn't need to know. I just needed to get out of there. Whatever explanation they might have wanted to give, it wouldn't have made up for . . . well, for that discomfort."

"I wonder what Edwin will do," Tom said.

"I already talked to him," I said. "I didn't think about him *doing* something, and I hope he doesn't. I called him just to let him know that it wasn't Malcolm who got us there and that Malcolm didn't ask us one question about Edwin. I wanted to ease his mind, about that at least. When I told him the rest, though, he wasn't happy. And he knows Clarinda fairly well, I think. Maybe I should have waited until tomorrow."

"No, tonight was good. If he was upset, he'll have the night to cool off. That's always helpful."

"I suppose." I paused. "What grown-ups do something like that? It was such a childish thing."

"Aye, but we don't know the history." Tom paused too. "Maybe it was meant to be a good thing, something that was meant to ultimately lead to asking Edwin to come back."

"I thought about that too, but they sure handled it poorly. It felt so sneaky."

"I agree." Tom had been angry as well, though he'd calmed. He was glad Hamlet and I had simply left. The others had probably ruined their own celebration anyway.

I hadn't told even Tom about the birth certificate, afraid a comment might accidentally slip when he was talking to someone at the bookshop, so I didn't mention Malcolm's offhand comment about Hamlet being somehow related to Edwin. I'd asked Hamlet about it, and he'd shrugged and just said people mistook him for Edwin's relative all the time. I had indeed once witnessed such a moment.

I wondered, though.

"Tell me about the happy couple," I said.

"Aye, they are quite adorable, though I would guess they are both sleeping off a good blabberin' this evening. Their families are thrilled for them, and they both have their health. I hope for many good years to come. They said they'd see me tomorrow. We'll see if they manage it."

"A honeymoon?"

"I didn't ask. I will next time."

A knock on the pub's front window jolted us both up and off the stools.

It was Wyatt.

Tom and I looked at each other as my hand went to my heart. Tom nodded at me and then went to unlock the door. Wyatt didn't come inside. Instead, he seemed to be speaking urgently to Tom.

I hurried to join them.

". . . Delaney over in Cowgate tonight? That's what I thought I heard. That's just up the way a little, right?" He was pointing.

I smelled something—a light smoky scent. I stepped around Tom and outside next to Wyatt.

"What's going on? Is something burning?" I asked.

"When I left Rosie at her flat, I was walking back this way. A fire engine sped by, and I noticed people were pointing to some smoke. They said a small old historical building went up in flames in Cowgate. I thought the chances were good that it didn't have anything to do with you, but you were my first concern. I'm glad to see you're all right. I've been trying to reach you."

I'd turned off my ringer for the dinner and had never turned it back on.

I looked at Tom. "I need to see."

"Let's go." Tom locked the door and we hurried to his car.

We could have walked up to the building in Cowgate, but that would have taken more time and we would have been cold. It was better in the car and we were there quickly.

My heart sank when I saw two fire engines and an ambulance blocking the entrance to the close that led to the Burns House. I couldn't see the small building, but even in the dark I could spot the smoke thickening the air, and it seemed to be rising exactly from where the building was located.

"Oh, no," I said as I got out of the car before Tom could come to a complete stop.

Tom and Wyatt were behind me as we ran over the cobblestones and around one of the fire engines. We could see all the way down the close now, and though there were other official vehicles in the way, the charred remains of the Burns House were visible.

It was gone. That lovely building that Edwin had renovated and then donated was now no more than a pile of ashes and burnt rafters.

"The fireplace," I said disjointedly. "Or maybe one of the food warmers."

I was trying to make sense of what I was seeing, but nothing was fitting into place.

"Delaney?" a voice said from the middle of a group of firemen.

I looked over, but had to blink away tears that had already filled my eyes to see who it was.

"Inspector Winters!" I said as I hurried to him.

He and I were friends, had known each other since I'd moved to Scotland. At first, he hadn't liked me much, but we'd grown close. He'd become close with all my Scottish family. So, when he took a sideways step and grabbed my arms to stop me from going any farther, I was thrown. Why would a friend do such a thing?

"What's going on?" I said as I sniffed away the tears.

"There's been a fire," he said as he inspected me, also sending Wyatt and Tom quick glances behind me. "Do you know something about this place?"

"I had dinner here this evening."

"Oh, Delaney," he said after a long pause.

"What's going on?" I demanded, probably far too vehemently for a police inspector's liking.

"Maybe I should have at least guessed," he said. "Come with me. Let's talk."

And, for the umpteenth time since moving to this beautiful new country, I went to the police station, this time with my husband and brother by my side. We were escorted to an interview room, one I'd come to know very well.

The news was bad, much worse than even the ruination of an old historical building.

This bad night was about to become one of the worst ever.

EIGHT

Inspector Winters told me not to say anything until he was ready. He brought us coffee and water and asked if we needed anything to eat. We told him that we didn't.

Despite the niceties, though, there was something different about the way he was behaving. I couldn't quite put my finger on it, but he wasn't his normal self. He was certainly acting more professional toward us than he had in a long time. Tom and I shared a look that told me he noticed it too.

When Inspector Winters finally sat in the chair across from me, there was a new weariness to his bones that worried me.

"You had dinner in that particular building this evening?" Inspector Winters began.

"Yes."

"*This* evening?" he repeated.

"Yes. I was invited to join a Burns group for their celebration. It's January twenty-fifth, the poet's birthday."

"Aye. What time did you arrive?"

"Hamlet came with me. We were there by five thirty."

"Where is Hamlet?"

"Home. Elias picked us up and we took him home first."

"When did you leave the party?"

"We left at about six thirty."

Wyatt raised his hand.

Inspector Winters looked at him. "Are you Delaney's brother?"

"I am. Wyatt Nichols. I'm here for a week, on business. We met briefly when I was here for the wedding."

"All right. What did you want to say?"

"If you're working on timing and such, I was walking back toward Grassmarket at around eight forty-five when I saw the fire engines drive by. I hurried to the pub, hoping to find Delaney. That's where I found her and Tom."

Inspector Winters nodded. "Why did you want to find Delaney?"

"I heard there was a fire in Cowgate. That's the name she mentioned as being the place she was going. I thought it was near-impossible that it was the same place, but I couldn't ignore my concern."

"And you were uncannily correct," Inspector Winters said.

"It's happened before," Wyatt said.

A part of me wished he'd stop talking now, but it was an interesting comment.

"What do you mean?" Inspector Winters asked.

"We're in tune with each other sometimes. I broke my ankle once, and she called immediately, telling me she thought something was wrong."

His recollection made me think of other occasions it had happened. Wyatt and I had picked up on each other's pain or emotions a time or two, nothing over-the-top, but he was correct.

Inspector Winters nodded. "Okay." He turned back to

me. "What happened at the dinner? Who was there? I need to have as many details as you can give me."

"Honestly, I wasn't there for long. It was a setup of some sort. Once that became clear, I wanted to get out of there."

"Setup? You were being set up?"

"Yes."

"Tell me everything."

Inspector Winters listened and took notes as I told him everything that had happened that evening. As I gave the names of the other people who had been in attendance, I saw something change in his eyes, but I couldn't understand which name had caused the transformation.

When I was done, I said, "Was it the fire from the fireplace?"

Inspector Winters set down his pen and then leaned back in his chair. "The fire is being investigated. We don't know how it started, but it's . . . suspicious. There . . . Delaney, there was a body inside the building."

My stomach plummeted. "Who?" I asked weakly.

"We haven't confirmed yet, but there was a wallet. The identification inside was legible. It belonged to Neil Watterton."

I hadn't known any of them before the dinner. When Hamlet and I left, I'd been angry at them all, felt used and betrayed. But, based upon that short time together, Neil Watterton had been the only one I might have considered wanting to get to know better. He'd been surprised by the revelation that I worked at the Cracked Spine. He'd been bothered by what had seemed to be behind me being invited. And he and Hamlet had shared some looks I couldn't read—I wasn't going to mention that to the police quite yet. No matter what, though, I wouldn't have wished a fiery death on any of them.

I swallowed the swell of tears that tightened the back of my throat. "Inspector Winters, that's horrible. Do you know anything else?"

He shook his head. "We don't, but the information you've given me tonight might help us solve it more quickly. Thank you. You've been a real help."

"But do you know if it was murder?"

"It's what we suspect."

I blinked, and my world went funny. I hoped I wouldn't faint. I told myself to keep it together.

"I'll know more by tomorrow, but I need to head out now and question these people." He tapped his notepad with his pencil. "Are you all going to be okay?"

I was afraid to speak again, so I just nodded as confidently as possible.

The three of us watched Inspector Winters stand and leave the interview room. We were wide-eyed and suddenly abandoned. As unobtrusively as possible, I took a deep breath and again told myself to keep it together.

"You helped, Sis, you really did. I don't think they had anything but a burnt building, a body, and an ID. This was good," Wyatt said.

"Are you all right?" Tom asked.

"I am. I am fine, but it's all pretty awful."

"Aye."

"At least you weren't arrested," Wyatt said, but then he cleared his throat. "Sorry, that was inappropriate."

My big-lug brother was still who he was. I was glad he was here, and that he and Tom, and everyone else I cared so much about, were all fine.

And, if I were being honest with myself, I too was pretty

darn glad I hadn't been arrested. But maybe it was too early to feel completely confident about that part. Time would tell.

We showed ourselves out of the interview room and then the station, the officer at the front sending us a tired wave.

"Home?" Tom asked when we were inside his car.

"Only if you don't need to go back to the pub," I said.

"I don't."

"Sounds good to me," Wyatt said.

"How was your dinner?" I asked him.

"Rosie and I had a good time," he said somberly. It didn't seem like a good moment to talk about having fun.

"Yes, she is the best," I said, exhaustion falling over me like a blanket.

"Home?" Tom asked again.

"Home," I said.

There was no place like it, particularly tonight.

NINE

In recent months, our meetings had become much less frequent, our complete staff meetings almost nonexistent. We'd managed a few things via group texts and phone calls, but for the most part the bookshop ran like the proverbial well-oiled machine. Today, however, Edwin, Rosie, Hamlet, Hector, and I were all there. And the sign on the door had been flipped to CLOSED.

Yet again, but with Hamlet's help this time, I recounted what had happened at the dinner. We hadn't heard if the body had been conclusively identified as Neil Watterton, but the burned building with the person's remains inside it was all over the news.

"Neil was very young when I was involved with the group," Edwin said. "He was friendly and seemed happy, smiling all the time. He loved books. He was a librarian when I knew him. He was always mild-mannered and minded his own business, from all I could tell."

"Where did he work?" I asked.

"At the National Library," Edwin said.

"Och, 'tis a wonderful place," Rosie said as she petted Hector.

"I can't believe I've never been," I said.

"I'm surprised," Edwin said.

Hamlet cleared his throat. "I've been, and I met Neil there."

Relief spread through me when Hamlet spoke up. I'd wanted to know what I'd seen shared between the two of them, but I wanted him to be the one to mention it, share the details.

"Aye?" Rosie said.

Hamlet nodded. "He helped me with some research a few months ago, for a class project."

"Did he know you worked here?" Edwin asked.

Hamlet shrugged. "It never came up. I was . . . it was just a class project."

We looked at him.

"Lad?" Edwin prompted. "Is there more?"

"He was a nice man. I'm sorry if he is truly the man who was killed."

There seemed to be more—an airy empty space left at the end of Hamlet's words. We looked at him again and waited, but he didn't say anything else, and Edwin didn't push. None of us did.

"Well, I sure would like to know what Charles's motive was for getting me, us, to the dinner last night. I don't believe that it was just because 'it was time.' There was more going on than any of us must have understood, and I'm none too happy about the cloak-and-dagger. It might all end up being things done with good intentions, but I want to know if something happened last night while we were there that might have led to murder," I said.

"Aye, just be careful in your search," Edwin said. When Rosie sent him raised eyebrows, he continued. "I'd like to know too."

I pulled out my phone. "Well, I already found a little something." Everyone sat forward as I showed them the screen. "Malcolm is about to open a new bookshop, in Cowgate."

It was a small article talking about the upcoming grand opening of Malcolm's Books. Malcolm Campbell had been out of the bookselling business for approximately twenty years, but now he was coming back, with a bookshop perfect for any bibliophile, at least according to the article.

"Good for him," Edwin said.

"I'm only surprised it took him this long," Rosie added.

"I might visit the shop," I said. Before anyone could protest, I added, "I really believe that Malcolm is no danger to me. He was genuinely caught off guard and unhappy about what the others had done. I'll be careful."

"Aye," Edwin said. "Maybe take someone."

I nodded. "Okay. And where is Clarinda's office? I'd like to talk to her again too."

Edwin hesitated, but then said, "I'll jot down the address for you."

"Clarinda Creston," Rosie said, as if she needed to test out how it sounded.

"Donald Rigalee was the man she defended, the killer." I looked at Rosie. I'd been so intrigued by the news about Malcolm's bookshop that I hadn't thought about looking closer at Rigalee.

"Aye, he works on the docks. He killed two fishermen. Clarinda ended up getting him off on investigation procedure mistakes, technicalities, but that's all I ken, lass," Rosie said.

"How about Charles? Where does he work?"

Rosie looked at Edwin.

"I know you are worried," I said. "But I'm careful. I'm still angry about being set up for something, and now I wonder if it ultimately had anything to do with murder. I'll find Charles, even if you don't want to tell me where to look."

"I know where Charles is," Edwin said finally. "I'll write down that address too."

Hector, seeming to want to contribute, turned on Rosie's lap, sent me a nod, and then curled back into a ball. He was back in his sweater, and his mere existence was enough to make any bad day brighter.

Hamlet peered up from his phone. "We have news."

We all looked at him.

He turned his gaze downward again. "'The body has been positively identified as Neil Watterton, Edinburgh resident for all his life and employee of the National Library of Scotland.'"

"Oh, I was hoping. . . . It's all so awful," I said.

Hamlet continued, "Police suspect foul play and are investigating it as a murder." He scrolled some. "'A witness on the scene reported that they saw Mr. Watterton enter the building at around seven thirty with another person.'"

"Man or woman?" I asked.

Hamlet scrolled more, swallowed hard. "It doesn't say."

I put my hand on Hamlet's arm. This was clearly upsetting him too.

"You and I were gone by about six thirty. Malcolm left immediately before us. I can't imagine the party continued. They probably cleared out quickly," I said.

"Probably."

"He went back tae gather something he'd forgotten?" Rosie offered.

"Who knows?" I said. "And who knows who he was with?"

"The killer," Rosie said ominously.

"Not clear yet," Edwin said. "Delaney, I know you're bothered by what happened, but I feel it's only responsible of me to remind you that a killer is on the loose."

I couldn't find the words to tell him, tell them, that now it seemed even more important to understand what was going on. I just nodded, tried to give him a look that told him not to worry, but I just couldn't let any of this go yet.

"Aye," Edwin said thoughtfully, reading my expression. "I also want you to remember this: Malcolm was as angry with me as a person could be. In his mind, I was the person who burned down his building, his bookshop, ruined his livelihood. I don't think he was ever convinced otherwise. That would not be an anger to take lightly."

"Och, aye, I have something aboot that," Rosie said.

"Aye?" Edwin's eyebrows rose.

"It was easy tae find." She pointed to my phone. "Just search for 'Malcolm Campbell bookshop fire.' There was an article, written a few months after the fire."

"I don't remember that," Edwin said.

"I didnae either. It was not front-page news by then, though. I found it last night when I was winding down, just looking at my mobile."

I searched as she instructed and found the article. I read it silently and then said aloud, "It was finally concluded that it was a random arson and perhaps something accidental. It was located right next to a close, one where a group of homeless people set up camp. It was thought that perhaps the fire was started by one of them, but that's about as much as was ever considered. There was nothing further."

"Not an electrical fire, then?" Edwin said.

"Doesn't appear so." I saved the link on my phone. I'd be curious about that location too.

Our bookshop had been closed too long, and someone tapped on the front window. Rosie stood and opened the door.

Edwin left shortly afterward, and I sat with Hamlet as we digested the terrible news.

"What are you going to do?" Hamlet asked.

"I'm so angry about Charles and Clarinda's manipulations to get us to that dinner, I need to know more about what's behind it. A man was ultimately killed, and that might not have anything to do with us or with Edwin, but I think Clarinda is who I want to talk to first."

"Want to call her?"

"Nope. I want to surprise her in her office. If she's there, she'll surely be upset about Neil, but I still want to know what was going on."

"Let me know what I can do to help."

"I will," I said.

I gathered my things and, with what I thought was Rosie's blessing, went to talk to one of the more famous criminal defense solicitors in town.

A conversation was probably much better than needing her services.

TEN

Clarinda was in court, according to the receptionist at her firm, which was located right off the Royal Mile. The old brick exterior of the building made me expect something quite different than the modernly furnished and decorated interior. Behind the receptionist, a group was gathered around a conference table inside a glass-walled room. A heated discussion was under way, but I couldn't make out any of the words, though the receptionist caught me trying to listen.

"Anything else?" she asked. She'd told me that Clarinda wasn't working a closed court case today and I could probably catch her at the courthouse if the matter was something that couldn't wait for a return phone call.

"No, I'm good. Thank you." I smiled and turned to head back outside.

The High Court of Justiciary was located in another beautiful historic building, made of pale brown and yellow stones. As you approached the tall front doors, you were greeted by a statue of philosopher and historian David Hume. He held a blank tablet on his knee, to represent skepticism. I was all about being skeptical where lawyers were involved, though I always appreciated having a good one when I needed it.

The inside reminded me of other courthouses I'd experienced, though this one immediately felt more formal because of the garments and wigs on many of the people walking around. The solicitors were required to wear what they called court dress, which meant robes and white wigs—perhaps a way to create an appearance of equality.

"I'm here to see Clarinda Creston," I said to the receptionist.

"See her? Are you here for court?" the elderly woman asked. She would have reminded me of Rosie, but she didn't smile quite as easily.

"No, I was hoping to catch her on break or maybe when she's done. Her office sent me over." I cleared my throat.

"Aye? Well." She looked at her computer screen. "Room 111, then. Maybe she'll take a break soon."

"Right."

"Go over there, through security."

I nodded. "Thank you."

I wasn't deterred. I wanted answers, and no matter what, I was out to get them. Still, I was glad I didn't have a metal nail file in my bag as it was searched and then sent through a detector.

Room 111 was a small courtroom, with only two benches along the back for observers. It would have been impossible for me to enter without being noticed. There were only three other people inside: the judge, a woman who peered at me over glasses on the tip of her nose; Clarinda, who, momentarily, seemed rattled to see me; and a man sitting at a table near a podium Clarinda stood behind. He lifted his eyebrows at me even more than the judge did.

"Can I help you?" the judge asked me.

"May I just watch?" I said.

The judge shrugged. "This is just a calendar-setting session, but if you'd like."

"My Lady," Clarinda said to the judge. "She is an acquaintance of mine. I suspect she's here to talk to me when we're finished."

The judge looked at me again. "Is that correct?"

"Yes."

"That's fine."

There wasn't much going on, as far as I could tell. It seemed to be basic time and date planning, though I didn't spot a clerk anywhere and the judge made her own notes. It was over before long. Police officers appeared from behind a doorway and escorted the man out through it as the judge adjourned the session and Clarinda came through to the gallery.

She took off her wig. "Delaney."

I stood. "Do you have some time we could talk?"

"My time is actually very valuable."

"Well, I figure you owe me."

She nodded a moment later. "I don't disagree. Let's step into a room. It's too cold to go outside, and I'll have to get back to work on the half hour."

The room she took us to was furnished with a four-person table and rich beautiful wood-paneled walls, but it was tiny. When we both sat down, it seemed a miracle that our knees didn't touch.

"I'm sure you've heard?" I said.

"What about the fire? Neil?" Clarinda asked, her tone clipped.

"Well. Yes."

"I have. And I'm fit to be tied. Someone killed Neil, and though I'm a criminal defense attorney, I will do all I can to see the killer comes to justice." She paused as she seemed to gather herself. "Someone killed Neil? It's all so very . . . horrible."

She was different than when I'd met her in the Burns House, the tam o'shanter atop her curls. She was serious, as would be necessary for her job. I had the notion that the time she spent in the Burns House were times she could let down her guard, relax, unwind.

Still, even though a part of me wanted to tell her I was sorry for her loss, I wasn't completely convinced that she hadn't played a part in it.

"When did you hear?" I asked.

"Last night, when police inspectors came to talk to me. It was awful. Delaney, why are you here? What is it that you'd like to ask me? You sought me out, today of all days, so I think something is weighing on your mind. Do you need an attorney?"

I hadn't even gone there. "No, I don't. Clarinda, though I just met you all last night, I recognized that Neil was a good guy too. When my friend and I left the dinner, it was because I was upset and didn't like what I thought was manipulation in getting me there. It was obvious that those sorts of intentions hadn't been made clear to Neil, and now he's dead. I want— need—to know what in the world was going on. Why did Charles suggest to invite me? Before you answer, I know you're an attorney and you know the law better than most everyone, but I'm truly not here about my feelings getting hurt. What I want to know is, did any contention occur that might have led to Neil's death, and is that something my friends and I need to be aware of, even be on the lookout for?"

Clarinda cocked her head and blinked at me a couple of times. "We all think everything is about us."

"Excuse me?"

"No, no, it's not bad, it's just the way it is. We can only judge circumstances via our own perspectives. There's nothing wrong with it, but I just needed a second to see things from your perspective, walk in your shoes, if you will. That's all I was doing."

I wanted to tell her that whatever it was she was doing, it sure looked like stalling to me, but I just waited patiently.

She took a deep breath through her nose and then let it out.

She said, "The history of our little group is spotted with some tragedies. At this point, a superstitious person might think we are cursed or haunted or some such thing, but it's simply the human experience. Last night, before the murder, it was all simply a terrible miscue of some sort. Aye, I knew that Charles had suggested you, but when I put it all together after we spoke on the phone, I thought it would end up being a pleasant surprise for Malcolm, not something . . . well, not how he reacted."

"Why? I know some of the history myself, Clarinda, and Malcolm was pretty upset at my boss many years ago. In fact, my boss might have thought Malcolm would never forgive him. Why would you think it would be a good surprise?" I worked hard not to sound incredulous.

"Because, Delaney, Malcolm had forgiven Edwin MacAlister. He'd moved on. He's opening a new bookshop and, even all these years later, he wanted to find a way to be friends again with Edwin."

"He did?" I said. "I'm having a hard time believing that."

"Why? Because *you* hold grudges forever?"

"No, Clarinda, because of the way Malcolm behaved. He left the dinner in a huff!"

"Well, that *was* unexpected, I have to admit." She frowned and held my gaze a moment. "But understand this: Not long ago Malcolm told me and Charles frankly that he wanted himself and Edwin to reacquaint. He spoke of time moving quickly and his memories of the good things, et cetera." She paused, and, for dramatic effect I presumed, said, "'Auld Lang Syne' and all."

I wanted to roll my eyes, but I didn't. "So Neil didn't know about Malcolm's wishes to mend fences with Edwin?"

Clarinda shook her head. "I don't think so. Neil is younger than the three of us. We all spend time together, but Neil isn't with us as much. And, aye, we spoke about bringing new blood into the group, someone younger and specifically female. I didn't mind being the only woman, but I thought it sounded like a brilliant idea. No one wanted to hurt you, Delaney. No one wanted to use you—aye, I suppose that's not completely true, but intentions weren't bad. We wanted a pleasant surprise for Malcolm."

"Even Neil saw that it wasn't pleasant."

Clarinda took another deep breath. "Aye, but we would have explained it all if everyone had just stayed put."

"And now Neil's dead."

Clarinda snapped her gaze back up to mine again. "Neil's death has nothing to do with anything that went on at the dinner last night."

"How can you be so sure?"

"When you left, the rest of us left shortly thereafter. Neil left first, not in a huff as much as just perplexed. Charles helped me with most of the initial cleanup. I was going to have the young men come in today and finish up. Then we left too. Before you ask me, aye, the fire in the fireplace was well put out, and I made sure all the food appliances were unplugged. It's an old building, and I normally keep a lot of papers inside it. I'm very used to making sure the fire hazard is minimal. We all have keys to the building, and Neil was no exception. He was spotted entering it with another person, and, well, Neil was known to take a date or two there. I suspect the police will figure out that a woman was with him. He was a sought-after bachelor, Delaney. You saw him. He was a handsome man and a lovely one too." Tears pooled in her eyes, but she set her jaw firmly. She wasn't going to cry.

"You think he was killed by a date?"

She shrugged ever so slightly. "Well, I simply don't know, but whoever was with him might at least shed more light on who the killer was. Neil was a good man, a librarian, for goodness' sake. But we all have secrets, and I assume he was no exception. These are the types of things I see all the time. People never share all of who they are. Never."

"Do you know any of his secrets?" I asked.

Clarinda shrugged again. "I don't, but remember what I do for a living. I have to be careful. What I've told you today are the facts as I know them to be. It's a murder. I'm not at liberty to dive any deeper or speculate. You understand that, don't you?"

"Sure," I said.

I also didn't think she'd been completely truthful with me. But she had no obligation to be. For all I knew, she could have lied about everything, which would have been her right, of course. I wasn't a representative of the court; she hadn't made any sort of oath to me.

And, really, if anyone could learn how to lie, wouldn't it be a defense attorney?

She stood, prompting the end of the meeting. She walked me back out to the front, but then turned to me as we stood near the security officers.

"I'm torn up because of what happened to Neil. It is one of the worst things I've ever experienced, but I have people who count on me. That's why I'm here today. Don't think I'm okay with any of it. I promise you, though, no one ever meant to make you feel uncomfortable."

"Thank you, Clarinda," I said.

There were no further words of farewell, no plans to get together again. Clarinda and I weren't going to be friends.

I watched her make her way back toward the courtrooms. I didn't leave until I saw her put her white wig back over her brown curls.

ELEVEN

Stay alert! Don't let someone's words blind you from their behavior. . . .

The bookish voice spoke the second I was outside the Justiciary building. I'd read the words not long ago. They were from a self-help, inspirational writer named Steve Maraboli. I'd read a couple of his books, seen a few videos. I knew his voice, so this wasn't one my mind had conjured. It was a memory of the real thing.

I looked back at the building. Had I missed something of Clarinda's behavior that I should have paid attention to?

I really didn't think so. Maybe it was someone else's behavior.

"Who?" I said quietly to myself. "What am I missing?"

No answers came, but that's the way intuition, gut feelings, sometimes worked, with a murkiness that hopefully made you pay attention just in case that big moment was about to reveal itself.

I did walk away from the courthouse with a few small regrets. Maybe I *had* been overly sensitive about what had happened at dinner. Maybe Edwin's sharing of his story had set me up to be too receptive or defensive.

But the part that was keeping me curious about everyone wasn't my gut instinct, it was something much, much stronger. More like a compulsion.

I walked up to the Royal Mile back toward Grassmarket, deep in my own thoughts, when I happened to see something that changed my course so thoroughly it seemed like a small tectonic shift at my feet.

Hanging—though only barely because one of the chains was broken—above a door just inside another close was a sign that read STRANGELOVE, YOUR FORTUNE TELLER.

I hesitated. I bit my lip as I considered the sign and the narrow door. There was nothing welcoming about either of them.

"Couldn't be . . . ," I mumbled to myself. I didn't think my cursory internet search had mentioned psychic abilities, but I hadn't dug deep.

I looked around. The only people paying me any attention were those I was standing in the way of, but no one seemed to be in too much of a rush.

I stepped out of the main walkway and into the close.

I had never seen this sign, this door before. I'd passed it hundreds of times by now, but my attention and my eyes had never been directed this way.

However, a déjà vu spread through me. I'd entered a door inside a dingy close before and had experienced one of the strangest things I'd ever been through. I still couldn't explain it. This wasn't the same close and definitely not the same door.

I lifted my fist and knocked.

I was just about to try the doorknob when a voice called from inside, "Com'in."

The door was unlocked, and it opened easily. A wave of

incense-thickened smoke greeted me and made me cough once. I cleared the smoke with my hand. It smelled like jasmine.

"Hello?" I said.

"Right 'ere, dear. Com'in, com'in."

At first, I just saw shapes, lines and curves, and some—though very little—lighting. But with just one step inside the door, the shapes took on definition.

It was a small room, about the same size as the conference room inside the courthouse, but made more compact by large swaths of fabric hanging on the walls. It was impossible to know if there was a window underneath any of the heavy dark material.

A round table with four cushioned chairs took up the middle space, and a purple-hazed crystal ball was situated in the center of it.

A woman sat on the far side, her robed arms atop the table, her arthritis-mangled hands folded in front of her. She was small and hunched some, with long gray hair falling over her narrow shoulders. The purple light from the crystal ball lit her wrinkled face. She smiled knowingly, and I couldn't help but return the smile.

The entire scene could have been from a fortune-telling 101 instruction manual, but even though it felt like forced theater, I liked it.

"Close the door, lass," the woman said. Her accent was as thick as they come, but her voice was thin with age. "'Ave a seat."

I did as instructed and then looked at her over the crystal ball. She was so tiny I had to sit up as tall as I could.

"I'll tell yer fortune, yer verra future." She waved her bent fingers over the crystal ball. "My fee a mere twenty pounds."

I reached into my bag but hesitated. I didn't believe in these sorts of things, but I did believe in the power of suggestion. I didn't want her to tell me something that would change my happiness, even mar it one tiny bit.

"My name is Delaney," I said, my hand still inside my bag. "May I ask your name?"

"Aye. Letitia Strangelove." She placed her hands back on the table. I was sure the light in the ball dimmed some. "I come from women who see things. Forever. We trace back tae the beginning of time. Ye're in good hands."

"I believe that, but I don't want my fortune told." I pulled my wallet from the bag. "I will pay you, but I just have some questions I wondered if you might answer."

"Aye?" Her smile fell into a straight line. "Place the money on the table between us. Ye'll ask yer questions, and if I answer, I'll take the money. If I don't, ye'll take it back."

"I don't mind paying you even if you don't or can't answer. I'm taking up your time."

"Och, 'tis the only way, lass. Place the money on the table."

I set the bills next to the crystal ball. Letitia eyed the money a moment. "What's yer first question?"

"Is your real name Letitia Strangelove?" I asked.

"It is."

"And do you, by chance, know a Dora Strangelove?"

Letitia sat up. "Why do ye ask?"

"It's a very long story."

Letitia scooted the money back to me. "Tell me."

Though she didn't turn on more lights or hide the crystal ball, Letitia and the room transformed. She was suddenly less ethereal and more just human.

And I was stuck. I hadn't even told my coworkers about the

birth certificate—well, asked them about it. I didn't want to betray any confidence.

But I'd touched a nerve with Letitia, that was obvious, and it was a nerve I wanted to explore.

"I work in a local bookshop, and it's a name I found on a provenance report. She was at one time the owner of a book we purchased. I have my suspicions about whether or not the book was purchased on the up-and-up. I wanted to talk to her." I was impressed by my lie.

Letitia deflated again. "Aye?"

"Yes."

"I don't know a Dora Strangelove," she said sadly. "But I used to. A long time ago."

I waited. I sensed she was gathering memories. I was right.

"She was . . . aye, I knew her when she was a young lass, but she left, disappeared many years anon," Letitia said.

"How long?"

Letitia didn't hesitate. "Twenty-two years ago, back in 2000."

Okay, so Hamlet had been three years old back then, or would be later in that year. But so what?

"I'm sorry," I said. "It sounds like you have missed her."

Letitia frowned and then shook herself some. "It's been a long time, lass."

"How was she related to you?"

Letitia paused a long time. "She was my granddaughter."

"Oh, I'm so sorry. What do you think happened to her? What were the circumstances behind her disappearance?"

A weariness clouded her eyes. "Lass, it's been a long, long time. I've no energy to remember those days anymore. It's best I don't."

"Of course. I understand. I'm sorry."

Letitia nodded. "A lad stopped by to inquire about her recently, and I've sensed her lately, as if she's been around. Ye havenae seen her, 'ave ye?"

"I haven't. I'm sorry. I'm going to keep looking for her, though. I'll let you know. Can you tell me about the person who stopped by recently?" Could it have been Hamlet?

"Nothing to tell. Just more misplaced hope. Would you tell me, though, if ye find her?"

"Yes."

"That would be lovely," Letitia said, sounding as if she might be working hard to keep her emotions in check. "Ye said ye work at a bookshop. Which one?"

"The Cracked Spine."

"The one in Grassmarket?"

"Yes."

"Not far, then. Good tae know."

"Very close." I had a vision of her walking in and somehow recognizing Hamlet. They'd be happily reunited. It didn't seem likely, but it played out in full Technicolor in my head, nevertheless. I listened for a bookish voice to tell me if I was making all the right connections. Could this be Hamlet's biological great-grandmother? That would be something. But the bookish voices were quiet, and it didn't feel like my place to spring Hamlet's existence on this old woman. I didn't know enough about any of it to say anything anyway.

"Och, ye see things too?" she said, bringing me out of my reverie.

"What?"

"Just then. The way yer eyes unfocused, the quirk o' yer mouth. I ken the look. Ye see things too. Ye ken ye do."

"No, not really. I just have a vivid imagination," I said.

Letitia leaned forward a small bit. "It's verra close tae the same thing, just a mere wish away."

I laughed. "I'm not sure it's a wish I want to make."

She nodded. "Smart lass. Once ye cross it, there's no going back." Letitia paused. "Now, I dinnae want yer money, but let me take a look." She scooted the money back toward me and then lifted her hands above the crystal ball again.

"I—"

"Shh. Hush."

I froze in place, though a big part of me wanted to leave. I really didn't want to be told anything that could change the magic my life had been since moving to Scotland.

Letitia smiled only a few moments later. "All is well, lass. Ye have a lovely life, and it's only going tae continue."

"Good to hear." I laughed.

Letitia lifted a finger. "There's one tiny thing ye need tae be aware of, though."

Uh-oh. "Oh?"

"Aye, but all I can see is something I cannae understand, except that maybe it's because ye work at a bookshop. Ye need tae be careful of men named Robert Burns, like the poet." Letitia shrugged. "It's what I see, but sometimes things arenae as clear as we would like. Nevertheless, there is no doot in my mind that all will be well with you. Ye are a lucky lass."

"I am."

"Still, take heed my words: ye need tae take caution around men named Robert Burns. Or mebee just Robert or Burns. Or poets?" She glanced at the crystal ball again. "I've nothing clear, but there is a distinct darkness with that name, and I want ye tae take care."

"I will," I said, bothered by the fact that it seemed she'd hit upon something that currently meant something in my life, something potentially valid.

"Take yer money, lass. Ye've given me a pocketful of hope today, always more valuable than a pocket o' coins. The memories arenae all good, but some of them are, and if ye find Dora, ye'll let me know."

"I hope it's not false hope."

"No such thing. It's just a matter of the stars coming together. Sometimes they do, sometimes they don't. We do our best either way."

"That's the truth."

I didn't take the money, couldn't have even if it had been the thing to do. We told each other thank you before I left and hurried back to the bookshop.

I was going to talk to Edwin about the birth certificate today, come hell or high water. Little did I know that either of those would have been much less awful than what I was met with instead.

TWELVE

Inspector Winters was inside the Cracked Spine, speaking in serious tones to Rosie and Hamlet. It took only a moment for me to key in on the fact that something was wrong.

Even the air inside seemed icier than normal. Absently, I picked up Hector as he greeted me and carried him to the desk. Rosie sat in her chair, Hamlet sat in one he'd brought up from the back, and Inspector Winters stood, wielding power, it seemed, over them both.

I didn't like it.

"What's going on?" I asked.

"Inspector Winters wants tae arrest Hamlet," Rosie said.

"It's not . . ." Inspector Winters said. He glared impatiently. "I just want him to come to the station to answer some questions."

"What questions?"

"If I could tell you that, we wouldn't have to go to the station."

"Just ask the questions," I said. "He doesn't have to leave."

"Look," Inspector Winters said. "I came here in good faith, by myself, because we are friends. But I'm also a police inspector, and something has come up. I need to talk to Hamlet, in an official setting."

"About what? Can you tell us that?"

"It's aboot the fire," Rosie said.

I looked at Hamlet, who shrugged.

I said to him, "You need an attorney."

"I don't think I do," Hamlet said.

Inspector Winters added, "I think it would be a good idea."

We all turned to him. This was more serious than I'd thought, and I'd sensed it was pretty serious.

"Okay," Hamlet said as he stood. "I'll go."

"I'll call Jack." Rosie stood and grabbed her mobile from her pocket. Jack had been Edwin's attorney for things that had come up over the years, but I thought he was in Glasgow. I didn't say anything. Maybe Rosie knew something I didn't.

"Very good. Have the solicitor meet us at the station. Come along, Hamlet," Inspector Winters said.

In a confused stupor, Rosie and I watched Hamlet leave with Inspector Winters. It took a small bark from Hector to pull us out of it.

"Are you calling Jack?" I asked Rosie.

"I'm calling Edwin. Jack's too far away."

About an hour earlier, I'd spoken to one of the best defense attorneys in town, but the conflicts of interest regarding her representing Hamlet drowned out any possibility of asking her assistance.

"What else did Inspector Winters say?" I asked when Rosie had ended the call with Edwin.

She shook her head and sat in her chair again. "Just that there were some questions as to Hamlet's whereabouts last night."

"What did Hamlet say?"

"That he went home after you two left the dinner party."

"Yes, Elias dropped him there first. I could have vouched for that." I looked out the front window, but Inspector Winters and Hamlet were long gone.

"Aye, but it was afterwards that Winters was wondering about."

"And Hamlet said he was at home, but he lives alone, so no one could vouch for him? Something like that?"

Rosie frowned and shook her head. "Hamlet said he didn't remember specifically."

"Well, that's possible, right?" It didn't really seem all that plausible, but he might have forgotten, I supposed.

"Lass, remember when I called ye last night, after I heard about the news of the fire?"

"Of course. I told you we were fine."

"I called Hamlet too, but he didnae answer."

"It was late by the time you called me. Maybe he was asleep."

Rosie gave me a long look. It would have been rare that Hamlet wasn't up until at least midnight.

"I know, I know," I said. "Did you ever ask him why he didn't answer?"

"I did. He said he didnae hear or see the call come in."

It was all possible. Wasn't it?

"What did Edwin say?"

"He'll be here in a moment."

Edwin arrived at the bookshop with at least a little good news. He'd rung another attorney he knew who would represent Hamlet fully. Lena Bilot was leaving the courthouse and heading toward Inspector Winters's police station. I wondered if she and I had crossed paths when I'd been at the courthouse.

It was a relief to know that *someone* would be there for

Hamlet, but once that task was taken care of, we couldn't help but dwell on the fact that *we* couldn't be there for him. Even I wouldn't try to barge my way into his questioning, though I sure considered it.

As we waited for news, Rosie and I took care of the customers. Edwin disappeared over to the dark side for a time, but I didn't know if he was visiting his office or the warehouse. The warehouse used to be his space. Now it was mine too, but since finding the birth certificate, I didn't like the idea of him being in there without me, even though I had hidden it well.

When he returned to this side and when business slowed—and Hamlet still hadn't called or returned—I hurried over to the dark side myself. I went directly to the locked drawer and opened it. The certificate was still there, right on top.

It was either time to put it back in its hiding spot in the file drawer or ask Edwin and Rosie about it. I stared at it a long time. It might not be any big deal, but it might be. There was a chance Edwin would be angry with me for not just talking to him first, but I decided I didn't want to leave Rosie out of it.

The fortune-teller had told me everything in my life was continuing on a good course, but what did she know, really? The allusion to Robert Burns could have come about simply because I told her I worked at a bookshop in Scotland. Or it could have come from something else.

I shook my head. It was ridiculous to think about what a fortune-teller had told me. I didn't believe in such things.

"Get it over with," I said to myself.

I grabbed the birth certificate and took it back over to the other side.

THIRTEEN

Edwin watched me descend the stairs on the light side.

"What's wrong, lass?" he asked.

Rosie appeared from the back with Hector in her arms.

"Nothing," I said.

"I don't believe you," Edwin said after he exchanged a look with Rosie. "You look upset."

"Aye, ye do," Rosie said. "We're all worried about Hamlet."

I took the last step. I was holding the certificate next to my chest. "I'm sorry. I don't mean to be upset. I am worried about Hamlet, but I found something, and it's been weighing on my mind. Maybe I should have just ignored it but . . ."

"Lass, there's nothing you can't tell us," Edwin said.

"I don't know," I said.

"Nothing," Rosie said. "I'll flip the sign."

I appreciated them taking the moment seriously and closing the shop, but I thought that might make it worse, make me more anxious.

"Do you mind just staying open? If Hamlet comes back, I don't want him greeted by a locked door. I don't want him to hear what I have to say, though, so we might have to abruptly stop the conversation."

They looked at me with almost identical expressions of concern.

"Let's go to the back." Edwin gestured for Rosie and me to lead the way.

Once we were seated, I felt like I'd made a terrible mistake. What right did I have to do this? Though I'd certainly felt like I had a right to know my biological grandfather, that was about me. This wasn't. This was none of my business.

The truth is rarely pure and never simple.

I smiled wearily at Oscar Wilde's bookish voice. It was a familiar quote, so maybe the words were just another memory, not a voice. Nevertheless, it was notably accurate.

"I found something," I said again. "I don't think I was supposed to find it."

"Where?" Edwin asked.

"In one of the file drawers in the warehouse."

"There is nothing there that is intended to be off-limits to you, lass," Edwin continued.

"I don't know."

"Lass, just tell us. Ye're scaring me a wee bit," Rosie said.

I nodded. "It's nothing to be scared about. I'm sorry. I'm just worried I'm stepping over a line, but unfortunately, and no matter how much I told myself to ignore it, I can't seem to let it go. I found a birth certificate."

"Aye?" Rosie said.

Edwin's expression went from concern and question to understanding. "I see."

Rosie glanced at Edwin, at me, and then back at Edwin. "Aye?"

Edwin nodded.

Rosie still seemed confused, but I didn't think Edwin was surprised in the least as I slid the piece of paper in his direction.

He lifted it and shared it with Rosie. A moment later, she also showed recognition in the form of a sad smile.

"Ye kept it in the warehouse?" she asked Edwin.

"I don't remember doing so, but it looks that way. There was a time when I thought we might want to do something more with it."

"Aye," Rosie said. "Meebe."

Together they looked at the certificate, seeming to both silently reminisce. I didn't want to disturb them, and just showing it to them had not only taken us to a point of no return, but somehow freed me. I still had questions. I held back, though. They'd come up for air in a minute.

Edwin was first. "You know who this belongs to?"

"I assumed Hamlet."

"That's correct," Edwin said. "By the way, his first name matching mine is simply coincidence. He and I aren't related."

"Okay. Does he know about it?"

"Och, oh no, lass, and ye willnae be telling him, aye?" Rosie said.

"Not if you don't think I should," I said, hoping Rosie might reevaluate her position. That had been my intention, after all, but maybe they could convince me otherwise. No matter what, though, I decided that if they truly didn't want Hamlet to see this now, even at his grown-up age, I would abide by their wishes.

Edwin frowned and his eyes unfocused as he looked off to the side a moment. He turned back to Rosie. "It might be time."

"Edwin! No, we cannae."

"If he searched public records, he could find this himself, though, couldn't he?" I asked. I'd acquired the legible copy easily.

Edwin sent me a slanted look. "Well, not really. He doesn't know of any connection to Edison or Strangelove. He thinks his last name is McIntyre, and I made sure it was made legal."

"Why is it a secret from him? I mean, if you want to tell me." I paused. Oh boy, did I hope they wanted to share. "I also understand if this is none of my business and that perhaps my curiosity has just gotten the best of me, but why doesn't he know the details on his birth certificate? Why the secrecy? Is his birthday really in August, not October like we've been celebrating?"

They didn't want to answer, but soon enough they nodded.

"Aye," Rosie said.

"Did you have another, different birth certificate manufactured? Don't people need them for things like driver's licenses and such?"

"Edwin has a friend . . . ," Rosie said. "At the records department."

"Why would you feel the need to lie to him?"

The bell above the front door jingled. Rosie made a move to stand, but Edwin put his hand on her arm. "It's your story to tell if you want to. I'll take care of the customers."

I was relieved that it hadn't been Hamlet who'd come inside but was surprised by Edwin's offer. He rarely helped customers anymore. I was even more surprised by the fact that this was Rosie's story to tell. I'd assumed it would be more about Edwin than her.

Edwin welcomed the customer, a middle-aged man, and they began to explore the shelves. I waited for Rosie to decide if she was going to continue. I thought I saw a pain cloud her normally cheery eyes. A part of me wanted to take the certificate, run back over to the dark side, and hide it again, but there was no going back. Either she would tell me or not. Of course, I hoped for the former but would accept the latter.

"Lass, ye ken I was married, aye?" she said quietly.

"I do. Your husband died."

"Aye, he did. After he passed, I found out he'd lived something of a double life."

"Oh, that had to be rough news."

"It was. Devastateen. I was broken apart, but once I moved past the shock, I became curious. I began to search." She smiled. "It was Christmas Day, 2005, a year after Paul had died, that I discovered some things. Similar to this moment, I was sent a birth certificate. My husband had fathered a daughter, someone I don't think he ever even met."

"You found her?" I prompted when she fell into silent thought again.

Rosie shook her head. "No, lass, I never did. She'd disappeared from her family."

The pieces came together in my head. It couldn't be. But it made sense, at least with what I currently knew. "Dora?" I nodded at the certificate that Rosie now held.

"Aye. Dora," she said. "Her mother was part of a family of women, the Strangeloves. They are . . . I guess I wouldnae call them gypsies, but they called themselves fortune-tellers. My Paul had a relationship with Dora's mother. Her name was Wilma. I found Wilma and her mother—"

"Is Wilma's mother's name Letitia?" I asked.

"Aye." Rosie's eyebrows came together. "Ye've seen her place up on the Royal Mile?"

"I have. I spoke to Letitia."

"Oh. Did ye tell her about this?"

"No."

"Good. I dinnae think they know to find me here, but I have-nae been hiding, just . . . well . . ." Rosie sighed. "Oh, lass, it's a terrible sad story. I believe it was Letitia who sent me the birth certificate, to my home, but she never admitted as much. I think they had been searching for Dora for a number of years and they heard about Paul's death, hoped I might have learned something and would be more willing to share once he was gone. I dinnae think that Wilma cared as much about finding Dora as Letitia did, but it was all to no avail, and Wilma's dead now, I believe. When Edwin started to help me search and we found Hamlet instead, a few years later, living on the streets in such a terrible way, we did what we could to guide him here, and then the rest of everything happened so that we could take care of him."

"He's your husband's biological grandson?" I asked.

"Aye." Rosie smiled. "From what I could figure out. We only have Dora's birth certificate where Wilma named him as the father. We've done no DNA, though we've considered it." Rosie laughed once. "I still have Paul's old brush with hair in it. Anyway, I don't know if Dora has ever resurfaced anywhere."

"I don't think she has." I paused. "Why didn't you just tell Hamlet the truth?"

"A few reasons," she said. "Dora's disappearance was suspicious, but I really don't know the details or what came of it. The Strangelove women don't like to keep men in their lives, but that's their odd business, I suppose. I have no biological tie tae Hamlet, so Edwin and I had to manipulate the situation, somehow get him to find and come into the bookshop. After that, it became easier, but he had a terrible start in life, Delaney. With no biological tie to the lad, no court of law would have listened to me if I wanted tae become his legal guardian. We just did what we thought best for him, and why tell him about his parentage if they didn't want him anyway? He knows who his family is; he knows how much we care about him. We don't need DNA for anything."

"Letitia hasn't come looking for him?"

"Not here, she hasn't. When I first talked to her years ago, she wanted to find Dora. She didn't even mention Dora's child— again, Edwin and I figured that part out ourselves, with the certificate you found. It was Edwin's idea to search the records more deeply."

"Okay."

"Aye. Do ye think we should tell Hamlet now?"

"I don't know, Rosie." I paused again. "But I can tell you, I resented not knowing something similar, and when I learned the news about my true biological grandfather, it was too late to do anything about it. It's still something that eats at me sometimes. It's not too late for Hamlet to at least know Letitia, if all parties are agreeable."

Rosie nodded. "I understand, lass, but Hamlet's mother all but abandoned him, left him as a bairn, two years old, we think, on the streets, perhaps sold him for money. It's a miracle he survived, and it was not because of any help from the Strangelove women."

I nodded. "I get it. I do. But Hamlet is a grown-up now. Maybe no harm can come from him knowing the truth. I promise you, though, I will not tell a soul about this. I would never want anything bad for Hamlet, so whatever you tell me to do, I'll do it."

"Let me think aboot it, lass. I need to . . . and, now, who kens what it means that the police want to talk to him aboot Mr. Watterton? Frankly, I'm more worried about that than anything."

"Me too."

Edwin sent the customer on his way, probably with more books than the man had intended to buy but was sure to enjoy, and rejoined us.

"Everything all right?" he asked.

"Aye." Rosie smiled at him.

"Of course. I'm sorry if I stirred up things I shouldn't stir up."

"Not to worry, lass. I believe that the timing of discoveries is purposeful. The universe decides."

I didn't disagree.

Edwin retrieved his phone from his pocket. "I'm going to text Lena, see if she knows if Hamlet will be released today."

"I hadn't even considered that he might not be released," I said. "That would be horrible."

"Aye," Rosie said. "Aye."

Lena didn't reply immediately, and when my phone rang, I had to redirect my concern.

"Wyatt?" I said as I answered.

"Sis, you busy?" he said.

"Not bad. What's up?"

"Can you come meet me?"

"Sure, what's going on?"

"I found someone I think you'd like to see."

"Who?" My mind had been so much on the Strangelove family that even though he wouldn't have any sort of knowledge of them, that's who I thought he was talking about. Had he found Dora?

"You mentioned that attorney and her client, Donald Rigalee."

My brain redirected quickly. "The killer?"

Rosie and Edwin looked at me.

"Yep. One and the same. Want to spy on him?"

I didn't, really, but I thought I should probably round up my brother anyway.

"Sure," I said with a little forced enthusiasm. "Where are you?"

I jotted the address on a piece of scratch paper Rosie sent my way. When the call disconnected, I told Edwin and Rosie what was going on and that I was going to take a bus to get my brother.

Based upon what he'd heard of this side of the conversation, there was no way Edwin was going to let me do that. Instead, we hopped into his car and he drove us to the docks.

FOURTEEN

We found Wyatt at an open-air fish-and-chips restaurant, a place with a large canvas top supported by poles. It wasn't a simple takeaway, but furnished with plenty of tables. You could enjoy a meal as you watched the very ocean where the food had come from, probably the same day, maybe within the hour.

Propane heaters blowing from each corner kept the place warm enough, and lots of older men who seemed to enjoy their fish-and-chips and some board games populated the restaurant.

Wyatt stood out among them in his button-down collar and necktie. He waved us over as we came through the entrance.

"Hey," I said.

"Howdy," Wyatt said. He shook Edwin's hand. "A good surprise."

"Lad," Edwin said.

"I ordered a platter of fish-and-chips to share. Should be here in a minute. I can't get enough of the vinegar. It's delicious, and the fish is so darn fresh. You don't get this in the Midwest. I've had some fresh fried catfish direct from a river, but the ocean makes all the seafood taste so much better."

I kept my voice low as Edwin and I both sat on stools. "You said you saw Rigalee?"

"I did. And he's still here." Wyatt nodded toward the other side of the restaurant, where a group had gathered around a game. "But don't be obvious about looking over there. He's the one on the left side of the table, playing checkers."

As casually as possible, I glanced that way. I hadn't really cared to see the man Clarinda had so successfully defended. I'd truly just come down to gather my brother. But now that we were there, I was intrigued, and there was a platter of food on the way, so it didn't make sense to grab him and run.

Rigalee didn't stand out among the rest of the men in the place. It seemed we three were the only ones not wearing warm winter hats and weatherproof coats atop rubber waders. This was unquestionably a gathering of fishermen, something off the tourists' beaten track. If tourists knew about the authenticity of place—and the characters inside it—there would be a continual line out the door.

On the other hand, no one seemed to care we were there, part of a group of infrequent but common interlopers who were lucky enough to have made the discovery.

"How in the world do you figure that's him?" I asked Wyatt.

"Heard some of the men discussing it. Apparently he's quite the checkers player."

Edwin glanced over and then back. "That's him."

A waiter, dressed as if he were a fisherman on break from casting lines, carried a tray of food up over his shoulder and stopped at our table. He set the tray in the middle. I hadn't realized how hungry I was, but my mouth watered at the sights and smells.

"Okay," I said as I grabbed a piece of fish and a paper plate from a stack next to the tray.

Wyatt kept his voice low. "The men I overheard spoke about him admirably."

"I don't know the story," I said, savoring the food.

"I don't either, but they called him a 'good man,' someone who did the right thing when it was necessary."

"Goodness, where was I?"

"It all occurred around the time of your wedding," Edwin said.

"That would explain it. Do you remember the details?" I asked, tempted to research right that minute on my phone but enjoying the food too much.

Edwin nodded and chewed. He loved a good fish-and-chips meal too. "The two men Rigalee killed were allegedly stealing from other fishermen."

"Stealing fish? That sounds like a difficult way to make a living."

"Poaching," Edwin said. "The fishing in the North Sea is mostly done with trawling. Pulling a big net through the water. The two men he killed had boarded a number of other boats and threatened crews with weapons."

"Sounds more like self-defense than murder to me," I said. "But Clarinda didn't use self-defense, did she?"

"No, the men were killed aboard their own boat, ramshackle though it might have been. Rigalee boarded their boat and killed them," Edwin said.

"Oh. What did Clarinda say the police did wrong?"

"They didn't search for any weapons aboard the boat. There were none in the open, but they didn't do a thorough search.

Rigalee claimed that one of them aimed a gun in his direction but then tossed it somewhere when Rigalee showed them his weapon," Edwin said.

"Sounds kind of weak," I said.

"Clarinda is very good at creating doubt, and even though it's not supposed to go that way, sympathies were not for the men who were killed."

"Why hadn't they been arrested for theft, armed robbery?" I asked.

"They had been. They'd even served some time, but they kept getting released."

Such circumstances must have been a universal story.

"It's pretty amazing that he's a free man," I said. "No matter how good his attorney was."

A cheer erupted from the audience watching the game. I looked over and saw Rigalee smiling as a couple of other men slapped him on the back. Money changed several hands.

I was caught staring. Rigalee's eyes locked on mine. I smiled quickly and looked away but couldn't help glancing back again. He nodded and smiled warmly. My imagination conjured him telling me there was nothing to be afraid of, that he wasn't going to hurt me, wasn't going to hurt anybody, unless they deserved it, of course.

He looked away, then stood to shake hands with some of the men who'd been around the table, cheering on the game.

He wasn't a big man, but he was wiry, with a medium frame and long gray hair sticking out from under his cap. He was neither young nor old, but certainly weathered. I could imagine him on the bow of a boat peering out into a dark sea, ignoring sleeting rain and uncontrollable wind while searching for land, his hand at his forehead shielding his eyes from the storm.

As he conversed with the other men, he seemed quick with a smile. No one else seemed to be staring at him, wondering if it was safe to be under the same canvas.

I was certainly now more curious about his case. The details were probably fascinating, and I would dive into a deeper search later, but for now I needed to stop staring and mind my own meal.

I didn't want to worry Wyatt about Hamlet yet, so I didn't bring up the morning's events. For a good half an hour we talked about normal things, like Wyatt's successful meetings, as well as what sights he still needed to try to see while he was in town. He felt like his work was almost done, but that didn't mean the company he worked for would shorten his stay. He could relax and enjoy if he wanted to.

He wasn't as into museums as I was, so Edwin and I gave him a list of other places that were more about the outdoor views.

By the time we finished the food, the rest of the place had mostly cleared out. I didn't know if the fishermen were headed back out to sea or to bed, because they woke so early.

Edwin and Wyatt were deep in a conversation about William Wallace as we made our way off the stools and toward the exit. I lagged behind, but as I sent another glace over to the table with the checkerboard set up and ready to go for the next match, I spotted something. It looked like a book had been left on the floor underneath the table.

I hurried over and gathered it. I'd leave it with the restaurant staff.

On any other day, or perhaps before I'd had a fortune-teller instruct me to stay away from men named Robert Burns, I would have found the book to be a delightful thing to behold.

It was a thin volume of Burns's poetry, the title something I thought had become lyrics to another song. *Scots Wha Hae and Other Poetry by Robert Burns* was embossed on the front cover. It wasn't a valuable book, but it had been well loved, read often, if the wear on the gray cover was any indication. An odd sensation of wanting to drop it back to the floor zipped through me. I didn't—I'm not sure I could ever do that to a book—but I certainly felt an internal disquiet. I think I even gasped a little.

"Excuse me," a voice said.

I jumped as if I were guilty of something. I turned to see Rigalee standing nearby—he kept a distance, as if being polite, but his coat was open and I could see the shirt underneath it. I told myself not to stare, but there was something familiar about that shirt.

He smiled and nodded at the book. "That's mine."

"Oh. Sure. Sorry." I handed him the book.

He reached for it but didn't take it from me immediately, keeping us both there holding it as he looked at me, his eyes still friendly but too inquisitive for my liking.

A moment later, he tucked the book under his arm. "You enjoy Burns?"

I laughed, way too nervously. "Who doesn't?"

"Indeed."

"Sis, we gotta go," Wyatt called from the entrance.

I was glad Wyatt hadn't used my name. I smiled and nodded at Rigalee again.

I hurried toward my brother. I didn't turn around to see if Rigalee was leaving too.

"Sorry about that," I said.

Wyatt put himself in between me and Rigalee as we made our way to Edwin's car.

"Goodness, leave it to my sister to make friends with a killer over a book," he said quietly behind me as we walked away.

I could practically hear the roll of his eyes. It was hard to blame him.

"What was that?" Edwin asked when we joined him in his car.

"Nothing, really," I said.

Wyatt sent me a look but didn't comment.

"Aye. It looks like Hamlet is back at the bookshop. He just texted me."

"That's great news!" I said.

"What's going on?" Wyatt asked.

"Tell you on the way." I got into the car.

I was more excited about Hamlet's release than bothered by the brief encounter with a known killer. At least that's what I kept telling myself—even after I noticed him standing outside the canvas tent and waving as Edwin steered us out of the parking lot.

FIFTEEN

Hamlet was rattled. His eyes were still glassy, his mouth a tight line, but he claimed he was okay, doing better.

"Lena was wonderful. Basically, she told me not to say much of anything," he said as we gathered around him.

"What did Inspector Winters ask ye, lad?" Rosie said.

"He asked me again where I was last night and what I'd done."

"What had you done? Where were you?" I asked.

"After the dinner, and after you and Elias dropped me off, I did go back out. I went for a walk, but I truly don't remember which direction I went. I was bothered by Delaney's invitation to the Burns dinner, bothered by the way they all behaved. I walk almost every evening, even during the worst weather. I have different routes I take."

It didn't seem possible that he didn't remember where he'd gone, but it didn't feel like the right time to doubt him aloud. "Did you tell him your normal routes?"

"I did, and then Lena told me to stop talking. Inspector Winters continued to ask questions. He asked if the police could search my flat, but Lena told him in no uncertain terms that they weren't welcome to do so without a proper warrant."

"That's good. Did he say what they're looking for?" I said.

"Not to me, no. Lena got more out of them. After we were done, she told me that Neil was spotted going back into the Burns House, and he was with someone. That someone looked like me. They would like to search for some sort of evidence that I'd been there at that time."

"Really?" Wyatt said. "Looked like you?"

Hamlet nodded. "Apparently. Male, about my build, with a ponytail. That's me in a nutshell." He shrugged, but I could tell that he was beginning to finally relax some.

"Did they ask you anything else?" I said.

"Aye, Inspector Winters wanted to know when my last visit was to the National Library and if I'd seen Neil Watterton when I was there."

"What did you say?"

Hamlet shook his head. "Those were questions Lena told me not to answer, but I was able to tell him that I've at least been there before."

"Why didn't she want you to answer?"

"She said it was because I hadn't been officially arrested, so I didn't really have to answer anything they asked. It was okay to give them that little amount, but she said to stay away from any specific details they might use against me later."

"Does she think ye'll be arrested, lad?" Rosie asked.

Hamlet fell into thought a moment. "I didn't even think to ask her that. I should have."

"Lad, you said you knew Neil?" Edwin asked.

"Right. He did help me with a project a few months back. But I've been in the library a number of times."

"Hamlet," I began, "I thought I saw a look of recognition between the two of you, at the dinner."

He shrugged. "I did think he looked familiar, but I couldn't place him right away. He might have thought the same."

"And you didn't tell this to Inspector Winters?" I said.

"No, Lena said that until I'm under arrest, I wasn't required to." Hamlet blanched and swallowed hard. "Do you think I'll be arrested?"

A chorus of supportive no's rose in the air. I was pleased they didn't sound too phony. We could only hope he wasn't arrested, but our reaction seemed to ease his new wave of concern.

"Aye," he said. "Thank you all." He turned to Edwin. "Thank you for Lena. I would have just kept talking because I know I've done absolutely nothing wrong."

"Ye're welcome, lad."

I looked around the table. We were a family, there was no question. Just like Rosie had said, there was no need for a birth certificate to prove that to anyone.

I thought about my grandfather as I looked at Wyatt. My brother had been as accepted and welcomed by my Scottish family as I'd been. My biological grandfather had been his grandfather too, but when I'd told him about my discovery, he'd waved it away.

It's not about biological family, Sis. Grandpa was our grandpa, no matter what the genes tell us. You'll never convince me otherwise. I don't care about the biology part.

He was probably right, but I wasn't ready to let go of the notion that Hamlet had a right to know the truth.

But not now. Not today. Maybe tomorrow. Tonight, we'd all go home with the truths we knew firmly in place.

Once home, behind our closed door as cold winds blew outside, Tom and I spent some time talking with Wyatt as he again recounted the events of the day, including what had happened at the restaurant. He played it down some, not quite sharing that I'd been almost alone with the killer for a good minute or so.

I'd thought about sharing with Tom the new things I'd learned about the birth certificate, but those details seemed much less important for the time being. I hadn't even shared with him yet that I'd come upon it. It would be better to save the news until Rosie and Edwin decided how much Hamlet should know.

When we said good night to my brother and made our way to our bedroom, shutting the door behind us, I asked Tom if I could bounce off him my impressions of what Hamlet had said.

"You think he was lying?" Tom asked me.

"I do, but I can't figure out about what," I said.

"Do you think he was the person with Neil, the one who was seen going into the building?" Tom asked.

"I really do wonder," I said.

"I've known him even longer than you have, lass. He's not a killer. You know that too."

"No, but what if he did go back to the Burns House? He can't have forgotten where he walked—that's the part that's really got me wondering, and the police too, I'm sure. But what if he and Neil did go back to the house?"

"Why?"

"Maybe he left something there and he's afraid to tell the police as much because he'll look like he somehow set the fire or saw the killer, I don't know." I swallowed hard. No matter what, I couldn't seriously speculate that Hamlet *was* the killer.

"I guess that's a possibility, but it seems far-fetched."

"I agree, but why didn't Hamlet just tell Inspector Winters the route he took?"

Tom nodded. "I see what you're getting at. He didn't even make up one, maybe because he could be more caught in that lie than the other."

"Exactly."

"But he's not a killer, lass. If something happened, it wasn't because Hamlet was murderous."

"I agree."

He wasn't. Hamlet was a good soul, a kind, peace-loving young man, there was no question. But doesn't everyone have a dark side? Hadn't Clarinda just mentioned that?

What was Hamlet hiding? It was either going to keep me up all night or I was going to have to try to push it away until I could do something more about it. What connection did he and Neil truly have? There was more there than he was admitting to.

"Want to go somewhere with me in the morning?" I asked Tom. "Early, before I head into work?"

"Aye, of course. Always."

A plan always helped, and now that I had one, I would be able to get some sleep.

It shouldn't have been a surprise that my dreams were filled with poems and fortune-tellers, visions of Robert Burns.

Even before I'd fallen asleep, though, I had decided that I needed to delve deeper into the poet and his life.

I thought that if Tom was with me, Letitia's warnings might not hold as much power.

SIXTEEN

Though I'd made a plan, I woke the next day vacillating between taking Tom to a couple of different places. I thought about the Robert Burns Monument located on Regent Road in Edinburgh, but with our limited time because we both had to get to work, I chose a different destination. It was inside the Writers' Museum where I thought the good stuff was located, at least the closest-by good stuff.

The Writers' Museum was founded to honor the lives of three Scottish writers: Burns, Walter Scott, and Robert Louis Stevenson. Located off Lawnmarket, it was not only a favorite tourist destination, but from all I could tell, locals loved it too. I'd been inside it only one time before and had wished for another chance.

The first time through, I had looked at Burns's things inside the museum, the most memorable for me being his writing desk. However, seeing Rigalee's shirt had sparked some vague memories of other items. A partial puzzle had formed in my mind, and it included the design on that shirt. I needed to see if I could find the other pieces and make them all fit together.

The museum opened at nine o'clock. Tom and I grabbed bagels and coffee on the way, but I was glad we had his car for this morning's excursion. It was cold outside.

An entryway paved with stones carved with quotes from famous Scottish writers led to the museum's front door. I'd dallied when I'd been there before, reading the stones—at least trying to. Some of the Scots was too difficult to translate, even when taking time to decipher it. But today I was all business, walking hurriedly over the words.

I didn't recognize the woman we paid as we entered, and she seemed to understand that we didn't need a spiel but were there to look at some specifics we knew how to find.

I led Tom to a room full of Burns memorabilia.

"Okay, somewhere here . . ." I said as I looked into the display cases.

"You're looking for a book?"

"Not really. Something handwritten, I think." Then my eyes found it quickly. "There!" I pointed as Tom sidled up next to me.

I'd looked right past a plaster cast of Burns's skull and the lock of hair that had belonged to his wife, Jean Armour, directly to an old parchment. Handwritten, the words weren't in a normal top-to-bottom, left-to-right fashion, but as if Burns had jotted down snippets of ideas at a number of different angles.

"I think that's notes for 'Scots Wha Hae,'" Tom said after inspecting it a moment.

"That's in the title of the book Rigalee came back for yesterday."

Tom nodded. "It's a song, but it wouldn't surprise me if it was a book title too."

"What do you know about it?"

"A fair bit, actually. It was an anthem of the Scottish National Party. It used to be sung all the time, but I don't think it is as much anymore. It's based upon a speech given by Robert the Bruce before the Battle of Bannockburn, where we Scots were once again saluting our freedom from England." Tom smiled. "Gaining, keeping, fighting for our freedom from England has been a reoccurring theme for a long time, if you hadn't noticed."

"Can you hum a bar or two?" I asked.

Tom looked around. "I'll—quietly—sing a couple of lines, in English. I'm not as good with the Scots as my da is." He looked around again, but no one was in sight. He cleared his throat.

Scots, who have with Wallace bled,
Scots, whom Bruce has often led,
Welcome to your gory bed
Or to victory!

His voice faded to silence. I said, "Oh, more of that, please. Even with the word 'gory' in there, I loved it." He had a wonderful singing voice, which I hadn't heard nearly enough of in our short marriage.

"Maybe later." Tom smiled. "But that's the gist of it."

"I think perhaps you should sing to me every evening. You can pick the songs."

Tom laughed. "We'll see what we can do. Is this why you wanted to come here today?" He nodded at the parchment.

"One of the reasons. There is one more. I'm not sure what form it will be in, but it will have something to do with archery," I said. "It's a sketchy memory."

"Aye?"

It was sketchy, but I knew I'd seen something about Burns and archery, though I couldn't pinpoint exactly what it had been. We circled around the display cases and ended up back near the handwritten lyrics.

"Oh, here!" I leaned in closer. "It's a diploma."

Tom joined me again, and together we peered into the case. He said, "Royal Company of Archers. A very distinguished group."

"What do you know about this?" I said, hoping he'd be able to sing again.

"Not much other than that they're well respected, even today."

There was an information sheet next to the diploma, and I read aloud.

"'Diploma admitting Robert Burns to membership of the Royal Company of Archers on 10 April 1792. Presented by the poet's sons, Lieutenant-Colonel James Glencairn Burns and Colonel William Nicol Burns. Admission to membership was a high honour as the company, formed in 1676, was a select and aristocratic group. Burns received the honour when he had left Edinburgh and settled in Dumfries.'" I looked at Tom. "Is the Royal Company of Archers still around?"

"Aye, I think so, but I think it's more ceremonial now, serving the queen or protecting her, something like that. Why?"

I bit my bottom lip. "I saw something yesterday. When Rigalee came back for the book, his coat was open, and I saw part of an emblem on his shirt. I didn't tell you this part because I wasn't sure, but now it's coming back to me. There were two arrows on the shirt, and I think I've seen that before."

"Where?" Tom asked.

I glance up at him. "I think Hamlet has a shirt with the same emblem."

"What do you think that means?"

"Tom, I have no idea, but there might be some sort of tie there. I need to see if there's a club or something. I don't think Hamlet is a part of any ceremonial group, but I wonder if there's . . . something else. I don't know anything except that shirt was familiar."

"Okay, but why would Hamlet and Rigalee having the same shirt mean anything?"

"Oh yes, there is one other thing."

Tom smiled and nodded.

I continued, "Because Neil Watterton also wore that T-shirt. He was putting on his costume when we met him. I saw the shirt then and didn't catch that it was familiar, not until I saw something similar on Rigalee. The memories have been coming together."

"And if they're part of the same group, Hamlet and Neil might have known each other better than Hamlet has let on."

I shrugged. "Maybe, and if they knew or know Rigalee, could that mean something else?"

"I don't know."

"Me neither, but I sure want to." I glanced at my watch. "I need to get to work. Thanks for driving us today."

"You're welcome." Tom glanced at the time too. "Anything else you want to try to see?"

"Well, there's probably a lot of things I'd like to explore, but I know you have to get to work too. Maybe later."

As we headed toward the front door, I said, "Sing to me some more?"

Tom laughed again. "Maybe later for that too, lass."

"I'm going to hold you to it."

I caught his smile, another that I loved seeing, the one that told me he was pretty close to as happy as I was about this whole marriage thing.

No one was as happy as me, I thought as we climbed back into his car and drove back down to Grassmarket.

SEVENTEEN

Hamlet wasn't in the bookshop when I arrived. In fact, Rosie seemed somewhat concerned that he hadn't shown up yet. He hadn't called her to let her know he'd be late.

It wasn't uncommon for him to be a little tardy, but on the morning after he'd been questioned by the police, it felt a bit suspicious, even if Rosie didn't want to say as much out loud.

Rosie didn't mention the birth certificate, and I didn't want to add to her concern, so I didn't either. I did, however, ask her about something else.

"Is Hamlet into archery?" I said as I crouched to scratch Hector's belly.

"I dinnae ken, lass. I wouldnae be surprised."

"Why?"

"Hamlet is verra athletic. Football."

She meant the game that I knew as soccer.

"I didn't know."

"Before university, he played with clubs. He's verra fast and a smart player."

I envisioned something similar to the Saturday mornings in my youth when both Wyatt and I had participated in sports. I'd been okay at soccer, but Wyatt had been built more for football, so after he'd mowed down a few soccer players, our father had switched him to the rougher game. Everyone seemed happier for the change. I wished I'd had the chance to see Hamlet play, cheer him on.

"I think I've seen him wearing an archery T-shirt or something like that before," I said.

"Meebe," she said as she fell into thought, distracted.

None of us thought he could ever commit murder, but just as I had, Rosie probably sensed something strange about what Hamlet had told us the day before.

The front door opened, bringing in a very cold wind but not Hamlet. Instead, a man I'd recently met came through. Charles Lexon. He moved hesitantly, and his expression was as sheepish as it could be.

"Help ye?" Rosie said to him.

I stepped around her and crossed my arms in front of my chest. "This is Charles Lexon, Rosie, the man who wanted me invited to the Burns dinner, for a purpose I still don't understand, unless it was simply to upset Malcolm Campbell." I didn't like my sassy tone, but Charles's mere presence did nothing but remind me of the fact that a murder had taken place after an event where I'd been made to feel uncomfortable and used.

"Och, Mr. Lexon. It's been a few years," Rosie said, though she didn't move forward to shake his hand.

She'd be polite, but not her most polite.

"Good to see you again, Rosie." He looked at me. "Do you have a minute, Delaney?" He looked around. "Is Edwin here too?"

I had wanted to talk to Charles. I'd thought about tracking him down to ask him questions but hadn't yet, and I didn't want him to think I'd forgive him that easily. I took a thoughtful beat before I answered. "Edwin isn't here, but I have a minute, I suppose."

There were currently no customers, and I only invited him to have a seat in the back because it would have been uncomfortable for us to be up front if a customer did come in.

Once we were seated, he began immediately. "I want to apologize for . . . what happened. I did not intend for things to go the way they did."

"Okay. Thank you." I folded easily now. I really wasn't one to hold a grudge. "Apology accepted, but what did you intend?"

He took a deep breath and let it out. "Certainly not a murder, and solving that is more important than my regrets, of course, but it was bothering me that what I did might have offended you. That's simply not how I operate. I thought . . . You spoke to Clarinda?"

I nodded, realizing the thick Scots accent he had used at the dinner was only part of his costume. His accent now was so light I wondered if he was even a native Scot.

"We both thought your presence would be a welcome surprise." He sat up taller in the chair. "Malcolm himself had been talking about wanting to mend ways with Edwin. We thought we were helping, but we should have at least let you in on the surprise. Maybe we should have simply invited Edwin, but hindsight and all."

"You probably should have just talked to Malcolm first, asked him." I shrugged.

"Aye, but . . . lass, I can't explain it well because you don't know us, but it was not meant as anything but a pleasant surprise. You'd have to understand the history of our friendships."

He waved his hand in the air. "Oh, I suppose that's not important. I just wanted to tell you I was sorry."

"What has Malcolm said?"

Charles shook his head. "He's not speaking to either Clarinda or me."

"I see."

"Delaney, if given the chance to do it all again, I would change everything." He paused. "I've even gone so far as to wonder that if we hadn't been so keen on surprising everyone, the dinner would have continued, and maybe . . . well, maybe Neil wouldn't have been killed. I don't know, but if that is the case, it makes our actions unforgivable."

I nodded, but my heart ached a little for him.

The man was a wreck. He was holding it together fairly well, but he was clearly hurting. If my accepting his apology helped ease that some—and if he wasn't Neil's killer, which I hoped he wasn't—I was willing to give him that much.

"Do you know anything about Malcolm's new bookshop?" I asked.

"Aye. It's not open, but he's setting it up. Lass, I know he wanted to talk to Edwin, mend their old disagreements. He said as much."

"Malcolm thought Edwin burned down his other bookshop. Does he still believe that?"

"I'm not sure, but I know he wants to let go of it."

"Edwin didn't burn down his bookshop, Charles. If Malcolm can't accept and believe that, I'm not sure they will ever be able to be . . . friends."

Edwin had done some unsavory things in his life, but I was one hundred percent certain he wasn't guilty of burning down his friend's place of business.

"I know, but I'd like to talk to Edwin myself."

"I'll let him know."

Charles's eyes told me he'd hoped for more. He'd wanted to talk to Edwin immediately, or maybe just expected that I would somehow guarantee that I'd get my boss to speak to him.

"How did you know about me?" I asked.

"I've been into the shop." He nodded toward the front. "Rosie wasn't in at the time, or I would have reintroduced myself to her. You were on a mobile call as you were playing with the wee dog. You were talking to someone about Burns, saying you had several of his books on the shelves. It felt fortuitous, actually."

I didn't remember that moment specifically, but I'd probably been on such calls many times. And I scratched Hector's stomach whenever the opportunity presented itself.

"I'll talk to Edwin." I paused. "What more can you tell me about Neil?"

Charles was surprised by the question. His eyes opened wider. "He was a good lad."

"Someone didn't like him," I said.

Charles frowned and shook his head. "I can't imagine that. He was a gentle soul, kind."

A description I frequently used for Hamlet.

"What happened after Hamlet and I left the party?"

"Not much. It was ruined, of course. Neil wasn't happy. Clarinda wasn't happy, but we calmed, cleaned up some." Charles sighed. "She thought you shouldn't have left or that we should chase after you."

I didn't feel the need to explain that I had to get away, so I just looked at him.

"You had a taxi waiting for you?" he asked.

I thought it strange that he'd noticed. "Yes, a friend."

"Were you scared to be there?"

"Not scared, but the whole evening was mysterious, Charles. It was odd."

"I'm afraid you're right, and again, I apologize."

"Thank you. Again, I accept." I paused. "Edwin says you're a businessman. What's your business?"

"I'm long retired, lass. I have been since about the time Edwin left the group, but I used to be in import/export, then commercial real estate. I read poetry and take walks most every day now. It's an ideal sort of life." He smiled. "I never married. Never found the right person."

"What ever happened to Malcolm's wife?" I asked.

"Maria?"

I nodded.

"Last I heard she went to the United States, but that was a long time ago."

I nodded again and looked at him. He seemed genuinely contrite, and my heart went out to him even a little more. Surely I'd participated in a surprise gone wrong somewhere along the way. It happened.

"Charles, was Neil involved in any sort of archery group?" I asked, both because I was curious and because it might give us a chance to move past this.

"That's a strange question."

"I saw his shirt underneath his costume, and it reminded me of something I'd seen before, something about archery."

He sat up straighter, seemingly glad to move on too. "I believe he was part of a club, though I don't know much about it. Of course, there are limited places such a club could gather.

I'm aware of one archery facility not far from here. Maybe he went there."

"Where is that?"

He lifted an eyebrow but didn't further question my curiosity. "Here"—he patted his chest as if looking for something— "I'll jot down the location."

I grabbed him a pen and paper, and he made a quick scribble.

"Was Neil ever married?" I asked.

"Only to the library. He adored his job there. He dated, but casually, as far as I know." Tears filled Charles's eyes.

"Oh, Charles, I'm sorry for your loss."

He nodded. "Thank you. It's difficult."

My heart sank. "You have no idea who might have wanted him dead?"

"No, lass, I cared about the lad, but even after all these years I didn't know him all that well, I'm afraid. Our times together were spent on Robert Burns, not on much of anything personal."

"What about someone who would want to destroy the building?"

"I've thought of that too but still came up empty. From my perspective, I know the building was valuable real estate, but we weren't approached by anyone who wanted to purchase it. Insurance will probably cover a rebuild if . . . well, if things get solved satisfactorily. But it won't be the same ever again. You can't duplicate that authenticity and build to the contemporary building codes."

I understood building codes a bit. The bookshop had run into some issues not long ago, and the mere thought of dealing with the bureaucracy tied to any of that left a distinctly bad taste in my mouth.

"The loss of life is the tragedy, of course. Edwin told me he originally bought the building because he somehow thought it had something to do with Burns. Did any of you ever find anything indicating that?" I asked.

Charles shook his head and smiled sadly. "I remember him talking about his dream, but that was a long time ago too. We never came upon anything, including a ghost. Do you know about something more specific we might have found? Has Edwin mentioned anything else?"

"No, nothing at all." I sighed again.

Charles reached into his pocket and gathered a business card, handing it to me. "Once again, lass, I'm so sorry I got you into the middle of all of this. Please forgive me, and let me know if Edwin will speak with me. I would enjoy seeing him."

I took the card that listed only his name and a mobile phone number. I liked it when people used real business cards.

"I will talk to him," I said.

"Thank you."

Charles made his way out of the bookshop, nodding at Rosie as he left.

"Everything awright, lass?" Rosie asked me when he was gone.

"He really is a nice man," I said. "I think he was misguided in the way he invited me to the dinner, but he is lovely."

"Ye sound like ye're trying tae convince yerself," she said.

"Maybe," I said. "I don't know. He seemed genuinely heart-broken." More so than Clarinda, I thought, but she had had a point—clients did count on her to concentrate on them when she was at work.

Wyatt came through the door. "Hello!"

"Lad!" Rosie said.

"Hey, Wyatt? What's going on?"

"I have no more work to do, so I thought I would come see you two."

His arrival gave me an idea.

"Wyatt, how about spending some time helping Rosie in the bookshop? I'd like to run a couple of errands."

"Sure! Wait, do you have any sports books?"

"I'm not sure, but I don't think so." I smiled at Rosie and then turned back to my brother. "Feel free to explore, though."

"Will do."

Rosie didn't need the help. I could have run the errand and left her alone, but since Hamlet wasn't there, I decided Wyatt would make a good substitute, for at least a short time.

I grabbed my coat, hat, scarf, and mittens, and left out the front door as Rosie and Wyatt were discussing the beloved Scottish addition to the world of sports, golf.

EIGHTEEN

I walked to Cowgate, though not down the close where the Burns' House had been; I couldn't bring myself to have another look yet. It was still really cold outside, but my destination wasn't far and I didn't want to wait the few minutes for the next bus. At least it wasn't raining or snowing—yet. I didn't know exactly where Malcolm's new bookshop was located, but I thought I could find it.

The article I'd found earlier didn't mention the address, and an internet search didn't help, but still, I'd figure it out. Like Grassmarket, Cowgate was a part of Edinburgh Old Town, centuries old and filled with historical stone architecture. Smaller shops were located along the bottom floors, with renovated flats above. It was highly sought-after real estate.

In my search I passed a cheese monger, clothing and jewelry shops, a small grocer, a place that specialized in suits of armor, a wedding dress store, and a bagel bakery before I came to the location that a few months ago I'd noticed was empty. MALCOLM'S BOOKS AND OTHER WORKS was painted on the front window.

"So not just 'Malcolm's Books.'"

I put my face up to the window and peered inside.

It was a small place, well packed with organized shelves. Even though it was an older building, there was no sense of history inside the shop yet, no feeling that hours had been spent discussing books with eager customers. Everything was still too pristine, too lined up. But the lived-in, homey comfort that a bookshop could offer would come with time.

I was disappointed not to see anyone at first. The sign on the front window said the shop would open for business the next week, but I'd hoped to find Malcolm inside.

Just as I pulled back from the window, ready to slip a note through the mail slot on the door, Malcolm appeared from the back. He was carrying a box, which he set down next to the cash register on the small counter.

I knocked on the window.

Malcolm squinted in my direction. His squint transformed into irritation when he recognized me. He didn't say a word, didn't even send me a gesture, but turned and walked away, toward the back of the building again.

"Well," I said to myself.

I wasn't going to be deterred, I decided. I moved from the window to the front door, where I resumed knocking and didn't let up.

A good long few minutes later, Malcolm marched to the door, unlocked it, and yanked it open.

"You're an annoying lass, aye?" he said.

I shrugged. "Some people do say that. Look, I'm sorry. I would like to talk to you. Please."

I thought he'd shut the door in my face. I considered putting my foot out just in case I needed to stop it, but no matter what I'd seen in the movies, it seemed like too painful an idea.

Fortunately, and for a reason I would never understand, a moment later he turned again and walked to the counter, leaving the door open. I took it as an invitation.

I followed him inside and then gently shut the door behind me. "Want me to lock it again?"

He didn't want to answer but nodded a moment later. "Aye. I'm not ready for customers."

I turned the bolt and then joined him at the counter. "Thank you, Malcolm, for seeing me. First of all, I want you to know that I had nothing to do with any sort of secret surprise for you. I was just as surprised. More, maybe."

"I didn't think you did."

"Okay. Well, then I'm not sure why you're angry at me."

"I'm not angry at you. I'm angry, and I feel no need to talk to you about it. And . . ."

"What?"

"You work for Edwin."

"You're still angry at him?"

"No. Well, aye, though not like I used to be. Lass, he took out a non-harassment order against me. I don't want to do anything to break that, and talking to you might mean I am. I'm beginning a new life here, and I don't want anyone to mess with it. I don't trust you or anyone who works with Edwin. I don't see why I need to."

"Oh. I see. Well, I didn't work for him back then, and I won't say anything." I sighed. "Look, I just want to talk to you a moment, if it's okay."

"Why?"

"Because I'm worried about a friend of mine."

Malcolm shook his head. "And I know this friend?"

"The young man who came with me to the dinner."

"What does he have to do with any of this?"

"I don't know."

"Lass, I have work to do."

I held up a hand. "Do you know anything about Neil Watterton being involved in an archery group?"

"Not a thing," Malcolm said a long moment later. "Why?"

"The shirt he had on underneath his costume. I think it was something about an archery club."

"That's very observant of you."

"I've seen something like it before. I was just trying to put it together."

Malcolm lifted his eyebrow again. "You know something about Neil's murder?"

I shook my head. "Not really, but I feel like maybe there's something that could help."

Our brief acquaintanceship transformed at that moment. Malcolm seemed to relax some; his shoulders fell slightly.

"What's going on?" he said. But this time his words weren't lined with anger or suspicion, just curiosity.

"I don't really know," I said. "What do you think happened to Neil? Why would someone kill him?"

Malcolm frowned. He was a big man with dark blue eyes that had probably scared me some, but they didn't scare me now. Now they were concerned. He reached over to the other side of the desk and grabbed a tall stool, bringing it back around to me.

"Have a seat, Delaney. Would you like some coffee or a cuppa?" he asked. "I don't have anything to eat, but let's talk."

"Coffee would be great. Thank you." I scooted up to the stool and watched as Malcolm disappeared to the back again.

When he was out of sight, I texted Wyatt.

I'll be longer than I thought.

He responded with: *No surprise. We're good. Take your time.*

Malcolm came back with two cups of coffee and then gathered a stool for himself. "Look, I don't know if I can answer any of your questions, but if you'd like to hear some about our group, I'll share. I don't really know what you're trying to do, but if you think you have some idea who might have killed Neil, and I can shed light, I'll do what I can."

"I don't know much of anything. I'd also love to hear what happened between you and Edwin."

"He didn't tell you?"

"I'd like to hear it from your perspective."

"All right." He took a deep breath, let it out, and then took a sip of his coffee. "Edwin and I used to be very close."

"He said the same thing."

"Aye. My other bookshop was in a rough neighborhood, and Edwin tried to convince me to move to an empty building around the corner from the Cracked Spine. He welcomed the idea of having both shops close to each other. He envisioned morning coffees, afternoon conversations."

"That didn't appeal to you?"

"Well, Edwin and I would talk, either on the phone or in person, at least once a day back then. We'd discuss books, politics, any manner of thing, really. We were very close friends, until we weren't. I didn't mind the idea of our shops being so close together, but I liked the neighborhood where mine was located. Sure, it wasn't the best area, but my customers found me, and . . . well, I'd started working with underprivileged youth over there, helping them with whatever books I could find. It doesn't matter now, but I want you to understand how close we were. If we'd been the type to use the term 'best friends,' I would have called us that."

"That changed when he bought the book from your ex-wife?"

He nodded again. "There was more to it, but, aye, he bought the book from Maria, and I was under the impression they were seeing each other romantically." He looked at me.

I wasn't about to tell him what Edwin said about that. I didn't want any words or meanings misconstrued. I kept my gaze unknowing.

"Anyway," he continued. "I was angry at him, very much so. The divorce with Maria was awful. She took me for just about everything. I don't know how I managed to keep the bookshop, but I think it was only because she didn't want it enough to battle for it."

"The courts don't split things evenly here?"

"They do, but only the items acquired during the marriage. Most everything I had, we had, came after the marriage. I bought the bookshop after we'd been married a couple of years, so it was part of the pot that was split. I had to pay her half its worth to keep it. Then it got messy regarding what went to who, back and forth. It was just ugly."

"I see."

"Oh, I suppose Maria did put up a wee fight for the bookshop, or half its assets at least, but she didn't battle hard, and when I offered her the book as part of a pile of things in exchange for her letting go of the shop, she agreed. I had owned the *book* before the marriage, and I had the provenance to prove it. Part of the deal, and this was recorded in the court, was that she couldn't sell the book for ten years."

"Why?" I asked.

Malcolm shrugged. "From this distance, I'm not sure I understand why I wanted that, but it made sense then. It was probably just something as simple as me not wanting her to have any more money. I was bitter enough to feel that. And asking that of her seemed to get under her skin, so I guess I liked that, the petty part of me did, at least."

"Okay."

"The most difficult thing about the friendship ending with Edwin was that he knew. He knew about the divorce, all the ugly details. He knew about not selling the book for a time."

I didn't think he did. He hadn't mentioned anything to me about that. Maybe he'd forgotten that part. "But he bought it from Maria anyway?"

"Aye."

I couldn't really imagine why he might have done such a thing, but if I were to guess, he'd done what he'd done from a position of honor, or at least what he'd interpreted the most honorable thing to be.

"I'm sure that was hurtful," I said.

Malcolm smiled. "My *feelings* weren't hurt, lass. I was pretty angry, though. It was betrayal, plain and simple."

"If I've learned anything, Malcolm, it's rare that something is ever plain and simple."

"Aye, I'll give you that."

"So, you confronted Edwin a number of times and he asked for a non-harassment order?"

"Not exactly," Malcolm paused. "The night of the dinner, we tried to be civil to each other, but after my bookshop burned down, and I was so convinced that he was the one to do it, I was verbally and visibly angry. I only confronted him once, and it was in the Cracked Spine."

"But Edwin is not the kind of person to do such a thing. I know he felt badly about the situation with Maria, but he didn't burn down your shop. I have no doubt."

Malcolm sent me an impatient look. "How long have you known Edwin MacAlister?"

"Not as long as you have."

"Lass, your boss did more suspicious and sneaky things before you were born than you've done in your lifetime, I'm sure. Aye, he has behaved better this last ten years or so, but he's lived quite the life. He's such an unusual man, Delaney. He'll do something so wonderful one minute that when he does something horrible the next minute, you're thrown for a loop."

I was aware of that, but I didn't want Malcolm to know as much. "But he wouldn't burn down anything, maybe most particularly a bookshop."

"Let's just agree to disagree. I've worked hard to forgive him, and that's not what I wanted to tell you anyway."

"I'm listening."

"When Edwin left the group, he gave us the building. He set up a corporation and put the building into it. Clarinda was the real managing member of the corporation. At first. But then Neil purchased it from her. It was legally his property, but he told us we could use it for the Burns House forever. Clarinda was there more than any of us, and Neil never complained."

Edwin didn't know about this series of transactions, and Charles, the man who'd once worked in real estate, hadn't mentioned it to me either.

"Aye, so she could . . . scribble."

"I saw all the paper, but it was all gone the night of the dinner."

"She always paid to have that taken care of, taken away.

The dinners are sacred to all of us, and we all want as much authenticity as possible."

"Hamlet, my friend, told me you furnished it like Burns's home in the museum in Alloway."

"Aye. Every year. Anyway, *over* the years, we've had some rough luck with the building. People have broken in, cats, rats, any number of critters. The heating system has been spotty, et cetera. It was an old building, not an eyesore, but probably turning too dangerous for its own good."

"So, it was bound to burn down?"

"Or, it was bound to be burnt down," Malcolm said, leveling his gaze.

"Insurance money?" I said a moment later.

"I think it's a real possibility. Was Neil killed by the fire or was it something else? I don't think the authorities have mentioned the actual cause of death."

"He might have wanted to set it but been killed first and then someone else set it?" I asked.

"Anything is possible. I haven't heard that he was shot or stabbed or strangled, or poisoned, for that matter."

I hadn't either, but I remembered Inspector Winters's words. "But the police are confident that it was murder."

"Aye, that's what they're saying."

"You think Neil needed the insurance money?"

"I know he did. Well, I know he needed money."

"Oh."

"He got in over his head with a house he bought, though I don't understand all the details." He paused, as if for dramatic effect. It worked; I listened with rapt attention. "It was something Charles tried to help him with, even though Charles's expertise was once in commercial real estate. Anyway, they seemed to have a falling out over it, but they kept it to themselves."

"Oh," I said, drawing it out longer this time.

"Aye."

"What else do you know? Did you tell the police about the issue with Charles?"

"I told the police all I know, and that's truly about it." He took a sip of coffee. "Neil *had* been distracted, maybe even by something else lately. I wouldn't have any idea what. I wondered if it was about his job or something personal. I just didn't know him that . . . deeply, I suppose. The last little bit he'd started carrying around some of Burns's poetry, and I found that somewhat odd."

"Books?"

Malcolm shook his head. "Handwritten copies."

"Clarinda's 'scribblings'?"

"No, that's what surprised me the most. And he claimed he hadn't written them down either. Someone else's scribblings."

"Whose?"

"I asked him and he just said a woman he knew."

"Something to do with his love life?"

"He didn't say anything else. I did ask him for more details, but he didn't want to talk about it. It was none of my business, really."

"I heard he would take dates to the Burns House."

Malcolm smiled. "Well, we all might have done that over the years. It's quaint. Light a fire, bring a bottle of wine. It's something different, but, aye, the building was Neil's. He spent more time there than any of the rest of us."

I nodded and took a sip of my coffee, digesting this news.

"Why did you ask me about the archery?" he said.

"Well, like I said, I saw his shirt and I've seen something like it somewhere. Wasn't Burns a part of the Royal Archery?"

"In fact, he was, and though I found the fact that he was carrying around the handwritten poetry odd, you'll never find a bigger fan of Burns than Neil." Emotion pulled at his voice. He cleared his throat. "I will miss the lad, but I'm not aware of his involvement in archery. There's a facility just around the corner from here, though."

"Charles gave me the address."

"Charles?"

"He came into the bookshop to apologize to me this morning."

"Charles has too much time on his hands. He should never have retired."

"You're still upset with him and Clarinda?"

"I am, but I'll get over it. They are friends, and you coming in to talk to me has helped. We'll need each other after this, I'm sure."

I inspected him closely, but the words seemed genuine.

"That's good," I said. "What will you do with your Burns group now?"

"I don't know, but I can't imagine we'll continue as it was. I suspect those days are now over, even if our friendships aren't."

A sensation washed over me. It was the same sort of distant tug at my attention that the bookish voices gave me, but I didn't hear anyone speaking. My intuition wanted me to pay attention—though to what, I wasn't sure. I studied Malcolm. Could it have been one of them who killed Neil? Our rocky acquaintanceship transformed once again. I hoped Malcolm didn't notice I'd suddenly become more alert, on guard maybe.

I wasn't scared, but I was probably as aware as I should have been in the first place. A murder had occurred. I worked hard to keep my expression neutral.

"Do you have any idea what happened to Maria? Is she still in the United States?"

"The United States? She never went to the States," Malcolm said.

I hesitated. "Where did she go?"

"I haven't spoken to her in years, but I suspect she's still in Scotland, though maybe not Edinburgh. She's not been a part of my life for decades, Delaney. She went one direction, I went another, but I've heard she's been around."

"Why did Edwin think she went to the States? Charles too?"

Malcolm shrugged. "It was probably a lie she told Edwin to get him to buy the book. She and Charles were never really friends. I don't know. We never discussed it."

Did Edwin know something about Maria that Malcolm didn't, or had Edwin been lied to? I wasn't sure if I would bring it up with my boss or not.

"I'm sorry, Malcolm," I said.

"For Neil?"

"Yes, and for anything I might have been a part of that was meant to trick you."

"Thank you, lass. And I apologize to you. You shouldn't have been brought into their manipulations, and I should have sought you out before you came and found me. It would have been the right thing to do." He paused. "As complicated as he is, it is what Edwin would have done."

I couldn't have agreed more. "Charles did tell me that you mentioned you wanted to talk to Edwin again, perhaps try to become friends."

Malcolm laughed. "All I said was that I was ready to move on to this new adventure." He waved his hand through the air. "I joked—joked—that I might even be ready to forgive Edwin."

If that was how it had gone down, both Charles and Clarinda had gotten it very wrong. I wasn't going to point that out.

"Would you *want* to talk to Edwin?" I asked.

"I don't think so, lass. I don't think it's necessary. Edinburgh is big enough for us both to go about our own ways, and it seems Edwin's not even working anymore."

"Not much, that's true. But you still might cross paths."

"I guess I'll deal with that if I have to."

When I finished the coffee, it seemed like it was time to go. Malcolm had work to do, and I did too. I held on to the sense of caution that had come over me, but I couldn't help but like him. He saw me to the door and sent me on my way with a friendly but still somewhat forced smile.

As I stood outside his shop and looked back in to see the bookshelves inside, I wondered if I truly had taken a liking to the man or if it was just the influence of the bookstore.

Books *had* been known to turn my head a time or two.

NINETEEN

It was very much like a gymnasium, minus the basket-ball hoops. Through glass walls behind the reception desk, I saw targets attached to stands at the far end of the big main space. At the other end, people were either walking around with bows and arrows or shooting arrows at the targets. It was surprisingly crowded.

Inside the front door of the building, I'd noticed a picture of the redheaded cartoon character from the movie *Brave*. Princess Merida, if I remembered correctly. A plaque next to the picture stated that "Scottish Archery Recreation" was inspired by the movie. A viewing had been held in a nearby school, after which many of the students became interested in giving the sport a try. A club was thus formed, then a location found, and more groups and a variety of clubs and teams, as well as open shooting times, had come about.

The names of all the teams that used the space were listed next to the princess, and I keyed right in on the name the Burns Team.

I approached the teenage girl sitting behind the reception desk.

"Can I help you?" she asked with a friendly smile.

"Yes, please. Who could I speak with regarding the Burns Team?"

"Oh. Let me look." She reached to a clipboard hanging next to her and grabbed it. She looked through the pages. "Neil Watterton is the captain of that group."

She must not have heard the news, but I didn't want to shock her.

"Anyone else? A co-captain or anything?"

She glanced back down at the board. "It doesn't list any other names, just the captain."

I nodded. "Okay, any facility manager I can talk to?"

"Not at the moment. Sorry. My manager will be back in an hour or so, though."

"May I look around?"

"Sure, but if you go in there"—she pointed her thumb backwards toward the gym—"you have to stay back behind the red line on the floor."

"I understand. Thank you."

She buzzed me through the doors that led to the target range.

Six of the ten spaces were being used by people shooting at the targets. I was surprised by the variety of the equipment, different sizes and a range of technology. I saw simple bows and bigger ones that I would have labeled battle-ready. The ages of the shooters ran from young teenager to senior citizen. I was more intimidated by the large bows than by the sharp arrows. The bows seemed awkward and heavy. I had no sense that I'd be able to successfully load an arrow, aim, and shoot.

This probably wasn't the sport for me. Nevertheless, it was fun to watch the others shoot at—and hit!—the targets.

I glanced over everyone's shirts, hoping to find one like I'd seen Hamlet, Neil, and Donald Rigalee wearing. There were no team shirts in sight. As far as I could tell, everyone was dressed in regular and comfortable street clothes.

"Want to try?" a young woman asked me.

"I don't think I could handle it," I said. "But thanks."

"Come on, give it a shot," she said with a smile.

I stepped toward her, making sure to pay attention to where that red line was. "Really?"

"Sure. If someone hadn't let me take a try a time or two, I never would have given it a go. Here, I'll show you."

It wasn't meant to be, though. Just as she was about to introduce herself, I saw something at the other end of the line of shooters.

A man with a ponytail was in the doorway of the locker room entrances. He turned and was walking inside. I was sure it was Hamlet.

"Oh, hey, sorry," I said to the woman as I kept my eyes toward the locker rooms. "I just saw who I came here to find. Excuse me."

I hurried away, apologetically, but making sure to keep my feet behind that red line of tape.

The locker room entrance was a wide opening, with signs indicating the men's room to the left, the women's to the right.

For a long moment, I stood there wondering if I should call out or just go in. I could pretend I'd missed the signs if I came upon anyone else.

"Hamlet?" I said as I cupped my hands around my mouth.

He didn't emerge, but another man did, an older one in a kilt. Kilts weren't as common as I'd hoped for in contemporary Scotland, but I didn't take the time to appreciate this one.

"My friend is in there. He's a young man with a ponytail. I really need to talk to him. Would you mind asking him to meet me out here? His name is Hamlet," I said.

I didn't want to risk that he might leave through an exit on the other side of the locker rooms, like I'd seen in some gyms.

"Aye, certainly," the man said with a thick accent before he turned and went back inside. I heard the rumble of voices, but couldn't make out the echoey words. He reemerged a moment later. "No Hamlet, lass, but there's a lad with a ponytail inside. He'll be oot in a moment."

"Thank you."

I didn't even consider that it might not have been Hamlet. I waited patiently, though I did glance back toward the woman I'd hurried away from. She was no longer there.

The person I'd seen soon came from the men's locker room. And it wasn't Hamlet, though anyone who knew him could have easily made the mistake—from behind.

"Hello," he said as he walked toward me. "Did ye think I was Hamlet?"

His accent was almost as thick as the kilt-wearing man's, and he didn't wear the team shirt either.

"Yes, I'm sorry. You look like him, at least a little."

Their faces didn't match at all. This man was clean-shaven, with playful freckles and light blue eyes, not brown like Hamlet's. Their brown hair color was very similar, though, and the ponytail was exact.

"We get that a lot," he said, extending his hand. "Al Maloy."

"Delaney," I said as we shook. "You know him, then?"

"Aye, we're on the same team." He nodded toward the line of archers.

"Burns?"

"Aye."

"Hamlet is on the team," I said absently, somewhat surprised and really wondering why he and Neil hadn't behaved as if they'd known each other like team members would.

"He is," Al said.

"Neil Watterton is the captain?"

"Och, aye, he was a time ago, but he hasnae been around for a year or so. Did ye hear the terrible news?"

"I did."

"So tragic. A good lad."

"Why hasn't he been around?" I asked.

"I dunno."

"He's still listed as the captain."

"Aye. No one else wanted the responsibility. We havenae met much over the last year, missed oot on all the competitions."

"And that's okay with you?"

Al shrugged. "Aye. I'm just here for the fun of it. I joined a club only to get the membership discount here."

"I see. Are you friends with Hamlet? I've tried to call him today, and no answer. We work together."

"At that wee bookshop?"

"Yes."

"Lovely place. I am friends with him, but I probably have the same number you do. I havenae seen him for weeks."

"Were he and Neil friends?"

Al's eyebrows rose. "Goodness, I'm not sure what ye're getting at, but I don't know. If I remember correctly, Hamlet joined on right before Neil left." His eyebrows came together. "Hold on. Is something wrong? Are ye worrit Ham is hurt or something?"

"No, not at all." I laughed lightly. "I was just walking by

here today. He'd mentioned this place before, so I thought I'd check if he was here."

"Makes sense," Al said as if it truly didn't.

"When's your next team get-together?"

"We havenae had anything formal for nigh on a year. I cannae imagine we will now, after what happened to Neil."

"Such a good guy," I said, watching his reaction.

"One of the best." Emotion cracked his voice.

"I'm sorry for your loss," I said. My next transition wouldn't be smooth, but I needed to take the opportunity to ask. "Hey, what about a man named Donald Rigalee? Is he a part of the team?"

"Och, no, but I know who ye're speaking about. The killer. No, he used to come shoot here sometimes, though. I remember seeing him around, but, no, he wasnae a part of our team. He was nice enough around here."

"Could he have acquired a T-shirt with your team name?"

"Not with our team name but maybe with the design. Everyone has the same shirt. You buy it up at the front desk and then have your team name ironed on. It's not all that sophisticated." Al paused. "I doubt anyone would have even noticed if he'd put a team name on a shirt, but who knows?"

I thought back to Rigalee's shirt. I didn't remember seeing a name, just that same bow-and-arrow logo I'd been noticing. It wasn't exactly like the one I'd seen in the museum with the Royal Company of Archers certificate, but similar. It seemed that even though Hamlet's was the Burns team, the same logo, though with different team names ironed on, was used on all the shirts, which made sense.

"Thanks, Al. I'm truly sorry for your loss."

"Ta." He sniffed. "I hope ye find Hamlet. Let him know I send a hello."

"Will do," I said to his back as he stepped around me and headed toward the exit.

I bit my lip and watched him a moment. I decided on one other stop before I relieved Wyatt from his duty.

TWENTY

Okay, so maybe Hamlet and Neil didn't really know each other well. Maybe they'd only worked together briefly on a university project at the National Library, or maybe what I'd seen pass between the two of them was simply vague recognition because of their common membership in the archery team, though Hamlet joined about the time Neil stopped being so involved.

But I couldn't deny to myself that it seemed like more than that.

And, despite what I'd said to Al, I *was* beginning to worry. Wyatt confirmed for me that Hamlet still hadn't shown up to work, and he wasn't answering anyone's calls. Had he gotten himself into something he couldn't get out of easily? Was he in danger? Had he done something horrible and was running away? My mind was conjuring unpleasant things.

I stood outside the National Library and gazed at the front façade. Made of large light-colored blocks of stone, the tall building was one of my favorites. No matter all the fabulous information inside it, the outside told a great story. And though I'd never been in there, I'd certainly admired the architecture.

One row of windows spread across the front, but they were small and not as impressive as many of the arched windows throughout the city. It was the sculpted additions that made the place so special. In a line, also across the front, was a row of carved allegorical figures.

Each of the statues represented a field of study: medicine, theology, history, poetry, justice, the arts, and science. The human figures, each in a pose representing its discipline, seemed to communicate that the entire world was right inside the building, waiting to be discovered.

Though my growing concern for Hamlet was real, I couldn't help but smile at the memory of when I'd shown my parents and my brother this particular building. My mother had loved it, my father hadn't thought much of it, and my brother had noted that the statues were "downright creepy."

I planned to tell him later that I visited the library with the creepy statues.

But as I went through the doors, I discovered that even with the carvings, the outside was bland when compared to the inside. A long dark wood table with chairs filled the middle of the impressive main area. Shelves, painted a dark green, took up two levels and were topped off by a paned light in the ceiling. A reference desk ran along one side of the bottom level.

The National Library was the legal depository for Scotland. It had the right to every book published in the United Kingdom, though it wasn't a lending library. Hamlet had mentioned that he'd visited here a few months ago to do so some research. I wished I'd asked him what he'd been researching.

There were some exhibits inside the library, including an excellent one on the history of golf; it was even decorated with artificial turf. Perhaps Wyatt would think it less creepy if I took the time to show him that exhibit.

A few people were seated, though well spread out from each other, at the long table as I made my way to the reference desk.

This was going to be difficult, but the transition from my curiosity about Hamlet to my concern for him kept me moving forward.

"Hello," a young man greeted me quietly from behind a desk. His name tag said LES.

"Hi," I said.

I didn't spot anyone else behind him, nor a place where there might be other rooms or offices.

"Can I help you?" He stood and walked toward me with a friendly smile.

"I hope so. I'm worried about a friend," I said.

The man's expression fell into concern. "How can I help?"

"Do you have a place where we could talk?" I asked.

His expression quickly shifted, and I could tell he was trying to calculate just how much of a problem I might be or how big a scene I would cause. I smiled, trying to communicate urgency but also wanting to let him know I wouldn't lose my cool. It must have worked.

"This way." He signaled me to the part of the countertop that lifted and let me pass through. He led me to a small break room in the back.

We didn't see anyone else along the way, and he didn't offer me coffee or tea, but gestured for me to take a seat at one of the two small tables.

"I'm the only one at the desk right now, so I don't have long. What's going on?" he said after he sat too.

"My name is Delaney Nichols, and I work at one of the local bookshops, the Cracked Spine."

"I know the place," Les said succinctly.

"I work with Hamlet McIntyre."

Les didn't comment as he continued to look at me. There was no hint of recognition in his eyes.

"Two nights ago, my friend Hamlet and I attended a dinner where Neil Watterton was present. Later that night, he was found killed in the same building."

Les didn't like this turn of the conversation. He squirmed and then crossed his arms. "Goodness, I'm . . . sorry. Neil was . . ." He cleared his throat.

I nodded. "I'm sorry for your loss."

"Aye," Les said. "Neil was a member of our archival team upstairs. He was a good man, from all I could tell. I didn't know him well. I haven't worked here long. I don't understand, though. Are you concerned about what happened to Neil or your friend Hamlet?"

"Both. I was hoping to talk to Neil's coworkers about his ties with my friend."

"Why?" Les looked as if he was both sad and confused as to whether he should be talking to me.

I forged on. "Someone who looks like Hamlet was seen entering the building with Neil the night Neil was killed. And Hamlet hasn't shown up for work yet today. That's not like him."

Les still had a pinched expression, but he kept talking. "Happens to us all, I suppose, running late and all, but I do understand your concern a wee bit better now. I can't tell you much of anything about Neil, but, aye, he worked with two people who might be able to help, if they're willing. Let me ring them."

He hesitated. "I don't know if they've talked to the police. They might pass along anything you say."

"That's fine. I will tell the police what I find too."

Les nodded, stood, and left the break room. I wondered if I should follow, but he didn't act as if he wanted me to. I stayed put.

He had a good point. It did "happen" that someone didn't show for work on time. It had even happened before with Hamlet. But I couldn't think of one other time that he hadn't sent me or Rosie or even Edwin a message as to why he was delayed. I hoped it was all just an oversight of some sort, but that's not what it was feeling like.

"Aye, come along," Les said when he returned. "They'll talk to you."

I followed behind Les's quick strides. He led us up a stairway and along the second-floor balcony until we came to a door. "They're in there. It's by appointment only, and one is scheduled soon, but they have a few minutes. Don't touch anything."

"I won't. Thank you. I can't tell you how much I appreciate this."

"You're welcome. I hope you find what you're looking for."

"I do too. Thanks again."

Les shrugged before he walked away. "That's what we do around here."

Ah, yes, the librarians' superpower. No wonder he'd helped me. Helping was in his DNA.

I considered knocking, but just turned the knob and peered in instead.

"Come in," a woman behind yet another counter said.

Her grim expression was all business. She was petite, though the dark hair piled on top of her head did give her some height, and she was pleasantly round, with laugh lines around her eyes even as she frowned. Her eyes were as dark as her hair, and they blinked with curiosity, as well as suspicion, behind thick glasses as I came through the doorway.

I introduced myself to her and a man who came around a set of shelves packed with oversized archival files.

I was familiar with this world. I'd worked in archiving in a museum in Wichita. I'd loved the job, the slow attention to detail being more an escape for me than something tedious.

"How can we help you?" the woman asked, though still with a suspicious tone and expression.

I wondered what Les had told them when he'd called.

"My name is Delaney," I began. "I was at the Burns dinner . . ."

"The one where Neil . . ." the woman said.

I nodded. "Well, that night, yes. My friend was with me. His name is Hamlet."

The man and the woman looked at me with tandem expectant expressions.

"I'm trying to figure out some mysteries. Maybe I'll understand who killed Neil too, but I'm worried about my friend. May I ask you some questions?"

They had to think about it for a few beats, but ultimately they nodded and then told me about themselves.

Barbara and Ethan Cunningham were not only coworkers, but spouses. I got the quick history regarding the beginnings of their employment at the library thirty years earlier, followed by their marriage a year after that.

They'd worked with Neil for over twenty years and thought fondly of him. In fact, I realized they probably thought of Neil as family. They were hurting.

"But I still don't understand why you're here, really," Barbara said, her accent light, as was Ethan's, "but if you have information about our Neil, we'd like to hear it."

"I don't have much, but let me tell you about the last few days," I said, then shared with them the reasons I thought Hamlet and Neil might have already known each other, those moments I thought I'd seen mutual recognition. I told them that Hamlet had now been questioned by the police, and he'd mentioned coming into the library to do some sort of research.

They listened intently.

"I see," Ethan said after he shared another look with his wife. "Well, I do remember your friend coming in to do research."

"I do too," Barbara added. "He and Neil weren't close friends, lass. I think I remember something coming up about archery at the time, but they didn't discuss much, just got to work. Your friend wasn't here long."

"Do you remember what the research was about?"

"Goodness, not really," Barbara said. "Ethan?"

"No." Ethan paused. "I don't know. Maybe. Give me a minute. I might have something."

Ethan disappeared behind the shelves again.

"Did you ever get the impression that Neil might be in some sort of trouble?" I asked Barbara.

"No, lass, he was such a good man. A hard worker, smart, aye, but also kind." She perked up a little. "He'd just sold a house that had been a burden on him, so he was lighter and happier lately."

"Did he get in financial trouble because of the house?"

"I don't know if it was trouble so much as . . . well, whatever it was, it seemed to have been remedied."

"Did he have a particular fondness for Robert Burns that he spoke to you about?"

"Oh, he loved Burns. He like to have his midday meal outside, particularly near the Burns statue on Bernard Street. Are you familiar with it?"

"Not the monument?"

"No, this is just a statue. There's a wee coffee shop near it that he enjoyed. He'd take his sandwich over there, grab a coffee, and then sit outside near the statue."

"Okay," I said, filing it away to research later.

"Aye, he would sometimes board the bus just to have lunch there. Ethan and I first thought it odd, and we discussed following him just to see if that's what he was really doing, but we never did. As time wore on, we didn't think much about it, just accepted that if he was late from lunch, we knew that's where he'd gone. Neil always worked extra hours. No one could fault him for taking a longer lunch."

"Did he live over there?"

"No. The house wasn't there, and after he sold it, he moved to a flat on the other side of Grassmarket. It's downtown." Tears filled her eyes. She sniffed and then grabbed a tissue. "Sorry."

"No need to be." I gave her a moment. "Gosh, Barbara, can you think of anyone at all who might have wanted to hurt Neil?"

"The police asked me the same thing yesterday. I couldn't think of a soul, and I can't again today. He was lovely, minded his own business."

"Did you hear of any issues he might have had specifically with the other members of the Burns dinner club he was a part of? Their names are Charles Lexon, Clarinda Creston, and Malcolm Campbell."

She shook her head, but a thought brought her eyebrows together. "No problems. Except . . . Ethan?" she called.

Ethan reappeared from behind the shelves. He was carrying a large, opened book. "Aye?"

"Was Neil talking about someone named Clarinda or Charles? I have a memory, but I can't pinpoint the specifics." She tapped the side of her head.

"Maybe Charles. I believe someone by that name helped him buy and then sell that house, but I don't remember anything else."

"That must be it," Barbara said, though not confidently. She looked at the book Ethan held. "What did you find?"

"I believe this is what your friend Hamlet was researching." He set the book on the counter and turned it so I could better read.

"*The Magic and Methods of Fortune Tellers*," I said aloud. Per Les's instruction, I didn't touch it.

"Aye, now I remember! They laughed about it," Barbara said. "I asked if it was for something Hamlet was studying at university, but neither of them gave a straight answer."

Ethan explained that the book wasn't all about fortune-tellers, but about scam artists of all kinds, and the ways they managed to fool people who were usually in some sort of desperate search for answers. The history of such characters in Scotland. This particular book even mentioned witchcraft.

"Is there an index? Any way to see if any specific names are mentioned?" I asked.

"Och, now that you say that, I think I remember your friend

saying the exact same thing," Ethan said. He turned the book around again. "But I don't remember the answer."

He thumbed through the book, slowing down toward the back. There was no index.

"What about the section on fortune-telling specifically?" I said.

Ethan found the section and pinched the pages between his finger and thumb. There was too much there to read right then.

"Would you like me to email you the pages?" Ethan asked when they saw my disappointment.

"You can do that?" I said.

"I can. I believe this book has been scanned already. No one will mind if I share the pages with you," Ethan said. He pushed up his own glasses. "If you'll do something for me."

"Anything."

"If you find out what happened to Neil, you'll come tell us. Everything. We need to know," Ethan said.

Barbara nodded. "Please, lass."

"I understand, and I don't know what I'll find, but I promise that if I find anything at all, I will tell you everything," I said.

"Ta, lass," Barbara said.

"Do you remember exactly when my friend was here?" I asked as I wrote down my email address.

"A few months ago is all I can remember," Ethan said.

That's what I thought he'd said too. Sometimes the universe is in synchronization. Had that been what happened here? Had Hamlet learned about his ancestry a mere few months before I'd researched it? Did he already know who Letitia was and what she had done right under his nose for years off the Royal

Mile? Had he been here to learn about her, about where he'd come from? Had he figured it out?

I wondered if Hamlet had somehow seen the birth certificate in the warehouse, but I knew I'd taken care to keep it hidden.

Had he seen Letitia, met her?

Did it matter?

And more important, did it mean anything regarding Neil's murder?

"Do you remember anything else from when he was here?" I asked.

They didn't, but they were sure about the fact that Hamlet and Neil had looked at the book Ethan brought up. Ethan would get the pages to me by this evening.

A knock sounded on the door.

"We have an appointment, but we'll be in touch," Ethan said.

I gave them my condolences as I left. I wanted to hug them both, but that felt inappropriate. I hoped I'd see them again, in some way or another.

I reached for my phone the second I stepped outside.

TWENTY-ONE

"Hello, Delaney," Edwin said when he answered. "Is everything all right?"

"I think so," I said speeding up my gait. I felt a few raindrops, but the walk back to the bookshop wasn't long. "But did you know that Hamlet hasn't shown up for work this morning?"

"I did, and I just drove by his flat, ran up, and knocked. He's not home, but there's no sign that something bad has happened to him. He's probably distracted, off to class."

"That's good," I said as relief flooded through me. It wasn't the perfect answer, but at least so far he didn't seem to be hurt. "I have another question, Edwin."

"Aye?"

"I found that birth certificate in a cabinet in the warehouse. Do you think that's where you put it?"

"I must have," Edwin said.

"But you don't remember putting it there?"

"I don't, lass, but it's been a long time. I might put something away today and tomorrow forget where that was."

"I know that feeling." I paused. "If you were to *hide* something like that today, or back when you spent more time in the warehouse, where would you hide it?"

"Probably in the warehouse. Or at home. Or in my office. Lass, the possibilities aren't endless, but the warehouse would be an option."

"Do you think you would have kept the birth certificate somewhere in the bookshop where Hamlet could find it?"

"That's a good point, lass. I very much doubt I would. That would probably be something I would keep at home. Do you think someone else put it in the file cabinet? Who?"

"I'm not sure."

"Where are you, lass?"

"Reaching for the handle of the bookshop's door."

"I'll meet you there."

"Och, lass, ye need a towel," Rosie said as I came through. "And ye're shivering."

"I'll be okay in a minute. Thank you." I took the towel Rosie grabbed from her desk.

I'd noticed the increasing rain and cold, but the conversation with Edwin had kept me somewhat distracted. I hadn't even stopped by Tom's pub. I did manage a glance through the front window, spotting my handsome husband serving an older couple some drinks. I wondered if they were the newlyweds, but I'd have to ask him later.

Wyatt looked at me over a stack of books he was carrying toward some shelves. "It raining out there, Sis?" he asked.

I smiled, not only because of the obvious answer to his question but at him carrying the books. It wasn't that he didn't enjoy reading, he just wasn't quite as bookish as I was, and this might have been the first time I'd ever seen him with so many books at once.

"A little," I said. "Edwin's on his way."

"Aye?" Rosie said.

"Did you solve the murder yet?" Wyatt asked as he set down the stack of books.

"Not yet." I used the towel on my face, hands, and then hair. "In fact, I've just muddled up more mysteries than we had. Heard from Hamlet?" I asked Rosie.

Her mouth made a straight line as she shook her head. "Not yet."

"Edwin drove by his flat. He's not home, but there was no sign that anything bad happened."

"That's at least something."

"Are you worried enough to call the police?" I asked her.

Rosie shook her head. "No, not that kind of worrit. I know the lad, Delaney. I'm worrit that he's afraid, for some reason, and I want him tae know that he can tell us anything and we'll protect him tae the best of our abilities."

I nodded. "Yes, we would." I nodded back toward Wyatt. "Everything here okay?"

Rosie smiled. "Yer brother is lovely. I'm not sure he'd be happy in a bookshop forever, but he's a pure delight. The customers find him a refreshing . . ."

"Big lug?" I said.

"I don't know that expression, but it sounds aboot right."

I was suddenly overcome by emotion again, so glad my brother was here. I missed my parents, but Wyatt's visit helped ease some of that. For a minute, those feelings, combined with my worry about Hamlet, overwhelmed me, but I shook myself.

I didn't have time to dwell on any of that, and I needed to warm up.

Edwin was there only a moment later, much less wet from the rain, because he always had a brollie—an umbrella—something I tended to forget, no matter how many storms I'd been caught in.

He turned the sign to CLOSED. "Let's talk."

We gathered in the back. Rosie wrapped a blanket around my shoulders, and Wyatt appeared with a mug of coffee before he sat down too. I'd warm up quickly now.

"I'm sure we'll hear from Hamlet in short order," Edwin began. "But Delaney has made a good point. Would I have hidden that birth certificate here in the shop?"

"Birth certificate?" Wyatt said.

"I don't want to be rude, but can I give you the details later?" I asked.

"Ye'll pick up on things," Rosie said.

Wyatt nodded.

"I don't think I would have. Do you still have it here?" Edwin asked me.

"I do. I'll go grab it."

The blanket still around me, I hurried over to the dark side, noticing even more the cooler temperature over there, but this time there was a sensation that something wasn't quite right. Instead of being in a rush, I slowed down and tried to figure out what might be out of place. I came to the bottom of the stairs on that side and looked around in the shadowy light.

No one else was there. I flipped on the lights in the kitchenette, as well as the loo, but found nothing unusual or unexpected.

I inserted the big blue skeleton key into the lock on the warehouse's ornate red door and turned it three times. I felt that horror movie sensation that I shouldn't go farther on my own or at least not without grabbing a weapon. But just like those characters, I moved on with curious stupidity.

The door swung slowly open, and I found the switch quickly, turning on the light above.

No one else was there, but there was clear evidence that someone had been. I spotted it immediately: the file cabinet drawer where I'd found the birth certificate was opened—only slightly, but there was no doubt in my mind that it hadn't been me who'd left it that way.

If my memory about anything was reliable, it was about the things I did in the warehouse. Yes, it was my space more than anyone else's and where I spent much of my time. But it was also my job, and the room was packed full of expensive treasures. No matter if it was where I was comfortable, I would always take what I did inside the room seriously.

I hadn't left the drawer open.

I walked to it and looked down into the files. Someone had gone through them, but I wasn't going to touch them myself. Maybe later, but not right now.

I walked to the desk, found the key, and unlocked the desk drawer. The certificate was there. If whoever was looking in the file drawer had been looking for it, they might have thought to check my desk but wouldn't know where I kept the key.

When Edwin had given it to me, he'd told me not to tell anyone, including him, where I kept it. It had been good advice.

I relocked the drawer and then the door to the warehouse as I hurried back over to the other side, the certificate clutched in my hand. The willies disappeared as I came out into the much warmer, better-lit area.

"Sis, you sure have an interesting job," Wyatt said. "Rosie and Edwin filled me in on what you found."

"Good, but now I don't know if I found it by accident or if someone—I'm thinking maybe Hamlet at this point—wanted me to find it."

I told everyone the state of the cabinet. It could have been Rosie or Edwin who'd disturbed the drawer, but I didn't really think it had been, and their denials seemed genuine.

"You would remember if you left a drawer open?" Wyatt asked.

"I would," I said unequivocally.

Edwin inspected the certificate. "Aye, I should have considered that I wouldn't have a copy of this unless it was pristine. This isn't something I hid, lass. I'm fairly certain. If I have a copy, it's in perfect shape, and I probably hid it in my house. I will look when I get back home."

"Why would Hamlet want ye tae find it?" Rosie asked.

I smiled. "Because he knew I'd research it. I couldn't help myself. Maybe he's looked into it some, but hasn't found all the answers. He knew I'd search."

"Why didnae he just ask?" Rosie said.

I fell into thought. "I'm not sure, but I bet it has something to do with him not wanting you two to know what he'd discovered. He would know you were aware of the history. I'm not sure, but that's a guess."

"A good guess," Edwin said.

Edwin's phone rang. We all looked at him with wide, curious eyes.

"Not Ham," he told us. Then he answered, "Edwin MacAlister. . . . Aye. . . . Thank you for checking. I'll let you know if I find him."

Rosie and I both sat up straighter. Hector didn't like the charge that suddenly filled the air. He perked up from Rosie's lap with a whine.

Edwin ended the call. "That was a friend from the university. I asked him to check Hamlet's classes, see if he could track him down. Unfortunately, he hasn't been in class today."

"It's time to call Inspector Winters," I said.

"Aye, I think so," Edwin said.

I made the call.

TWENTY-TWO

There wasn't normally a waiting period for the police to file a report for a person who might be considered missing. However, Hamlet was a grown man and there was no indication that he'd been hurt.

Looking at it from another angle, though, Hamlet had been questioned by the police, which now made his potential "disappearance" suspicious, so the police were willing to at least get Hamlet's name and a description spread throughout the city's police communication.

"He's probably fine," Inspector Winters said after he made a call and then explained what he'd done.

"Do you think he's hiding from you?" I asked. "Do you have any real evidence that he was the person with Neil?"

Inspector Winters shook his head. He sat on a corner of Rosie's desk as the rest of us stood around him. "Just an eyewitness who saw someone with Neil. I don't know if Hamlet is hiding from us. I don't really think he has a reason to, unless there are things we don't know yet. I hope not."

"Who's the witness?" I asked.

"I can't share that with you, lass, but we are confident they weren't involved and didn't lie to us."

"Can you tell me how Neil was killed? You're sure it was murder, right?"

"Aye, we're sure." Inspector Winters frowned and then looked at Rosie as if for approval to speak of such things. She nodded. "Blunt-force trauma to the head. We don't have the weapon, but his lungs did not indicate that he died from smoke inhalation. He was killed before the fire was set. It was most likely set to try to destroy the body and any other evidence."

Rosie said, "Do ye think that the rest of the people at the dinner might have been dealt the same fate if they'd stayed longer?"

"Oh, it's impossible to know, Rosie, but I doubt it. Strength in numbers an' all."

"The dinner stuff had been cleaned up?" I asked.

"Clarinda said she threw away most of the food in a bin near the building, and the rubbish had been gathered before we could take a closer look."

"That's convenient," Wyatt said.

I looked at Inspector Winters. I didn't want to be the one to throw Hamlet under the bus, but I also thought some information might help find him.

"Neil and Hamlet were on the same archery team, though Hamlet joined just as Neil was becoming less involved, it appears," I said.

"Aye?" Inspector Winters stood. "Tell me what you know."

I told him everything I'd learned about the archery club and my visit to the library. The police had talked to Barbara and

Edgar, of course, but they'd had no idea about the archery. Inspector Winters was duly impressed, as was my brother.

Inspector Winters left after making notes, telling us to call him the second we saw Hamlet and that he'd do the same.

I plopped down in one of the chairs when he was gone. I was exhausted.

"Lass, go home, get some rest," Edwin said. "Wyatt, take your sister home. We'll start again tomorrow."

"Thank you, Edwin, but what do you really think is going on with Hamlet? I'm truly worried," I said.

Edwin shook his head. "Whatever it is, he hasn't done anything wrong. It's not in him."

"What about his biological family?" I said. "Is it in them?"

"They aren't bad people," Edwin said. "Well, they aren't murderous."

"Fortune-tellers usually aren't living honest lives," I said, though I remembered how Letitia seemed to key in on something that was currently relevant to my life: Robert Burns.

"No, but . . ." Edwin paused. "They've not hurt him, even if he told them who he was. It's only Letitia now anyway, and she couldn't hurt anyone."

Again, I thought about Letitia and what I'd interpreted as her sense of loss. "I don't think so either. Edwin, what happened to Dora?"

"As far as I know, she just disappeared."

"Left Hamlet on the streets and disappeared?" I asked.

"Aye, that's the story. He was about two."

I was tired. Bone-deep tired. I worked hard to stifle a yawn, but all that did was contort my face.

"Go home, lass" Edwin said. "Get some rest."

"I think that's a good idea."

Wyatt and I walked up to the pub and let Tom drive us all home. My blue house by the sea was a haven, particularly tonight.

I fell into a deep sleep, though it wasn't without dreams, and one of them woke me the next morning, with a whole new idea.

TWENTY-THREE

"He's looking for his mother or trying to figure out what happened to her," I said to Tom and Wyatt over breakfast.

"Really?" Wyatt said.

"Aye, that sounds like something Hamlet would do," Tom said.

"I think he's in trouble or something, though," I said. "Or he'd ask us for help."

"Instead of just leaving the birth certificate in the file cabinet?" Wyatt asked.

"That's another thing." I pointed with a piece of buttered toast. "I remember saying to everyone, a few weeks ago, that I was going to tackle the file drawers during an upcoming week. Hamlet might have used that as a chance to put the certificate in there."

"Why is everything such a secret?" Wyatt asked. "Remember when you found that stuff about our biological grandfather? Why in the world don't people just talk about these things? It is what it is, you know?"

"I do, but those things can be sensitive issues for people.

Remember, our grandmother had to have been unfaithful for what happened to have happened."

"A million years ago," Wyatt said. "I mean, I can understand not wanting to broadcast it way back when, but after all that time, who cares?"

"Time moves quickly. Life goes on," Tom said.

"So why would this be particularly difficult for Hamlet?" I asked.

"Well, when it's your mum, things can get . . . sensitive," Tom said.

"And would any of this have anything at all to do with Neil?"

"I can't see how," Tom said as he slipped another piece of toast on my plate.

I fell into thought as I chewed. "Neil was surprised about who we were, our connection to Edwin that night. He and Hamlet didn't *really* act like they knew each other, but I saw . . . something. Do you suppose they were both faking it for some reason?"

"What reason?" Wyatt grabbed more bacon.

I had nothing.

After I'd woken up with the fresh idea that Hamlet was either looking for Dora or trying to find out what might have happened to her, I started the day with a glance at my email. Just as Ethan Cunningham had promised, he'd sent me copies of the pages of the book he'd shown me.

The section had been about the "scam" of fortune-telling, particularly as it had come about and then transformed in Scotland. Fortune-telling, of course, had its beginnings in witchcraft, which had been the reason for many a murder in the country. Being labeled a witch usually led to nothing better than a torturous and painful death.

But some fortune-tellers had been deemed good; at least they had not been accused of practicing witchcraft. The smart ones figured out that if they only "saw" good things for royalty, they would fare better than those who saw bad things or didn't ingratiate themselves with powerful people. In the pages that Ethan sent, I only found a few paragraphs devoted to the Strangelove women:

We believe that Letitia Strangelove was born in or around 1939, but it's a mystery as to where she came from and who her parents were. She never married but gave birth to a girl she named Wilma. Together, they told many fortunes, using their signature purple crystal ball. Some say that Letitia has—as of this printing, she's still alive—an uncanny sense of the future, but Wilma's act was purely that, an act. Wilma might have caused more trouble than any of the Strangelove women, including her daughter, Dora. Wilma died from natural causes, but we don't have any further information.

We don't know who Dora's father was, but we do know that Dora might have been the most gifted "seer" in the family. Our investigations have turned up that Dora might have even been able to pick lottery numbers. She disappeared mysteriously in 2000, leaving behind a child: a boy, who also disappeared. They have never been found.

Some say they see Dora's ghost roaming the streets of Edinburgh at night, most of the time near a statue or a monument or a museum that somehow highlights our beloved Rabbie Burns. It was said that Dora loved anything that Burns wrote.

"Of course she did," I'd said quietly to myself after reading the paragraphs.

That was all there was, and it didn't tell me much. I tried to put myself in Hamlet's shoes and feel what he'd felt when reading it. The Burns connection seemed to be important, but I couldn't guess where that might have taken him, unless it was toward something Neil Watterton was involved in. I couldn't pare it down to anything more specific, though.

Even before reading the pages, I'd texted Edwin and Rosie, asking if they'd heard from Hamlet. They hadn't. I'd also told Tom the details about finding the birth certificate and its contents.

I would call Inspector Winters later in the morning, see if he knew anything more.

"Want to come with me to check on Hamlet's flat?" I said to Tom and Wyatt.

"I would love to, lass, but I've too much to do at the pub," Tom said. "Want the car?"

"No, the bus is easier, but thanks."

"I'll go with," Wyatt said, as he grabbed yet another piece of bacon.

"After I do a little more research." I stood up from the table. "I'll be quick. I'm running up to my library. My laptop is up there."

I kissed Tom and told him to have a good day. Wyatt offered to clean up the breakfast dishes. I shouldn't have been shocked. My brother was a grown man, after all. But I was still surprised by his offer and wondered what the end result of his efforts would actually look like.

Tom had built me my very own library in the attic of the old house. He hadn't altered the pull-down ladder that led up there, but the alcove space had been transformed with shelves of books, comfortable seating, and good but mellow lighting.

He'd even included a couple of portable heaters, one of which I turned on first thing.

I took a seat in one of the oversized chairs and opened my laptop.

"Okay, Dora Strangelove, who were you, really?" I said aloud as I began a new search.

There wasn't much about her, most of the links leading to something about the Marvel movie *Doctor Strange*.

But a few pages in, I found two small items.

The article's headline read "Local Fortune-Teller Goes Missing." Underneath a picture of what looked like a bedroom, it said:

> *Edinburgh woman Dora Strangelove has gone missing. Her family claims she has a two-year-old male child with her. Ms. Strangelove, sometimes considered homeless, last resided in a small flat. Please call the police if you see her.*

An address was also listed.

I took a photo of the picture. I knew it was located in a rough neighborhood.

A photo of Dora was also included, and I suddenly knew where Hamlet got his fine features. Though, of course, more masculine, his nose and cheekbones came directly from his mother. She was a beauty, there was no doubt, even though the picture (taken a year before she disappeared) couldn't hide her world-weary eyes.

The other item I found was a copy of an old flyer about the Strangelove women and their ability to tell your fortune with clear accuracy, guaranteed! I cringed at the uncomfortable sales pitch, but we all had to make a living, I supposed. A sketched purple crystal ball with disembodied hands hovering above it filled the middle of the page.

There was nothing else with the flyer, but the link took me to a familiar website. At least I knew the shop attached to the site.

Just around the corner and up Victoria Street from Tom's pub was a place I'd visited a few times since moving to Edinburgh: the Cadies and Witchery Tours. In fact, as far as I knew, they still displayed the card holder made from the skin of notorious body snatcher and murderer William Burke.

The staff offered tours and the small shop sold unique items befitting the haunted tours, which were done with perfection, based upon my own experience. The ad mentioned the shop, but it looked to be a forgotten page, a long-broken-off link that might have been attached to a site at one time. There were no other links, nothing to take me back to a home page or anything other than the search page.

I printed out the flyer and grabbed it before doing one more search, just in case. I found nothing. Though Dora had gone missing more than twenty years ago, I felt a wave of sadness that there wasn't much about the disappearance of a young woman and her toddler son.

I turned off the heater and then hurried back down the ladder. Tom had mentioned his concerns about how safe the ladder was and wondered if he should remodel further, changing the ladder to stair steps. I'd encouraged him to leave things as they were. I loved everything about my library.

He was already gone when I made it back downstairs. Wyatt had done as he'd said he would and the kitchen was spotless.

"Thanks," I said, keeping my surprise well hidden.

"My pleasure," he said. "I love your house."

"Me too."

"You're doing great, Sis," he said with a big-lug, proud-brother smile.

"You're not doing so bad yourself," I said.

Wyatt took a deep breath and let it out. "I know. We did okay."

I laughed. "We did."

"We're going by Hamlet's house?"

I thought a moment. "Yes, at least first."

"Can we get in?"

"I know where a key is," I said, feeling guilty. "So does Edwin. I didn't ask him if he went inside yesterday, but he mentioned knocking. He probably peeked inside."

"Are *we* going in?"

"I don't know yet. I'll decide when we get there."

"Works for me."

I texted Rosie and Edwin that I'd be late, and they said they didn't mind. They were glad Wyatt was with me, though.

It was still cold outside, and rain was on its way, but we made it to the bus stop about a half block from the house without needing the umbrella that Wyatt remembered to grab. Hamlet lived near the university but not in university housing. Edwin had found him a small flat above a coffee shop. The scent of brewing coffee made its way up to his place in the mornings. He often commented that it was a wonderful way to wake up.

A narrow stairway was tucked in between the coffee shop and a tailor's place. The tailor inside was old and hunched over but always sent me a friendly smile when I caught his eye.

"How many apartments are up here?" Wyatt asked as we climbed the stairs.

"Just Hamlet's. I think the space above the tailor's is used for storage."

"I'm not sure Scotland was built for people my size."

"It wasn't." I laughed. "But you'll be okay."

I turned back to glance at my brother. His wide shoulders fit just fine in the stairwell and then in the landing outside Hamlet's flat's door, but it was true that the walls seemed a little closer than he was used to.

I knocked on the door, pounding harder than I usually would. "Hamlet, it's me."

"There's no one in there," Wyatt said.

"Yeah, I don't think so either."

"You should go in."

"I should?"

"Yeah, I would. If he told you where he keeps a key, and if you're worried about him, go in."

I was easily convinced.

At the top of the stairway was a narrow banister. I reached out to the closest of the three balusters and found the key taped there, in the spot Hamlet had shown me.

I grabbed the key and showed it to Wyatt, who nodded me further along.

Though Hamlet was artistic in nature, he wasn't into interior decorating. His flat was furnished with the barest minimum of furniture and lots and lots of books. They filled a few floor-to-ceiling shelves and were stacked on the coffee table in the small front room, as well as the small kitchen counter behind the living room.

He enjoyed cooking, and he fixed dinner for himself and friends frequently, but there was no indication that a meal had been recently cooked on the small stove. The microwave was spotless too and the fridge mostly empty, though a few basics that were still fresh sat on the shelves.

The small loo showed no signs of recent use, and it was difficult to know if anyone had slept in the unmade bed over the last two nights.

"He hasn't been here, I don't think," I said.

"Everyone's left him messages. He would have called," Wyatt said as we stepped back to the front room.

"I think he would have."

"He's hurt or he's hiding." Wyatt cringed when he saw my expression. "Sorry, hate to make you think that."

"I'm already thinking it." I put my hands on my hips. "There's got to be something here to tell us what he's been up to."

"I don't see a desk or a television."

"No, he likes to go to films, but if he wants to watch something at home, he watches it on his laptop."

"That's what we need. His laptop."

I bit my lip. "That's too intrusive."

"No, it's not. Do you know where he keeps it?"

I shook my head. "I would think out in the open somewhere."

"Let's search." Wyatt stepped around me again and went directly to the couch.

I joined him as we even lifted cushions and checked underneath. We moved to the kitchen and opened the three cupboard doors. No laptop.

But in the bedroom, right under the bed, we hit pay dirt.

"There's a sock under here too, but let's leave it," Wyatt said as he grabbed the computer.

"The police might want the laptop."

"If they had a warrant, they'd've come in here and got it," Wyatt said. "Back to the couch."

Wyatt tucked the laptop under his arm and led us back to the couch. He lifted the screen. We were greeted by a picture of Hector and a slot for a password.

"I was afraid of that," Wyatt said.

"I don't know it," I said. "I couldn't even guess."

"Right. Well, let's try the usual suspects. Birthdays, etc."

As I spouted off dates, we weren't greeted with success. I even included the birthday from the birth certificate, but that didn't do any good either.

But as we sat there, my eyes wandered over the rest of the room. Books everywhere. Some people would find it messy, but I just found it comforting. My eyes landed on the second shelf of one of the bookcases.

I hopped up from the couch and inspected the shelf.

All the books were by Robert Burns. None of the editions were valuable, but they were old, well used, often read.

However, there was one book with a piece of paper sticking up from its top. I pulled it from the shelf. It was a compilation: *Complete Poems and Songs of Robert Burns*. I'd seen many copies of it at the Cracked Spine. I might have even sold a couple.

I opened to the page with the paper, which turned out to be a drawing.

"Who's that?" Wyatt had come up behind me.

"I don't know."

A pencil sketch, it was of a woman standing outside, on a street corner, I thought. As the subject of the picture, she seemed to be emoting, maybe acting a part. Her short hair was messy, her eyes full of pain or concern.

"Did Hamlet draw this?" Wyatt asked.

"I have no idea," I said. "He could have. He's good enough,

but it doesn't seem like his style, which is more abstract. I don't know, though."

The background was made up of small shops, businesses, but none of the signs were clear, just scribbles to represent words.

Still, though . . . something familiar was in the background, off to the side and meant to be in the distance, I thought.

"What is this?" I said as I put my finger on it.

"I have no idea."

And then, with the spark of something close to a lightning bolt, it came to me. I gasped.

"I know exactly what it is."

"What?"

"Come on, let's go."

I took a photo of the drawing with my phone and then put the sketch and the book back where they belonged. I had Wyatt take the laptop back to the bedroom, and we hurried out to the bus stop.

TWENTY-FOUR

"I think we've found it." I held up my phone displaying the sketch. We were right next to the old Assembly Hall, which must have once been a meeting place, probably replaced by the new Assembly Hall, which was about ten minutes away. I'd been to a lecture inside the new one. A grand building, built with the older architecture of Edinburgh and Scotland kept in mind.

It had started raining, so we stood under an awning that, though not in the exact spot that offered the view from the sketch, was close enough for us to know that we'd found the right area.

We were near the Robert Burns statue that Barbara and Ethan Cunningham had told me about, the one where they said Neil would eat lunch. I'd thought the edge of the sketch was one side of the statue. It seemed I'd been correct. Actually, I'd been by this spot before but hadn't digested the fact that the statue represented Burns. Apparently, when it came to erected statues, the number of Mr. Burns's effigies held third place in the world, at least of non-religious figures. Christopher Columbus and Queen Victoria were ahead of the bard. This was a fact that Wyatt had looked up on the way over.

"Okay, but who is the woman?" Wyatt asked.

I had an idea who she was, but it was a big stretch. I wanted to find her before I speculated out loud. I'd been holding up my phone, comparing my photo of the sketch to the real view. I dropped it to my side and looked around. A few people were out and about, most of them under umbrellas.

"I've seen a number of performing street artists throughout town. I wonder if she's one."

"I don't see any out here now, but maybe because of the weather," Wyatt said. He nodded across the square. "There's a coffee shop. Maybe we could wait out the rain in there?"

"Let's go."

The monument was a figure in bronze, standing atop a base of red sandstone and red granite. The bronze Burns was dressed very much like the costumes worn at the Burns dinner. Carvings and engraved plaques took up each of the four sides of the base, and the name BURNS had also been carved into the granite. It was an impressive sculpture.

Inside the shop, we ordered coffees and found a table near the front window. I was only one sip in when I heard the background music being played in the shop. It was "Auld Lang Syne," and it was well past New Year's. I looked around. The coffee shop was decorated with sketches of Burns, as well as pictures of his books and sheets of music. This place was all about Burns.

"Hang on," I said. "I'll be right back."

I made my way to the barista. More customers would be in shortly; there was no time to waste with extra small talk. I pulled out my phone and showed him the sketch. "By chance, do you know her?"

"Aye. Well, I don't know her, but I recognize her. She's out there quite often." He looked out front as his forehead crinkled. "But I haven't seen her for a week or so, maybe."

"She's a street performer?"

"Aye. All Burns. That's why she stands near the statue. She recites his poems and sings the songs, with spot-on accuracy, from what I've heard. I think she moves around sometimes, though. Spends some time by the big Burns monument too, the one on Regent Road."

I nodded and put my phone back in my pocket. "Do you know her name?"

"No, not at all."

He'd written our names on our coffee cups. "Has she ordered coffee here?"

"Aye." He smiled. "We just call her Burns. And we never let her pay."

I nodded and bit my bottom lip. "Do you know where she lives?"

"Sorry, lass, I have no idea. I get the impression that she might not have a permanent home. I don't know, though. She's not addled in the brain." He tapped the side of his head and smiled again. "But she's not . . . I don't know, lass. She's not like you and me. She struggles with . . . even eye contact."

I nodded and then scrolled to a picture of Hamlet on my phone. "Have you seen him around here?"

"Aye. Hamlet. I know him. We took some classes together at university, and he's been here a time or two." But the barista stopped suddenly, as if he might not want to keep answering questions.

"Have you seen him today or yesterday?"

He hesitated. "No, it's been a while."

"Did you ever see Hamlet talking to the woman?"

"Lass, I don't know who you are. Why so many questions about Hamlet? He's a good lad."

"He's a good friend of mine," I said. "We work together, but he hasn't come to work for two days. We're worried."

"Aye?" The barista scratched the side of his head. "I can see why you'd be worried, but no, I haven't seen him. Do you want me to have him ring you if I do?"

"Actually, I'd prefer if you'd call me, and I'll come right over. Any chance you'd do that? I mean him no harm."

The barista looked at me a long moment. If he was in tune with his intuition, he'd know I wasn't out to do anything but help Hamlet.

"I don't know. But here, write down your name and number." He handed me a pen and a napkin.

I left my contact information, with my mobile number, as well as the one for the bookshop. I hoped he trusted me enough to call me if he saw Hamlet. "Thank you."

He nodded as he took the napkin I slid over the counter.

Distracted, I made my way back to the table and told Wyatt what I'd learned.

"You think that's his mother, don't you?" he said when I was finished. "Dora?"

"I do, and it makes sense, kind of, or at least I'm making it make sense in my mind."

"I understand, and I see it too."

I remembered the flyer about the Strangelove women. "Come on, I have one more place to stop by before I get to work."

"Let's go."

We waved at the barista, who sent me a cautious smile. I was sure he wasn't going to call me, but even if he told Hamlet about me, maybe that would be an extra nudge for Hamlet to let us know he was okay.

Oh gosh, I really hoped he was.

The Cadies and Witchery Tours shop was crowded. A tour was being organized, and I could tell Wyatt would have enjoyed it, but he wouldn't join in right now. I wondered if Tom had asked him to keep an eye on me or if he'd decided to himself.

"Can I help you?" a young woman from behind the counter asked.

I glanced at her name tag. "Betty, hi." I held up my phone displaying the picture of the old flyer. "I know you're busy, but I have a question. I found this on the internet. At one time I think it was linked with this place's website. The business name is on the flyer."

She took the phone and looked closer. "I didn't know we worked with the Strangelove women. Must have been before my time. I've been here about ten years."

"You know the Strangelove women?" I asked.

"Well, I think there's just one left. Letitia has a place up off the Royal Mile."

"Wilma was her daughter, Dora her granddaughter?" I said, hoping to prompt something more—anything more.

"Aye, I think those were their names, but it was a long time ago. Letitia's worked on her own for . . . I knew about the family when I was a little girl, but the others have been gone for a long time." She fell into thought. "I don't know that I remember the particulars, but, aye, I saw Letitia not long ago. She was walking up the Royal Mile, toward her place, I suppose."

"Do you have any idea what happened to Dora?"

"I . . . that's right, Dora's disappearance was a mystery.

Goodness, I haven't thought about that for a very long time. No, lass I have no idea, couldn't even speculate. Why?"

"I need to find a friend. I think he's somehow related to the Strangelove women."

"Oh, that could be a problem in itself."

"Why?"

"You said 'he.' They weren't known for welcoming men into their lives. They were such a strange group back then." She cocked her head as she fell into thought again. "They probably would have been thought of as witches back in the day, and their reputation twenty years ago wasn't much different. They were feared in some circles."

"Because they would, what, cast spells?"

"Kind of." She shrugged. "We're a superstitious lot, us Scots, but it really did seem that the Strangelove women, at least Letitia, could tell the future. Many people talked about their experiences with her. That's right! When Dora disappeared, it was speculated that someone Letitia had told a bad future to had grabbed Dora and harmed her."

"Any names mentioned?"

"Goodness, not that I remember."

I thought about the small amount of information on the internet. "They weren't liked?"

"Not really. They were respected and feared, but not really liked back then. And I don't know if I'm remembering this fairly, but I don't think the police worked very hard to find Dora."

I cringed. I didn't want to say one bad thing about the Scottish police, and in my experience the officers and inspectors I knew never slacked on the job.

"No, no, not in a bad way," Betty corrected when she saw

my expression. "It's just that . . . they looked, but, oh, ignore me, I don't know what I'm saying."

"It's okay. It was a long time ago," I said, though I wasn't exactly sure what I meant by that. "Any chance you know where Letitia lives?"

"I don't," she said.

I wasn't sure I believed her, but I also understood her not sharing an address with a stranger. I didn't know any other way to quickly make myself more familiar.

"Thanks, Betty," I said as more people started to file in for the next tour.

We didn't take a lot more time, but I managed to show Wyatt the Burke skin card holder. He was properly intrigued.

As we waved goodbye to Betty, she held up her hand as if she wanted us to wait. She was helping a couple, so we hung out by the door. When her transaction was complete, we went back to the counter.

"I have something," she said as she turned and pulled an old shoebox from a shelf behind her. She brought it around and rifled through it, finding a card.

"This man came in not long ago asking about Dora. Seriously, something must be in the air, because over the past ten years, as far as I know, only you and he have come in. You might want to talk to him, join forces."

I took the card and read aloud. "'Matthew Edison.'"

It was all I could do to contain a cheer. This was the name of the father listed on the birth certificate. I'd thought about trying to find him, but there were so many Matthew Edisons. It looked like we'd caught a break. Here he was, just waiting for us to track him down at the most surprising of places.

"Thank you, Betty," I said, still managing to keep my emotions in check.

She was inspecting me, probably wondering what we were up to. She rubbed her arms. "Aye, you're welcome. Whatever is going on, I hope it all works out."

"Us too," I said as I looked at Wyatt.

"Us too," he agreed.

TWENTY-FIVE

Matthew Edison was a business owner. He owned a shop that specialized in tartans—kilts, scarves, women's skirts. If there was something that could be made with a tartan pattern, it appeared that Matthew's shop could create it, at least according to his website.

Wyatt and I had hurried back toward the bookshop, this time stopping by to say hello to Tom. Taking advantage of a lull in Tom's business, Wyatt and I sat up at the bar as we shared what we'd been up to and used the time to research Matthew's business.

We also found a picture of Mr. Edison. And while Hamlet looked like his mother, there was something about . . . I couldn't pinpoint it, but maybe it was something about Mr. Edison's crooked smile or maybe his cheeks—yes, I could see how this man could have been Hamlet's father.

"If Hamlet found the birth certificate, he didn't have to search far to find Mr. Edison," Tom said.

"I don't know," I said. "I'd searched for him when I first found it, and there were so many men with that name that I was overwhelmed. It took the business card from Betty to narrow it down to this one. Maybe Hamlet hasn't figured it out yet, or maybe he's only searching for his mother. I wish he'd just talked to us. I hope he's okay."

"Me too," Tom said.

"Everything all right at the pub?" I asked, thinking I hadn't asked about his day for a while.

Tom smiled. "Everything's fine, love. I'm just worried about Hamlet."

"Me too."

After updating Tom, while Wyatt enjoyed a bowl of pretzels, my brother and I made our way back to the bookshop.

Rosie and Hector greeted us.

"Anything from Hamlet?" I asked.

"Not a word," Rosie said. She nodded toward the back. "Edwin is here. Did you find out anything?"

"I haven't found Hamlet," I said as Edwin appeared from the back of the shop. "Does anyone mind if I call Inspector Winters again?"

No one objected.

Inspector Winters came over to the bookshop again, but he had nothing new to report. He listened and took notes, though. I didn't lie about where I'd found the sketch of the woman who might be Dora. He seemed to agree that since Hamlet had told me about the key, it was fine that I'd used it. Briefly, I wondered if maybe he wouldn't be so agreeable if we'd managed to get into the laptop. But we hadn't.

The part that surprised me most was that Inspector Winters recognized the woman in the sketch. Back when he'd first become part of the police force, he'd walked a beat, and he'd seen her around the statue a few times.

"She was really very sweet," he said when he thought back. "I never knew her name."

"Do you know where she lived?" I asked.

"I didn't, but I haven't worked over there for many years. I'll check with others."

"I don't know if any of this has anything to do with Neil's murder," I said.

"But you don't want Hamlet to get in trouble," he said. "I understand, and you all know I would do whatever I could to help him, but I do have to do my job."

We all nodded, though each of us with a different expression. I was grim, Wyatt the most understanding. However, Rosie and Edwin were clearly doubtful about the inspector's words. We would all go to extremes to save Hamlet from getting in any trouble; I hoped even our friend who also happened to be an officer of the law would do the same.

"Lass, what was the address of Dora's flat again, the one listed in the article?" Edwin asked.

I pulled up the picture I'd taken on my phone, the one from the article I'd read noting where Dora might have lived at one time. I'd included that discovery in everything I'd shared with everyone.

"Aye," Edwin said as he looked at it.

"What?" I said.

"I thought so," Edwin said. "I can't imagine this means anything at all, but directly across that close right there"—he pointed—"was where Malcolm's bookshop was located."

"Really?" I said, but I was the only one who thought this discovery was the least bit interesting.

"A strange coincidence," Edwin said.

"Is it?" I said. "I thought there was no such thing."

But everyone thought it was simply that, a coincidence. Even Inspector Winters simply wrote a quick line in his notebook about it.

He told us he would do what he could to find the street performer and continue to search for Hamlet.

After Inspector Winters left again, I couldn't let go of the set of circumstances that everyone else thought made for a coincidence. I was sure something bigger was going on. What could tie Hamlet, Neil, and Malcolm's bookshop together? I'd convinced myself that Dora was the connection, even if I didn't understand how or why. With Edwin and Rosie's blessings, Wyatt and I set out for more exploring, beginning with a look at the tartan shop.

I was surprised by Wyatt's first words to me once we'd boarded another bus. "Hamlet *might* have killed Neil," he said.

"Why do you think that?"

"Something's clearly up," he said. "And he's on the run."

I cringed. "I'm not going to believe he's on the run yet. And Hamlet couldn't kill a fly. In fact, I've watched him trap creatures just so he could free them to the great outdoors."

"Yeah, well, we can all be driven to murder."

"Really?" I looked at him. I believed that too, but I was curious if there was more he wanted to share.

His eyes widened and he put his hand on his chest. "I've never killed, but if someone threatened someone I loved, I could do it." He winced. "Maybe."

"Yeah, I know what you're saying."

We fell into silent thought as the bus made its way toward the tartan shop. I was so worried about Hamlet that I couldn't have stayed inside the bookshop to work.

I had to *do* something; I had to keep looking.

We disembarked and tucked our chins down as we walked another half block to the shop.

Disappointing us both deeply, it was closed.

"Who closes on Fridays?" Wyatt asked as we peered in the front window.

"Tartan shops, I suppose." I looked for a sign with a phone number one could call if they had a tartan emergency, but there was nothing posted.

"I think we've been thwarted," Wyatt said.

"I think you're right." I bit my bottom lip.

I thought about leaving a note, asking for someone from the shop to call me. I could slip it under the door. I decided I would rather talk to someone in person as I stood on the stoop and peered through the window at the top of the door.

All the items inside were appealing—lush and giving the impression they were comfortable and soft, though I knew some of the woolens weren't as soft as they were itchy. I wished for a moment inside with a cup of hot chocolate.

"Now what?" Wyatt asked.

We stood under the shop's awning, which gave us a slight reprieve from the bitter wind. I plopped my hands on my hips and then recrossed them in front of me.

Painters and poets have liberty to lie.

Mr. Burns himself had come back to say a few words. I loved the sound of his voice, the sound my imagination had conjured. Artists and their self-honest lies. *I hear you, Rabbie,* I thought, *but I'm not sure what you're trying to say. If it's Hamlet who's lying, I don't want to know.*

He didn't respond.

I had another idea. "Want to go look at the space where Malcolm's bookshop used to be?"

"The place near Dora's alleged apartment?"

"Yep."

"You know how to get there?"

I thought a moment longer, putting the route together in my head. "I think so."

"Lead the way."

No business had replaced the bookshop in the space where it had been. Even two decades later, it was still a burned-out shell of a building. The windows were blacked out, but Wyatt and I could peek through worn spots in the paint. You could still see the charred walls and ceiling inside, though there were no books, no furniture.

"How is this possible?" Wyatt said. "They should have taken care of this a long time ago. I'm surprised it hasn't brought the whole building down."

I looked up at the two stories atop the lower level. "Maybe that's the point. Maybe if they did anything to it, that would bring the building down."

My engineer brother looked at me incredulously. "That's not really the way it works."

I shrugged. "Then it just wasn't important."

"I guess not."

We couldn't get inside the building. Not only was the door locked, but it was also boarded over.

The close next to the building was dark and clearly a place where people set up tents or bedrolls. Neither Wyatt nor I had any desire to explore the dark alleyway.

But the squat building on the other side of the close made me more curious. This was the place where Dora had lived?

An elderly, hunched-over man came out through the front

door. His winter gear was old but seemed to do the job well enough. Without any hesitation, I approached him.

"Hello," I said. "My name's Delaney, and this is my brother Wyatt." I signaled over my shoulder as Wyatt came up behind me.

"Aye?" the man said warily. His rheumy eyes showed a combination of fear and suspicion.

I felt terrible that I'd scared him. "I'm so sorry to bother you, and I don't mean to, really, but I'm doing some research on the local Strangelove women. Do you know them?"

His eyes transformed immediately to sad understanding. "Aye, lass. Well, many years anon now, I ken sweet Dora."

"You did?" My voice didn't hide my excitement.

"Aye."

I sighed. "Is there any chance we could buy you a coffee and ask you some questions?"

He looked around and then seemed to deflate some. "It's not an easy task getting myself ready tae go oot, lass. I need tae get tae the store."

"I'll do your shopping," Wyatt offered. "Just give me a list, point me toward the store, and I'll get it done."

"Aye?" he said, the suspicion back and lining the one word.

"Absolutely. I'm good at shopping."

I didn't quite know what to do. I appreciated Wyatt's offer, but I was sure it was all very strange being approached by two curious Americans. I tried to smile in a way that would ease any of his concerns.

It took him a long moment, but probably not as long as it would have if it had been warm outside.

"All right, then. Come in; I'll give you a list. I've a kettle at the ready. We'll have a wee bit of tea inside." He looked at Wyatt. "Ye'll do my shopping?"

"Of course."

He shook his head before he turned and led us back into the building.

He guided us up a flight of stairs and to his one-room flat.

"Name's Clyde McCannon," he said as he unlocked and opened the door.

His room was compact but well organized, and he seemed immediately comfortable in the space. A tiny stove, with a filled kettle atop it, took up a corner. On one side of the stove was a small refrigerator and on the other was a sink and some counter space. Similar to the setup I'd seen in the Burns House, Clyde's few dishes were stacked on wood shelves out in the open, and the room reminded me of the picture of Dora's flat.

I didn't know if the couch pulled out and into a bed or if he just slept on it as it was, but there was no sign of any other sleeping spot, no bedding in sight. I thought he could have tucked away some sheets into a narrow closet next to the smallest bathroom I'd ever seen. There was no tub, but a shower where even a half turn to rinse would be tight.

Clyde ignited the burner under the kettle and gave Wyatt a wad of bills, a grocery list, and directions to the store.

My brother nodded and hurried away, leaving Clyde and me alone. I sensed he still thought this was all very weird, but once he was seated on the couch with his tea, he didn't seem to be bothered.

"Good light in here," I said.

"Aye. This is a corner room; I get two windows. The front one, and the one that leads to the close. I keep those curtains shut most of the time, but the front window has a nice enough view." He took a sip of tea. "In fact, this use tae be Dora's room."

"Oh," I said, surprised and intrigued by the fact. "You knew her well?"

"As well as anyone, I suppose. I lived up a flight at the time. Dora was only here a few short months, but she had a young lad, and we all wanted to make sure they were well taken care of. We did the best we could."

"What do you remember about her?"

He hesitated. "Lass, why are you asking these questions? I'm not put off by your curiosity, but I'd like to know why you're here, why you care."

I bit my bottom lip. "Clyde, I might know her son. I can't be sure yet, but I might." I was pretty darn sure, but it didn't seem right saying that much.

Tears filled his eyes. "I was hoping you'd say something like that. He's alive? I've had hope all these years."

I nodded. "If he's who I think he is, he's alive and well."

Clyde blinked away the tears. "If you've come upon the truth, may I meet him?"

"Yes, of course. I'll bring him by."

"Well then, aye, I'll tell you what I can. Dora was lovely, sweet, trying tae care for her child, but it was difficult."

"Why was it so difficult?"

"All she could do was tell fortunes," he said with a shrug. "Not enough money in that tae make it on yer own, and she didnae want tae be around her family anymore. They werenae welcoming of the lad. Well, her mother wasnae. I think her grandmother was, but it didnae matter. I dinnae think I ever understood the issues."

"After she disappeared, did you ever see her again?"

Clyde shook his head slowly. "No, I always suspected she was kil't, though chances were good the lad was too."

"Why? Did someone see or hear something?"

"All I saw was her and the lad leaving the building. I didn't see which way they went." He shrugged again. "Never laid eyes on her again."

"You saw her leaving the building the day she disappeared?"

"Aye."

"What . . . what was she like? Scared or anything?"

Clyde smiled sadly. "I'll never forget it. She was determined, that's the best I can explain. Determined. I asked her if something was going on, and she just said that she was putting an end to something that was bothering her, and she left."

"Did you tell that to the police?"

He laughed once. "Of course, but I dinnae think they cared much. We're a poor group here, lucky tae have what we have."

I nodded, but I didn't like hearing again that the police might not have done their jobs well. "Determined?"

"Aye. I'd never seen her jaw set so firmly, her spine so straight. I wish I'd gone with her, but she clearly didnae want my help."

I found the picture of the sketch of the woman on my phone. "Clyde, I'm wondering if I might have a line on her too. Could I show you a picture?"

"Aye." He reached for some glasses in his pocket and put them on as I held the phone out for him to see.

"Could that be Dora?"

His eyebrows came together. "I dinnae ken, lass. Dora had long hair at the time, brown eyes. I can't tell much from this except she looks . . . old."

"Right. If this is Dora, I think she's lived a rough life. What do you think, could this be her?"

Clyde frowned and finally nodded. "Aye, it could be, I suppose, but I'd need tae see her in person tae know for sure."

"I understand. I hope I find her."

Clyde sat back on the couch. "She could be alive? That would be . . . wonderful, and the lad too?"

I nodded and smiled.

"He's awright. Gracious, this is all such good news."

A noise sounded from somewhere outside.

"Och, that's just my neighbors. They're known to get in a row or two." He nodded toward the side window.

I stood and made my way to it. I peeled back the edge of the curtain and looked down and into the close. Two men were arguing, but I didn't see any weapons. I was just about to let go of the curtain flap when my eyes landed on a window across the close, one that wasn't covered by a curtain. It appeared there was a flat there too, directly above the burned-out remains of the bookshop.

"Who lives there?" I asked Clyde as I nodded.

"No one. It's been empty since a fire took the shop below. In fact, it happened about the time Dora disappeared."

"Did you think the two events might be tied together?" I looked at him.

"Not really. It was the second thing, ye ken? Bad things happen in threes, and I kept waiting for the third thing. That's why I remember it so well."

I nodded. "Did they ever figure out how the fire got set?"

"I dinnae ken. I might have heard they thought it was from someone living in the close."

"It's so strange that the flat wasn't harmed."

"Well, the shop owner had to move. It was deemed unsafe, that much I do remember."

"But the building's never been fixed?"

"No, lass, it's not a priority. We're not a priority."

I turned again and pulled back the curtain a little more to glance into the other window. I was looking at a kitchen, one bigger than Clyde's single room, but still not luxurious. I could see a table with two chairs tucked underneath, a much bigger stove, and an empty refrigerator with the door left open.

Had Malcolm and Maria lived right there? They must have.

The best-laid plans of mice and men often go awry.

Hello again, Rabbie, I thought. Here was probably one of his most famous quotes of all. He was absolutely trying to tell me something.

I sure wished I understood what it was.

"Lass?" Clyde said.

I turned back to him. "Did you know the shop owners back then?"

"Aye. Lovely man. Gave me a few books when I was down on the ill-luckit."

I knew he meant unlucky. Rosie had used that Scots term before.

"What about his wife?" I asked.

"I dinnae remember her at all," he said. "Weel, I do a wee bit, but she was just never a part of the bookshop, that I recall."

I sat down again. "Clyde, could you tell me more about that time? Maybe about the bookshop."

Clyde nodded and then gave me a verbal sketch of what life had been like in this neighborhood twenty years earlier.

It wasn't much different than it is now, but he focused on the fond memories. He mentioned again that the bookshop owner—I reminded him that his name was Malcolm—had always been welcoming.

"In fact, I think he welcomed Dora and the lad to sit in a corner and read any time they wanted," Clyde said. "He allowed us to read without buying a thing."

I wondered if Edwin and Rosie knew about that, but I didn't think they had. If I remembered correctly, Rosie found out about Hamlet when he had been slightly older, and I was the one who'd come across Dora's old address.

What a small world it had been. They'd all been right there, in front of each other in one way or another, but they just hadn't known—until it was too late to save Dora and Hamlet from those horrible years.

Wyatt came through the door just as it seemed Clyde might be tiring. My brother and I put the groceries away as Clyde showed us where everything went.

Afterward, I showed my brother the view out the window, and Clyde offered him some tea, but it was with a weary tone.

Wyatt declined politely, and I wrote my name and phone number on a piece of paper. I told Clyde to call me if he needed anything.

As we left, I spotted the bills Clyde had given Wyatt to purchase the groceries. My brother had left them tucked under the tea box on the counter. Wyatt had purchased the groceries.

"That was really great, Wy," I said as we boarded another bus.

He shrugged and smiled at me. "It was the least I could do.

Poor guy, just wanted to go to the store, but my determined sister had to have some answers."

Determined. There was that word again. I smiled back at Wyatt and pondered what in the world Dora might have needed to take care of.

TWENTY-SIX

We boarded another bus, but we were both at loose ends, unmoored. Hamlet was out there somewhere, and I wanted to know if he was okay. Wyatt was just as unsettled as I was, and he left me at the bookshop so he could visit Tom or just "tour around or something."

Rosie, Hector, and I watched him make his way up to the pub. His big frame took on the wind with authority.

"It's good tae have him here, isnae it?" Rosie asked.

"Yes. It's always good to have family around."

"Och, not always, lass," Rosie said as she turned away from the window and made her way to her desk chair. "Sometimes it's much better tae have family living far away."

"You speak from experience?"

"'Twas a long time ago, but my mother-in-law and I didnae get along." She smiled sadly and shook her head. "Silly stuff, really, but we never quite . . . got into sync, aye?"

"I get that."

"Ye're a lucky one tae have such a lovely family. Even Tom's father, Artair, is a good man."

"He is . . ." my mind quickly wandered—no, jetted—down an altogether new path.

"Delaney?" Rosie said as Hector trotted to my feet and looked up at me.

It wasn't a bookish voice speaking to me. It was that memory of Artair at dinner, when he spoke about Robert Burns. He was going to check on something, but I'd been so distracted at the dinner that I couldn't remember what it was.

"I was thinking about something Artair once said, something about Burns Night dinners and how many he'd been to."

"What about it?"

"I'm . . . I'm not sure." I picked up Hector and smiled at Rosie. "I think I have a question for him, but I can't remember what it was."

"Ring him." Rosie lifted the handset from the old phone on her desk.

I did exactly that, but it wasn't a surprise that he didn't answer his office phone. Artair was rarely by his phone, and he turned his mobile off while he was at work.

"You probably need tae go see him in person," Rosie said when I placed the handset back on the cradle.

"I . . . I just got here."

"G'on, lass. I'll call yer brother back down if I need the help."

"Thank you, Rosie." Hector kissed my cheek, and I kissed the top of his head before I put him back on the floor.

I bundled up once again and set out, texting my brother that he should head back to the bookshop when he could, if he wouldn't mind.

I didn't think he would mind a bit.

It wasn't surprising that, along with almost every other

building in Edinburgh, the university's library was lovely. The outside wasn't bad, but the real draw was the columns inside topped off with a domed ceiling. Today, I hurried past all the literary busts, one next to each column, and made my way to Artair's office.

He wasn't there. I stopped a passing librarian, asking her quietly if she'd seen him.

"Aye, he's in the far corner, working on . . . well, I'm not sure, but he has a project."

He loved projects.

I thanked her and resumed my hurried pace to find him.

"Hi," I said when I emerged from between some shelves. I told myself to slow down and breathe, if only so I didn't startle my father-in-law.

Artair was building a man. Out of paper.

"Lass!" he said happily but still quietly. "Hello, how are you?"

"I'm okay. Are you making a mannequin?"

Artair was holding a wadded-up piece of paper that was covered in words. It must have originally been a page in a book. He frowned at the sculpture—it resembled an alien more than a human, but I got the gist.

"It's an interpretive piece. Something about humans being made or built with words, or some such thing."

"Oh! I get that now."

"Now." Artair lifted a bushy eyebrow. "It's going to need a sign or a plaque or something, or everyone's going to be confused. Sometimes I take on things that I probably shouldn't."

"I love it," I said.

Artair smiled knowingly. "Ta, lass." He put down the paper. "What can I do for you?"

"I'm sorry to bother you, but do you have a minute we could talk in private?"

"I would love to take a minute away from this. Let's go to my office."

We made our way back toward his office again. Artair had a slight hitch in his step, and I'd come to find it so endearing that I watched for it. He claimed it wasn't painful, but just one of those "old things." I wanted to thread my arm through his every time I saw it—though I refrained from doing so inside the library.

His office was more overflowing with books than any bookshop I'd visited. They were everywhere: stacked, piled, shelved. It was a wonderful room.

We sat around a small table—after he cleared two chairs of the books that were atop them.

"Everything all right?" Artair asked when we sat.

"Yes, all is well with Tom and me. I'm here, though, because I'm worried about Hamlet, my coworker."

"Aye. A good lad. Tom's told me some of what's happening. I hope it all ends well."

"Me too. Artair, do you remember our dinner earlier this week?"

He laughed once. "Of course. I'm not that forgetful yet."

I sobered. On the way over, I'd had another idea, but it wouldn't make for a pleasant conversation. "Artair, you've heard about the fire, the murder?"

"Aye. Neil Watterton. Such a tragedy." For a moment, tears pooled in his eyes, but he blinked them away.

"You knew him?" That's what I'd wondered. They had very similar jobs in the same city.

"Aye. He was a librarian. Over the years, we crossed paths."

"I'm so sorry for your loss, Artair," I said. "I met him the night he was killed."

Artair nodded. "I knew that too. I was so relieved you weren't hurt. Elias was there with his taxi, wasn't he?"

I nodded.

"Did the police find the killer yet?"

"No, but . . . Hamlet and Neil might have known each other. Their membership in an archery group overlapped some."

"Okay," Artair said.

"And the group that held the dinner, it was originally formed by Edwin," I said.

Artair fell into thought. "Goodness."

"It was an honor to be invited, and I brought Hamlet along. It was somewhat of a setup, though. Another man, Malcolm Campbell, and Edwin had a tragic falling-out years ago . . ." I watched Artair's expression change. "What?"

"Malcolm Campbell, the bookseller? The one whose shop also burned down some years back?"

"One and the same."

"Give me a minute." Artair stood and went to his desk. Without sitting down, he punched some keys on the keyboard, soon printing out a couple pieces from the printer on the corner of the desk. He grabbed them and brought them back to the table. "Lass, I've been to so many Burns Night dinners, I couldn't even count—I've been to them even when they weren't held on the proper night. I know many people who love and want to honor the man. It's probably just a Scottish thing, but we do enjoy our history."

"I've noticed."

"I've never attended a dinner with Neil and Mr. Campbell. I didn't even know about that wee building, which is saying a lot. I know most of every inch of Edinburgh. Nevertheless, I know Malcolm too. And I remember his tragedy."

"He thought Edwin burned down his bookshop."

"I didn't know Edwin back then, and I'm afraid I don't know Malcolm well enough for him to have confided in me, but I have this." He stood in front of me and held it to himself. "This is part of what I was trying to remember at the dinner, lass."

"Really?" I sat up.

I expected him to show me something about the burned shop, maybe an article or something, but that wasn't it at all. He handed me a letter.

I read through it so quickly that I had to begin again to catch the details. It was dated February 2, from three years ago.

Artair,

I hope this finds you well. Thank you again for your time and assistance with the discovered manuscript. I didn't think it was Burns either, and I appreciate your wisdom and expertise in determining that it truly wasn't.

I need to make you aware of something that's come up though. You might not have any reason to be concerned, but I didn't want you to be blindsided either. The friend who brought it to me is not as convinced as you or I. I'd kept his name under wraps so as not to influence anyone's determinations. You might have heard of Malcolm Campbell. He once owned a local bookshop. It came upon a terrible tragedy when it burned up in a suspicious fire.

Since that time, Mr. Campbell, having suffered a number of personal setbacks, has been attempting to regain his footing. He brought the manuscript to me, asking for help in authentication. That's when I brought you into the loop.

It seems Mr. Campbell doesn't want to accept our determinations, which would be fine. I told him to feel free to talk to as many people as might offer him proper assistance. However, in his anger and frustration, he has made threats that he would sue me for everything I've got, or some such thing.

Honestly, I feel his outburst was just a moment of anger that passed as quickly as it flared, but I did tell him your name, and I would not be surprised if you hear from him. Again, I didn't want you to be blindsided.

Apologies for bothering you with any of this. I should have just dealt with Mr. Campbell myself. I know him well enough to have been able to predict this outcome, but, alas, I was excited about the possibility of a new discovery and I have always respected your opinion.

Please let me know if you need anything further from me. And, as always, dear Artair, thank you for your help and continued friendship.

Fondly,
Neil

I looked at Artair. "Did you ever hear from Malcolm?"

"No, never."

"Why did Neil write you a letter? Why not a phone call?"

"That was just Neil. He was proper, formal, paid attention to details. It was probably his way of being thorough."

"What was the manuscript?"

"That's the part that was stuck in here." He tapped the side of his head. "The name, Weatherby. The manuscript was just some scribbles, but they sounded very much like Burns. The beginnings of a poem about a sheep herder. The name of the main character was Jacob Weatherby McBurney."

"Oh yes, even that sounds very Burns."

Artair's eyebrows came together. "Should I show this to the police? It's like my subconscious picked up on who you were going to have dinner with. A wee bit of soothsaying, aye?"

I made the quick decision not to let Artair in on the other fortune-tellers currently in the mystery, at least not until we knew more.

"Maybe," I said. It didn't seem right throwing Malcolm under the bus, and he did seem to have moved on to what was shaping up to be a good life, but maybe this was motive for Neil's murder. "Yes," I said more decisively. "Do you want Inspector Winters's number?"

"I have it." He patted his pockets but there was no phone in any of them. He stood up to search the desk.

"Did Neil just give the manuscript back to Malcolm?" I asked.

"I never inquired. I didn't make a copy of it either." Artair held up his phone proudly. As he looked at it, he continued, "I see I missed a call from you, as well as others. I really should carry this dreadful thing with me, shouldn't I?"

"Only if you want to. I'm glad to see you in person anyway."

"Me too, lass."

Artair sat in the chair across from me again. "Are you sure Neil and Hamlet might have known each other?"

"I think so, but I feel like I'm missing the . . . big connection."

Artair nodded somberly. "I'll call the good inspector."

I nodded too and stayed to eavesdrop on the call.

TWENTY-SEVEN

There is no doubt I looked stunned as I exited the library. I stood there, frozen for a moment, right outside the front doors. I didn't even move the first time someone said, "Excuse me." But my moment of shock had nothing to do with my time with Artair or his succinct call to Inspector Winters.

I'd received a text from Hamlet:

I'm fine, Delaney. Meet me at the coffee shop by the statue. XO.

It was unquestionably a moment of truth. One like I wasn't sure I'd ever felt before. The right thing to do would have been to call Inspector Winters and let him know about the text. I should have called Edwin and Rosie—and Tom and Wyatt, for that matter—to let them know about it too, or at least tell them that I'd heard that Hamlet was fine.

But I wasn't going to call any of them.

My loyalty to my other friends was no less solid than it was to Hamlet, but I would have ignored the right thing to do for any of them if I thought I knew what, well, the righter thing to do was.

I was worried about him, though hearing from him certainly eased my concern a bit.

Without notifying anyone else, I responded:

Give me fifteen minutes.

The public transportation fates thankfully were with me, and a bus arrived quickly. I was walking into the coffee shop near the Burns statue twelve minutes after I'd sent the text.

Hamlet sat at a corner table. He sent me a weary smile and then lifted one of the two coffee cups on the table in salute. I glanced at the familiar barista, who sent me a somewhat furtive but knowing nod.

I sat in the chair across from Hamlet as I visually accessed him. Yes, he did look tired, but he was fine, unharmed.

"Hey," I said.

"Hey," he responded.

I took the cup he offered. "We are very worried about you."

"I know. And I'm so sorry."

"What's going on, Hamlet? You can tell me anything." In fact, I thought he could probably tell me he did kill Neil and I'd keep his secret forever. But maybe that was because I was as sure as I could be that that wasn't what was going on.

He took in a deep breath and let it out slowly. "A lot is happening, Delaney. More than I think I can handle."

"I can help. We can help. Do you need the police?"

Hamlet nodded. "Aye. I wasn't sure, and I had to figure a few things out, but I could talk to Inspector Winters now."

"Okay," I said, wondering why he hadn't and wishing he'd called him before texting me. "Should we call now?"

"Could you and I just talk first?"

"Sure." I put the coffee down and folded my hands on the table. "I'm listening."

"I found my mother," he began.

Even though I thought that was part of what had been going on, it was still a shock to hear him speak the words, so heavy with emotion.

I didn't even think twice about letting him know what I'd come upon. My promise to Rosie and Edwin didn't seem nearly as important as helping salve the pain he was in. "Hamlet, I, uh, I found a copy of your birth certificate."

Hamlet's eyes widened, and then he laughed once. "In the cabinet in the warehouse?"

"Yes."

"I put it there about a month ago."

"Why?"

Hamlet shrugged. "I was using you."

"I don't understand," I said, even though I thought I might.

"I thought you'd find it and bring it to us, demanding to understand it."

"I kind of did that, but I left you out of it until I got some answers."

Hamlet shook his head slowly. "I should have predicted that's how you'd do it. You talked to Edwin and Rosie?"

"I did."

"Well, that didn't go quite as planned."

"Did you rummage around the file again yesterday?"

Hamlet nodded. "I snuck into the shop the night before to see if you'd found it. I was just going to take it if you hadn't. I surmised you had, but I still wasn't sure what to do."

I was glad he said it had been he who'd disrupted things.

"You should have just confronted us all with it if you had questions."

"I couldn't," he said. "I think I was scared."

"I get it. So you originally found the certificate in the bookshop? When?"

He shook his head again. "No. Remember when I had to run out to Edwin's house when he and Valerie were on holiday last year?"

"Kind of."

"He asked me to search a specific drawer in his desk for an address of a friend in Australia. The file on me was right behind it, labeled 'Hamlet.'"

"Goodness. That had to be a surprise."

"I couldn't resist looking inside it. Then I was shocked to my core, Delaney. You know, I never even thought about searching for a birth certificate. My earliest memories are of living with different people in different run-down places where we weren't supposed to be. There was never any blood family, just down-on-their-luck people moving around and hiding together. When I found the certificate and saw the names of the parents, I snapped a picture and then printed it out later."

I swallowed hard. He'd had a terrible existence as a child, but I couldn't dwell on that at the moment. It wasn't that Hamlet didn't have a right to know the truth about his past, but I wasn't sure how much of it I was supposed to tell him. He hadn't brought up Rosie at all—of course, he must not know that connection yet.

"Then what?"

"My birth father was a challenge. There were so many Matthew Edisons to choose from. I approached a couple, but neither of them ever knew Dora Strangelove, or they said they didn't."

I nodded and bit my tongue regarding the Matthew Edison who most certainly had known Dora. One thing at a time.

"Anyway, I put my attention toward finding Dora," Hamlet continued.

Hamlet looked out the window toward the statue. I glanced that way too, but the street performer wasn't there. No one was there, not even any passersby. He turned back to me.

"I know Letitia Strangelove is a psychic just off the Royal Mile. I went to talk to her. She's Dora's grandmother, my great-grandmother, but I didn't tell her who I was, just that I was hoping to find Dora. She was hoping the same, but claimed not to have seen her for years. She thought Dora was probably dead, but . . ."

"Go on," I said. I'd been wondering if the "lad" had been Hamlet.

"I mentioned the story to an acquaintance." He looked at me, his eyes sadder than I'd ever seen them.

I figured that one out quickly. "Neil."

"Neil." Hamlet nodded.

"I'm still not understanding the time frame of events here, Ham. I know this is hard, but just tell me."

"Sure. Neil and I knew each other because he worked at the National Library. He helped me with lots of research, not just a few months ago about fortune-tellers but before that too. He'd been the captain of an archery group I'm a part of, but we never met there. Anyway, it was a few months ago, at the library while I was researching local fortune-tellers, that I told him I'd found the birth certificate and thought it was mine, told him about my childhood. He helped with the research, but then a couple of weeks ago called me saying he might know someone named Dora Strangelove." He looked out the window again. "She's a street performer. Neil used to come over here quite often to listen to her. It took him a while to put it all together. She reads Robert Burns's works, and there was not a bigger fan of Burns than Neil Watterton."

"Okay, but why the secrecy?" I asked. "There was no real indication that you two knew each other at the dinner."

"I didn't know he'd be there, and he didn't expect to see me. We weren't close friends, Delaney, but had common interests, I suppose, but not because of friendship. He didn't even know I worked at the Cracked Spine. He knew me as a student," Hamlet said. "And we'd . . . something had happened two days before, and neither of us wanted to acknowledge that we knew the other just in case . . ."

"Back up. What happened?"

Hamlet nodded again. "Something happened to Dora. She disappeared."

"Oh. Okay."

"And the police thought Neil had something to do with it."

"What?"

"I was walking into the library with him when they stopped us. I was meeting him there that time. When the police approached us, Neil didn't want anyone at his workplace knowing, so he asked to talk to them at the station instead. In those few moments, I could tell he didn't want them to know we talked to Dora . . ."

"Wait. Stop there. You talked to Dora?"

"Aye. Right out there." He nodded. "I finally got up the nerve to talk to her, and Neil came with me. He gave her his card, asking if she recognized him. She said she did, that she'd seen him watch her perform for years, during his lunch. He'd left her plenty of tips, so she seemed willing to talk to us. We told her we had an old but delicate matter to speak to her about. We asked if we could buy her coffee, but she declined, just wanted to know what was going on." Hamlet paused again. "I guess there's no way to be overly diplomatic when telling someone you might be their son, but Neil began with asking her if she remembered ever having a child."

"Maybe that was too direct?"

"Aye, it wasn't good. She looked at both of us. When she looked at me, her eyes filled with an eerie recognition. And then she ran off. We scared her."

"She just needed to process it."

"Maybe. Neil said we'd try again another day. He seemed very bothered by the interaction."

"He was scared?"

"Not then." Hamlet shook his head. "He was just worried, I guess. We both felt like we'd handled it poorly, but there was something about Dora. She's probably mentally ill, Delaney, and we might have added to that."

"Oh no, Hamlet, you didn't. If she's not well, anything can set off bad moments. You weren't mean to her. You were just being curious."

"Maybe. And then, the next day, when we were headed toward the library and the police stopped us, Neil sent me away. The police didn't stop me, just Neil. When we spotted each other at the dinner, I don't know, we both just kept the secrecy in place. And he was caught off guard by me even being there, you too."

"Okay. Go on."

"This is the bad part."

"I'm listening."

"It was me who went into the Burns House with Neil the night he was killed. But I didn't kill him!"

"I know you didn't kill him, Hamlet. But why were you there?"

"He wanted to tell me about his visit with the police. Apparently, Dora went missing from the place she'd been staying. She left her meager things there, as well as Neil's card. They'd wondered if he knew anything. He told them that he didn't and that he'd just given her his card, just in case she ever did need something. He wanted to keep me out of all of it. He also asked me how you and I were at the dinner, how well we knew Edwin."

"I see. He was suspicious of us being there?"

"I'm not exactly sure, but once we had that brief conversation, I left, walked home. That's all I did."

"Why didn't you tell the police?"

"Two reasons, Delaney. The police had wanted to talk to Neil about Dora, and I wasn't sure he'd shared all those details with me. Additionally, I was unquestionably one of the last people to see him alive, and that never looks good. It was all so . . . I felt guilty even though I truly wasn't."

"Okay, okay, I get that. What have you been doing?"

"Searching for Dora," he said as if it should be obvious.

"Why?"

"Because, doesn't it seem a possibility that she's the one who killed Neil?"

"No . . . I mean, I don't know."

"The business card, Delaney. He wrote the Burns House address on it, thought she might like to see it. I don't know, it made sense then, and I'm so worried that my biological mother is a killer—or maybe she's been harmed too."

My heart fell. "I think there are other possibilities, Hamlet. I doubt Dora killed Neil." As I said the words, I wasn't truly sure of anything, but I hoped that Dora would show up again, that she hadn't befallen a fate similar to Neil's. "Where have you looked for her?"

"Not far from here. She . . . not lived, but stayed down that way for a while."

I followed his glance. There was nothing to see.

"Should I call Inspector Winters?" he asked.

The answer was yes, but I didn't say it quite yet. "Let's go take another quick look."

"You sure?"

"Hamlet, I'm not sure of anything, but a quick look first wouldn't hurt."

"Aye. Let's go."

I left a tip in the jar on the counter as the barista and I shared another nod. I suspected he'd somehow encouraged Hamlet to text me, but he wasn't going to confirm.

TWENTY-EIGHT

It was not a good place.

Hamlet and I stepped into the building, making our way in through the front door, though it wasn't easy. The door hung from only one hinge and had to be lifted to be moved. But with the expertise of someone who'd done it before, Hamlet handled the task quickly.

"It's not safe in here," I said as we stood in the wretched entryway.

"It's not as unsafe as some." Hamlet shrugged. "The building's in good shape. It won't fall down on us. It has electricity, which is unusual. Normally, the power's off in abandoned buildings."

"Who's paying the bill?"

"No idea." Hamlet shrugged.

He walked around a pile of garbage on the floor and started up the stairs. Three steps up, he turned back and looked at me. "This way."

I nodded and followed, wishing we either had a weapon or had just called Inspector Winters, but knowing my curiosity was going to win this round.

If not for the windows next to the front door, there would be no light to allow us to see. An exposed fixture held no bulb. There was no heat. It was freezing inside, our breath fogging as we climbed up to the third floor. As we bypassed the second level, we heard noises come from a room a few doors down, but Hamlet ignored them, so I did too. Well, I tried to.

"She was staying here for a few months," Hamlet said as he took the landing on the third floor.

"In this cold?"

"There are some space heaters in the rooms."

"That doesn't sound safe."

"It's at least warmer," he said as he stopped in front of a door. "Whoever owns the building either forgot to have the electric shut off or the electric company missed it." He smiled at me in a way that made him look older than he ever had. "These sorts of situations are good discoveries, but they never last forever. People find out, then folks get kicked out. For whatever reason, though, this one has been working for some time."

He knocked but received no answer before he turned the knob. I followed him inside. It was nothing like Clyde's small place. This was literally just one tiny room. A dirty mattress had been stuck in a corner. Clothes were strewn everywhere, even exceptionally close to a space heater—I was relieved when I saw it was unplugged. A hot plate and a pan sat, almost primly, in another corner, and a lamp with no shade but an un-illuminated bulb in another.

"This was her room," Hamlet said.

"Why did the police think she was missing?"

"There's a man in the building who keeps track of everyone. I don't know, some people just take on the role. We'll talk to him when we leave. He's the one who called the police."

"Wasn't that quite a risk? I mean, the police now know about the situation in this building."

"Caro—that's his name—has a few contacts with the police who keep secrets well. There are some sympathetic officers who know that sometimes they should look the other way."

"Would that maybe be why Inspector Winters didn't know about the police talking to Neil? Maybe it hadn't been officially recorded."

"Aye, maybe."

We were silent a moment as we both took in the room. It was unpleasant, but it would have provided shelter.

"They found Neil's card in here?" I asked.

"That's what Neil told me."

"Does it look any different than the last time you investigated it?" I asked.

"No. There's no sign anyone has been here since I last looked. I don't think the police are stopping by again. They're counting on Caro to call if he sees her again."

I nodded. "Should we talk to him?"

"Aye, let's see if he's learned anything new."

I followed Hamlet out of the room and down to the first floor. Caro's room was in the back of the building. I suddenly realized that we weren't in an old apartment building, but a place that used to house business offices. From the old sign still on Caro's door, it appeared that a tax solicitor once used to work from behind it.

This time, when Hamlet knocked, someone answered.

Caro was a big, meaty man, bald, with piercing blue eyes that told me he wasn't about to suffer fools or take any crap from anybody. He sent me a critical squint and nodded at Hamlet before he opened his door to let us inside.

His room was organized, though no less austere than Dora's, even down to the shadeless lamp.

"What can I do for ye, Hamlet?" he asked, his booming voice scratchy and raw.

"This is my friend Delaney. We were just wondering if there's anything new regarding Dora?" Hamlet said.

We each grabbed an old folding chair, opening them before sitting in a triangle. There were about ten other folding chairs against the wall, and I wondered where they'd come from. Maybe they'd just been here, being used by the tax solicitor's clients before the building's current inhabitants.

"Lass," Caro said in my direction.

"Good to meet you," I said, though for the first time in my life, it seemed an odd, way-too-polite thing to say considering the circumstances. No one else seemed to notice.

"I haven't heard from her," Caro said. "I've no idea at all where she is, but I'm officially worried now."

"Would you mind telling Delaney the same things you told me about when you last saw her?" Hamlet asked.

"Aye." The word rumbled so much it seemed to shake the walls. "Last week, she came back to her room in a bothersome way. She's a sad case, lass, not well, but able to fend for herself for the most part. She's kind, so we all keep an eye out for her."

I nodded.

"I followed her up to her room, but she wouldn't talk to me," Caro continued. "I shouldn't have let her kick me out of there, but I did. Then, when I went to check on her in the morning, she was gone. I didn't fret too much, but when she didn't return that day, nor was there the next morning, I called my lads at the police station. They came over, not in any rush, I might add, but they did show up and looked through her room. I wasn't aware they took anything, but Hamlet told me they must have taken a man's card—the man who was killed."

I nodded again.

"I told Caro that I think Dora's my biological mother," Hamlet said so easily my heart panged a little as I wished he'd been able to do the same with all of us at the bookshop.

"I see. What did you make of that?" I asked Caro.

"I knew her first name, but I was not aware of her last. The Strangelove women have been around Edinburgh for a long time. Witches, some say, but we're a superstitious lot, and we tend to want to give mysterious labels to everything."

"That's true," I said.

"It's not unusual, you know, to have given up a bairn for adoption. I know plenty of girls and women who've done the same. Things happen, and they can't be cared for out here."

I looked at Hamlet and then at Caro again. I swallowed hard. "I don't think Hamlet was put up for adoption. I think Dora just left him with other people."

"Aye, and that happens too, but I wouldn't know the circumstances. I've only known her for a few months, maybe half a year, and we've never spoken about such things." Caro fell into thought a moment. He looked at Hamlet. "She lived here for a while, lad, but I think she was in the shelter down the road before that. I told the police about the shelter, but you might want to talk to them."

This was news to Hamlet, I could tell, and I was grateful we'd stopped by.

"Thank you," Hamlet said to Caro.

They shared a look. Whether because this was Hamlet's second visit about Dora, or maybe because of what I'd said about her just leaving her baby behind, or possibly just their shared experience, the two men had connected.

Caro was well spoken, clean even in the dingy surroundings. So many things can happen that can cause people to fall on hard times. For some, it wasn't a big leap to go from relative comfort to homelessness. I knew that, even if it was something I didn't allow myself to dwell on often.

The moments I thought about Hamlet and what he went through during the first part of his life were gut-wrenching. Here, in this instant, I saw the common bond, and though it wasn't the sort of bond people wished for, it was still strong. Maybe one of the strongest.

I didn't even really understand why, but I thought it was a good thing we'd come to visit Caro today.

"Now we know more," I said as Hamlet and I stepped back outside.

"I'm glad I brought you here. I know it's time for us to call Inspector Winters, but would you mind running by the shelter with me first?"

I nodded. I had the same thought. "Let's hurry."

We hurried.

TWENTY-NINE

The shelter was located in another old office building, though this one was a more modern structure. Three stories made of cement-like stone extended up from a bottom level filled with two businesses: a shoe shop and a small market. Under each narrow window on the upper floors was a strip of some construction material that had been painted bright teal.

We entered through double-glass, blacked-out doors. Once inside, I wondered if walls had been cleared away or if this bottom level had always been one big space, about half the size of a gymnasium.

Two rows of beds lined the sides of the room. There were probably about thirty beds total, but at the moment only three were occupied, one with someone sleeping, two with people sitting. No one was trying to be quiet, but the sleeping person seemed to not be the least bit bothered by noises.

An elderly man walked toward us. "Can I help you two?"

I introduced myself and Hamlet. He said his name was Stanley.

His handshake was warm and so were his inquisitive eyes. He was one of those good-vibes people.

"We are looking for a woman named Dora," I said, purposefully leaving out her last name. "She's a street performer. She reads Burns's works."

"Aye, I ken who ye mean." He glanced at the second bed back on the left. It was unoccupied, but something was taped to the wall behind it. He looked at us again. "I havenae seen her for nigh on a couple months. But she's been known to disappear for a while. We keep her bed for her."

"She was staying here?" I said.

"Sometimes. If we ever get too full, she stays elsewhere and lets others sleep in her spot, but we havenae been too full for a couple of weeks. I keep expecting her to show up again."

Hamlet and I looked at each other before I continued, "Do you know where else we might be able to find her?"

"I have no idea, lass. I'm a wee bit worrit, but these things do happen."

"Can you tell us about her?" Hamlet asked.

"What do ye mean?"

Hamlet shrugged. "I think she and I are related."

Stanley inspected Hamlet as I spent a moment wondering if he'd needed to be quite so honest.

"She's lovely," Stanley said a moment later. "Full of a good heart, but . . . she's haunted, ye ken? She has lived a difficult life maybe. I've told her she is welcome tae tell me anything at any time, but she doesnae talk much. She adores her Burns." He rubbed his chin. His eyes brightened as he looked up again. "Would you like to see the picture taped on the wall? It's been there for as long as I can remember her spending nights here."

"Aye. Ta," Hamlet said.

Stanley led us to the bed, where we both had to get close to see the small snapshot. It was a color photograph, square in shape, taken probably ten years earlier. Or that was my best guess.

I gasped but caught it before it was too loud. Hamlet also made a noise, something like *hmmm*, but with more surprise.

It was a picture of the outside of the Cracked Spine as Edwin was walking inside.

"About ten years ago, you think?" I asked Hamlet.

"That's about right," he said.

Dora Strangelove had a picture of the Cracked Spine above the bed she slept in.

"She knew," I said to Hamlet.

"That's my guess too," he said.

"Knew what?" Stanley asked.

When he saw our uncertainty regarding what to say, he waved off his own question. "Never mind. Sometimes it's best not to know everything. In fact, most times it's better that way."

I took a photo of the picture with my phone before Stanley escorted us back to the door.

"Will you let us know if she shows up?" I asked. I jotted my number on a napkin I had in my bag.

"I don't know," he said. "I might."

I nodded. "That's all we can ask. Thank you."

"Thank you," Hamlet added.

"Ye're welcome. Will *ye* ring me if you find her?" He handed me a flyer from a stack on the front counter that listed the shelter's phone number.

"Absolutely," I said as I tucked the flyer in my bag.

Once outside again, I began, "Hamlet—"

"I know, it's time to ring Inspector Winters."

"It is."

Hamlet pulled out his phone, took a deep breath, and then made the call.

Upon Inspector Winters answering, Hamlet told him we'd meet him at the bookshop. He ended the call just as I thought I heard Inspector Winters say that he needed to meet him at the police station instead.

"I want Rosie to know I'm okay, so he can come to me," Hamlet said.

"I get that."

It took less than twenty minutes by bus to get back to the bookshop. We were surprised Inspector Winters hadn't beaten us there, but everyone else was happy to see us.

Rosie and Hector, of course. Wyatt too. And Edwin, who'd spent more time in the shop in the last few days than I could remember him doing since I'd moved to Scotland.

Relief filled the air, and then everyone spoke at once.

"Hamlet is the one who hid the birth certificate," I said.

"I'm sorry I didn't just confront everyone." Hamlet hugged Rosie.

"Och, lad, we shouldnae kept any secrets," Rosie said, though I sent her a side-eye, hopefully letting her know that her husband's involvement was still a secret. She seemed to understand.

"Time just moves on, and I didn't even think about it," Edwin said. "We should have, though. We should have let you know."

"Hamlet, what a relief," Tom said as he came through the door. I'd texted him on our way to the shop.

"Good to see you, Hamlet," Wyatt said when there was a lull in the conversation. Even my brother was relived.

Inspector Winters was too, though in a much less jovial way.

"You'll come with me," he said to Hamlet when he came through the front door. "Someone call his solicitor and have her meet us at the station, but we're going to do this right." Inspector Winters wasn't immune to all the critical eyes now looking at him. "It's the best way for him too, I promise."

He had a point, even if the rest of us didn't want to hear it.

"Don't say a word until your attorney gets there," Wyatt offered. "Not one word."

"Ye tell 'im," Rosie said quietly, even though Inspector Winters must have heard her.

When they left again and the solicitor had been called, I filled everyone in on what I'd learned today. It was an exhausting story, and they were none too happy that I hadn't let them know Hamlet was okay the second I knew, but their real interest seemed to be regarding the picture taped above Dora's bed.

"Of Edwin, not Hamlet?" Rosie asked.

"It didn't feel like a picture of Edwin, just one of the bookshop as he happened to be walking inside."

Rosie nodded.

Tom and Wyatt ran up to a favorite takeaway restaurant to gather dinner for everyone, and Edwin signaled me to the back of the bookshop.

"I'm remembering something," Edwin said.

Rosie, Hector, and I followed Edwin to the back.

"The manuscript you told us about, the one Malcolm gave to Neil to evaluate. The one Artair saw too," Edwin said as he opened one of the file drawers where Hamlet kept his things.

"What?" I said as I gathered Hector and sat in a chair.

"Hamlet has a copy too. I've seen it. I remembered the character's name. Did you mention the manuscript to Hamlet?"

"I didn't even think about it. We were looking for Dora, not talking about Malcolm."

"Here it is," Edwin said as he retrieved a file and looked at the name on the tab. "'The Ballad of Jacob Weatherby McBurney.'"

"I don't understand. Is this the manuscript or a copy?" I asked.

"I don't know, lass," Edwin said. "I don't even know how Hamlet acquired it. Similar to Hamlet's exploration of my files at home, I was rummaging through these one day, looking for some old sketches, and I found it. I read it back then and now remembered it. It's quite good."

"Is it Burns?"

"I don't think so, but I never even considered that it might be." He frowned. "No, I don't think Burns wrote it, but I can understand why someone might speculate that it was. Or . . ."

"What?" I asked.

"*Hope* that it was. There are a number of people like me, always looking for treasures, Delaney, and there would be very few treasures as valuable to any Scot as something long lost from Robert Burns. Hope can alter reality."

I thought a long moment. It seemed such a stretch that this manuscript had anything at all to do with Hamlet's troubles, but I didn't want something that might point a light at Neil's real killer to go unnoticed. "I think we need to talk to Malcolm about it."

"Edwin cannae," Rosie said.

"Actually, maybe it's time to mend those fences," Edwin said to Rosie.

"I know where his new bookshop is located," I offered.

"Do ye think he's there this evening?" Rosie asked.

"I think he's there all the time. He's trying to get it ready to open," I said. I turned to Edwin. "But are you sure now's the time for you to talk to him?"

Edwin fell into thought. "Neil was killed for something. I don't think it was because of this"—he put his finger on the manuscript—"but I think we need to explore it. I trust Inspector Winters, but the circumstances . . . Hamlet's going to be honest now, and once the police know he was one of the last people to see Neil alive . . . well, that never goes well. Let's make a visit to Malcolm and just ask what this was about."

Edwin had been feeling the same things I was. We were all probably worried about Hamlet being "railroaded" even if Inspector Winters worked hard for that not to happen. Or perhaps we were just all so worried about him maybe being guilty that we were exploring any small lead, hoping to make someone else look guilty.

Tom and Wyatt were back only a few minutes later. We all ate something, though I wasn't hungry, as Edwin and I told them what we were going to do. With a kiss from Tom, a "Be careful" from Wyatt, and a "Get the answers" from Rosie, Edwin and I were off—to one of our mutual favorite places on the planet, a bookshop. But we both knew this time our visit might not be greeted in a friendly manner.

The lights were on inside Malcolm's place, but we didn't immediately see anyone inside, as we stood side by side, looking in the window that took up the top half of the door. The shelves were more organized than they were the last time I was there, though I wasn't able to see the specifics. The place looked almost ready for customers.

"Oh," I said as we saw Malcolm emerge from the back. He didn't see us, his focus on a book he was holding.

He cut quite a figure. With his broad shoulders and long-ish hair, he reminded me of someone who could wear a cape well.

"Should we knock?" I asked when he still didn't notice us at the door as he made his way behind the narrow counter.

"I suppose," Edwin said.

I tapped on the glass. Malcolm turned immediately, not attempting to hide how he felt about us being there. His expression was full of nothing less than contempt as he shook his head.

"Malcolm. Please. We need to talk to you for a minute," I said, hopefully raising my voice just enough.

He stood still a moment and then took a deep breath. He shook his head again, but this time he made his way toward the door.

He unlocked the latch and pulled the door wide. "Edwin has an order of protection against me. I could be arrested just by allowing the two of you inside."

"That expired years ago," Edwin said. "I never refiled. Malcolm, it was for the best for both of us back then. Tempers were simply too hot to be trusted. I would tell you I'm sorry, but I don't think you'd believe me. And though I am sorry, it's for something that's difficult to fully explain."

"You're right. I wouldn't believe you."

"No, I know, but I am requesting the opportunity to find a way for us to move forward without any further nastiness. Would that be acceptable?"

Time ticked by slowly as Malcolm considered Edwin's words. I worked hard not to speak up and tell them it was simply time to move on, just get over it, whatever *it* truly boiled down to be.

Malcolm turned and walked back to the counter. He didn't shut the door on us, so we took it as an invitation to go inside.

"Thank you," Edwin said as we approached the other side of the counter. "We were good friends at one time, Malcolm. I'm happy for you, happy you have this new shop. I swear on everything that is holy to both you and me, I did not burn down your other one."

Malcolm pursed his lips and regarded Edwin. "I don't know if you did or you didn't, but I still have my suspicions, and I have worked hard to forgive you"—he held up his hand, but I didn't think Edwin was going to interrupt—"for so many things."

If Edwin was angered by Malcolm's proclamations, he didn't show it. It wasn't often that my boss was humbled, but I sensed this was one of those moments, and it was genuine.

"Thank you," Edwin said.

The moment stretched again. Finally, I cleared my throat. We needed to move this thing along.

"Malcolm, do you remember this?" I pulled the file from my bag, set it on the counter, and opened it. Inside was the copy of the manuscript about Jacob Weatherby McBurney.

His eyebrows lifted. "Aye, of course. Where did you get this copy?"

"It was in the bookshop. The Cracked Spine. In a file," Edwin said. "I came upon it not long ago, but I have no idea how we ended up with it."

"I don't know either," Malcolm said.

"I talked to my father-in-law, Artair Shannon, about it," I said.

"Aye? A good man," Malcolm said distractedly. He looked up at me. "Why is this so important that you and Edwin have come to ask me about it?"

"I don't know yet," I said. "We're trying to figure things out."

"What things?"

"Maybe who might have killed Neil," I said.

"How would this lead to . . ." Malcolm's eyebrows came together.

"Would you just tell us the story of this manuscript? Why were you so sure it was written by Burns? Where did you get it?"

"It's been a long time," Malcolm said.

"Do you mind?" I asked.

Malcolm frowned. "Maria sent it to me."

"Your wife?"

"Aye. Ex-wife. She said she wanted to make amends for selling my book to Edwin."

"And she told you it was written by Burns?" I asked.

"Aye. She was sure of it."

"She sent it from America?" I asked. "Or from here?"

"As I told you before, I don't think she went to America. She didn't send it directly to me. Well, she sent it to me through Clarinda. Maria didn't want me to know where she was, so she sent a post to Clarinda, asking her to give me the manuscript."

"Clarinda?" Edwin said. "She gave it to you?"

"She did." Malcolm nodded. "Clarinda was her solicitor back then." Malcolm smiled, but not pleasantly. "Maria grabbed her before I could, and I didn't object. Anyway, Clarinda gave it to me. There was a note in Maria's handwriting. The words were words she would have used. I still . . . I still have it, I think. Excuse me a moment." Malcolm stepped away from the counter and went to the back of the shop again.

Edwin and I looked at each other.

"I don't know that this will do us any good," I said.

Edwin shrugged and then nodded at the file I'd put on the

counter. "This is odd, Delaney. We'll ask Hamlet about it too, but it is odd."

Suddenly we heard distressful, loud noises coming from the back.

"Help!" Malcolm called in between yells that verged on screams.

Edwin and I took off immediately, speeding down a narrow hallway and then through a doorway that led to a large storage room. Smoke filled the air. It took us a beat to find the flames. Malcolm was in the back corner, attempting to douse a fire with a throw rug. Edwin grabbed another rug, and I grabbed a half-full coffeepot.

I threw the coffee on the fire right before both Edwin and Malcolm managed to put their throw rugs over it. The combination did the trick.

"Are you okay?" Edwin asked Malcolm as they both crouched to make sure the fire had been put out completely.

"I'm fine," Malcolm said, his voice high and wired.

It hadn't been a big fire, but one that seemed to have just been set. I stood behind the men and looked at the two big boxes that had been ruined.

"What in the world?" I asked aloud.

"Someone set it," Malcolm said. "They must have come in the back door. If I'd waited another thirty seconds to come back here, this whole place might have been destroyed; we might have all been killed."

We'd have probably gotten out the front, but I did agree that the fire had been put out just in time. It was all a bunch of paper. Cardboard boxes filled with books. Malcolm's timing was perfect. Maybe too perfect, I thought. But I didn't like considering even for a moment that he had set this fire.

I finally noticed the back door. It was wide open. I hadn't given much consideration to my own safety, and I still didn't. I hurried out the door, hoping to catch someone running away.

The door led to a close that was more an alley than most of the others I'd experienced. There was no one around. I pulled out my phone and illuminated the flashlight app.

There was plenty to see: discarded items—some garbage, some old furniture. But there were no people, no one running away. If they had already, we were too late to catch them.

My eyes landed on something on the ground about twenty yards away. There was something familiar about it. I hurried to get a better look.

"Delaney," Edwin called from behind me. "Come in. We need to call the police."

Yes, we did, but first I had to understand what I was seeing. It was a hat, a tam o'shanter, though not the one I'd seen Clarinda wearing. This one was older, dirtier, though it wasn't easy to tell when it had been dropped there. It very well could have been a few moments earlier.

"What is it?" Edwin said as he stepped out of the shop and came to join me.

"A hat," I said.

"Aye, a tam," Edwin said.

"Does almost everyone in Scotland have one of these?" I asked.

"I don't know. I do," Edwin said. "It's probably not a stretch to think that all Scots know what it is. Leave it, though. Let's leave it and call the police. They need to get on this immediately."

I nodded, not even bringing up my fleeting thought that Malcolm might have been his own arsonist.

But I didn't need to. I could tell by the way Edwin behaved, the look in his eyes, that he was right there with me. Or maybe even a few steps ahead.

We stepped back inside, just as Malcolm was dialing 999.

"Someone tried to burn down my place tonight," he said into the phone as he sent Edwin a concerned look.

I was glad when Malcolm, after his eyes narrowed again at Edwin, continued with what seemed an answer to another question. "No, I have no idea who set it."

THIRTY

Malcolm didn't accuse us of setting the fire, and we didn't accuse him. We told the police our stories, all of us leaving out any sort of past issues, at least as far as I could tell. I didn't hear Malcolm's statement, but no one seemed any more the curious about Edwin afterward. The police didn't bring up the order of protection, which made me think that Edwin had truly let it expire. I would ask him later.

I still wished to see the letter Maria had written to Malcolm and included with the manuscript, but that moment had passed, and it would have been not only inappropriate to ask, but probably weird.

Malcolm was devastated. There'd been little damage done to the shop, but he'd come this close to losing another one, by the same method. He was now also fighting paranoia.

I overheard that the police had found some footprints in the close. I wondered how there'd been any footprints back there, but there was no way to explore on my own. I was, however, bothered that I hadn't noticed them myself, and then, briefly, I wondered if Edwin and I had been the ones to leave them.

We'd cross that bridge if we came to it.

The police relayed a sense of concern, but they were visibly relieved about the small amount of damage. Even the smoky smell would dissipate pretty quickly, and the structure of the building hadn't been compromised at all. They were quick to notice that the fire had been caused by a simple match, nothing else. They didn't behave as if they were suspicious of any of us, but they might have been. They couldn't offer Malcolm full-time protection, but they said they'd send officers by to check on things throughout the day and night, for at least for forty-eight hours.

Malcolm would probably hire his own security and place cameras everywhere.

When we were dismissed by the police, we told Malcolm we were sorry for what had happened, but there were no further conversations about Jacob Weatherby McBurney or Neil—or Maria.

Edwin and I were silent as he drove me home, both of us still processing what might have happened. I texted Hamlet but didn't receive an immediate response. We could only hope that he'd been released, and all had gone well with Inspector Winters.

"Do you think Malcolm set that fire?" I asked as I reached for the car's door handle when Edwin pulled in front of my house.

"I don't." Edwin shook his head. "Briefly I thought it was a possibility, but now I don't think so at all. His distress was genuine."

"I agree. But then who in the world set it, and was this their second go at setting a fire to a bookshop owned by Malcolm?"

"Those are the new questions to add to the growing list."

"Thanks, Edwin," I said a long moment later.

"For what, lass?" he asked.

"Everything," I said as I got out of the car. I leaned back in. "Good night, boss."

Edwin smiled sadly. "I'm sorry for the turn of events, but I'm glad you're here, Delaney."

"Me too."

I watched him drive away. I was relieved to be home, frustrated about no answers, and worried about Hamlet.

Thank goodness I had Tom, who was inside our blue house by the sea, with a dinner plate in the fridge that I could warm up and a fire in the fireplace that would warm me up.

"What a day!" I said as I came through the front door.

Tom shook his head slowly and greeted me with a kiss and a cup of hot chocolate. "Come have dinner. Hamlet didn't kill anyone, love. You know that, I know that, I even think Inspector Winters knows that. It will be fine. Come have dinner, and we'll work on the mystery when we're done."

It was what the doctor ordered. A relaxing and delicious meal, a warm fire, and my husband.

After we'd eaten, cleaned up, and found comfortable spots on the couch, Tom said, "I talked to my da earlier, and he said the manuscript was a beautiful story about a tortured man."

"I haven't even read it," I said.

I stood and gathered my bag from where I'd dropped it beside the front door. I carried it back to the couch and pulled out the file I'd managed to retrieve from Malcolm's counter.

The writing was old-fashioned script. I even noticed that in some spots the letter s looked like an f, which happened in Old World English.

"It was given to Malcolm through Clarinda, which . . ."

"Aye, you said." Tom lightly nudged my elbow. "Go on."

"You know, I wondered if it might not have happened that way at all. I wondered if Clarinda wrote it and then made up a story to go with her work. She 'scribbled' inside the Burns

House. It's what she liked to do. It's not a stretch to think she did this."

"Malcolm didn't suspect that?"

"I don't think so. He didn't say that he did, at least, though we didn't have enough time to really talk about it. I thought I'd talk to Clarinda tomorrow, but I'm not sure this has anything to do with Neil's murder, and, really, isn't that the most important matter here?"

"Aye." Tom leaned back into the couch. "If Neil was killed because of this manuscript, why?"

"The only reason I can think is that it's fake and he was going to somehow expose its author."

"But this was from a while ago. I suspect he was killed for something else."

"I guess I've mostly been trying to get to know him through his connection to Hamlet. I just don't know much else."

"Lass, I'm going to say something, and it's going to bother you."

"What? There's nothing you could say that would bother me that much."

Tom shrugged. "Okay, here goes, then. Though I don't think Hamlet killed Neil, I do think that he's more deeply involved with whatever is going on than anyone wants to believe."

"I don't want that to be true."

"And yet, I think you believe it too. That's why you're looking at the connections."

"I think it's what the police believe."

"Maybe you do too? A little?"

"Okay, maybe a little." Though I still didn't want to. "Let's see if we can read this thing."

Jacob Weatherby McBurney was a man down on his luck. Way, way down. His shoe was ripped, his coat shoddy, and his last coin had lost its shine. Nothing was going his way. Then one day, he meets a child who seems to be happy even though he has nothing either.

As the story of their time together goes on and then comes to a close, we learn the child was actually Jacob, come to ask him about his own future. Adult Jacob, not knowing he was talking to himself, gives the child hope by telling him how life is good, no matter the things you acquire, that you should always look on the bright side. The child skips away, and Jacob realizes who he was speaking to. Suddenly he sees that at least only one shoe is torn, the coat can be sewn, and even coins that don't shine can still buy you food. He has everything he needs and always has.

The words and rhythm were comfortable and clever.

"Lovely, but this doesn't much help, does it?" Tom asked.

"Well, it might," I said with a smile. "I'm not a language expert, Tom, but I've done enough archiving to know that these words aren't exactly the words that would have been used by Burns. I can't pinpoint the specifics, but I bet I know a couple of people who can. I bet that's what your father thought when he first read it. And the two folks who worked with Neil. I don't know what all that means, but if he showed this to them, they might have also told him that this wasn't really from Burns."

"And who knows where that might have led, after he told Malcolm?"

"Where indeed. Unfortunately, we didn't get to talk to Malcolm much about it, but if he'd been angry back then, like the letter Neil wrote to Artair said, he sure seems to have gotten over it. Read it one more time aloud please."

Apparently it wasn't just my husband's singing voice that I felt I could listen to forever, or at least for the rest of our lives.

Tom smiled and then read it again.

THIRTY-ONE

I let the sun warm my face for a good long minute. It was cold outside, but there wasn't a cloud in the sky, and I couldn't possibly let the moment pass without enjoying the warm rays on my skin. Winter wasn't quite as harsh here as I'd experienced in Kansas, but clouds and rain or snow were almost constant cold-weather companions in Scotland.

Still, though, I was in a hurry to get to the bookshop. I'd already received a text from Hamlet saying he was on his way in. Then a text from Rosie saying that he'd arrived. We were all on close Hamlet watch.

"Ready?" Wyatt came up behind me.

"You going with me today?"

"Absolutely. I'm sure Rosie will need my help at the bookshop. You and Hamlet will be off doing something."

"I really do work hard," I said.

"I know. I know you, and you don't know how to not work hard. This is important, though. Hamlet's a good guy. I don't want him framed or anything, you know?"

"I agree. Thanks, Wyatt."

"Of course."

I'd thought about what had occurred to me regarding Neil's library coworkers and had come to the conclusion that I needed to talk to Hamlet before I did anything else, to ask him how it had gone with Inspector Winters. I was grateful he'd been released. We all were.

I turned my face away from the sun, and Wyatt and I set off for the bus stop.

Today, Hector didn't greet us as we entered. Instead, he and Rosie were in the back with Hamlet, probably unwilling to leave his side for the foreseeable future.

"Hey," I said when we joined them. "You okay?"

Hamlet nodded. "Fine. I told the truth, Delaney. The police know it was me going into the Burns House with Neil."

I sat. "Well, you're not under arrest, so it must be okay."

Hamlet shared a forced smile with Rosie. "I don't think it's okay, but it could be worse, I suppose. I didn't kill him, but I'm not sure they'll find the real killer. They've got absolutely nothing else. They still might come for me."

"Did Rosie talk to you about the manuscript?"

"She did. I have no recollection of how it got into the shop," Hamlet said. "I don't remember reading or filing it, but that doesn't mean I didn't."

"There's no record of us purchasing it either," Rosie added. "It might have just been given to us."

"And you don't remember that happening?" I asked Hamlet.

"No, not at all. I really don't remember anyone saying they suspected Burns had written it. That would have been cause to call Edwin."

I nodded. "We should tell Inspector Winters about it."

"I'm not sure it means anything to their investigation."

"What did Lena say?"

Hamlet shrugged. "That it was good I told the truth, though I don't really think she believed as much. I think she just said what she thought she should."

"Did you hear about the fire last night?" I asked.

"I did," Hamlet said. "I'm so glad no one was hurt. It happened when I was still being questioned, but it feels wrong to be relieved about that."

"I get it," I said. "Inspector Winters should know about that fire."

"If his fellow officers didn't tell him, I did," Rosie said. "I called him first thing. Had to leave a message. I told him about the manuscript too. Weel, I told him he might be curious about it. I havenae heard from him yet."

"Good." I should have known Rosie would do what she thought needed to be done.

"Hamlet, how well do you know the couple who worked with Neil at the library, Barbara and Ethan Cunningham?" I said.

"I don't really know them at all. I met them when I was there researching, but I didn't have many conversations with them."

"Do you think Neil could have shown them the manuscript?"

"I don't know. Probably. I sensed they were close."

Rosie nodded and looked at me. "Delaney knows how to authenticate things. I imagine they do too, but that might not matter."

"I think you and Delaney should go up and talk to them," Wyatt interjected. "You didn't get the answers from Malcolm that you were looking for. Maybe Neil talked to them about Malcolm giving him the manuscript."

"I agree." Rosie nodded.

I looked at Rosie and Wyatt. "You think it might be important?"

Wyatt nodded enthusiastically.

Rosie nodded once. "Lass, you two go. Honestly, I dinnae care if you go to the library or not; you two go for a walk, get some air."

"Sis, you're wound tighter than a drum." Wyatt looked at Hamlet. "You've been through the wringer. It's all good. Rosie and I got this."

"Okay, if you think—" Hamlet said.

"We do," Rosie said.

Hamlet and I took off for the library. Once we were outside in the cold, it was obvious that Rosie and Wyatt had been on to something. The fresh air was good, and having a task was even better. We stuck our heads into Tom's pub on the way and sent his employee and good friend Rodger a quick greeting. Tom had left the house early to meet a supplier and would probably be at the pub by the time we headed back to the bookshop.

At the library, I was glad Les was at the counter again. He recognized me immediately but didn't seem to know Hamlet. Keeping my voice low because today there were lots of people around the big table, I asked if we could talk to Barbara and Ethan.

Les stepped back from the counter and used the phone on the far desk to call the room upstairs. Only a moment later, he nodded and sent us on our way.

Both Barbara and Ethan were there, in front of the counter to greet us, their wide eyes hopeful and curious.

"Do you know anything new about Neil?" Barbara asked.

"I'm sorry, we don't," I said as I closed the door. "Do you guys remember Hamlet?"

"Aye. Lad." Ethan extended his hand. "Come in. It's crowded in here, but Barbara and I will move to the other side of the counter."

As they went around, I second-guessed my decision to come talk to them. They wanted news about Neil just as much as, if not more than, everyone else.

Nevertheless, I said, "Do either of you know anything about a manuscript Neil had, something he thought might have been written by Robert Burns?"

"No," they both said quickly.

I pulled the papers from my bag and showed them.

They both shook their heads as they glanced at Jacob's strange adventure.

"No, lass, he never once showed this to us," Barbara said. She looked at Ethan, who also shook his head.

There was no need to ask if they were sure. It was clear they were telling the truth.

"Thank you. We're sorry to bother you," I said.

I didn't know what it would have meant if they'd seen the manuscript, but the fact that they hadn't did make me wonder about Neil not showing it to them.

"This is a copy," I said. "But if he'd given you something that looked like an original . . . would you mind taking a quick look at this and see if it could have come from Robert Burns's time?"

They both nodded and slipped on reading glasses. They looked at the manuscript for only a few moments.

"No, lass, this is much more contemporary," Ethan said quickly. Barbara nodded in agreement.

"The language?" I asked.

"Aye," the couple said.

"I thought so too." I paused. "Thank you."

How had Malcolm not known? He didn't work in a library, but he'd owned a bookshop, he knew words. Edwin had no doubt it wasn't authentic.

"We're sorry we don't have better news regarding the manuscript," Ethan said, pulling me out of my reverie.

I smiled. "It's okay. Thank you."

Barbara's eyes opened wide as she looked at Hamlet. "Oh, lad, I might have something for you."

She turned and made her way around the big shelves, returning only a few seconds later. "I found this." She handed Hamlet a piece of paper with a copy of a photograph. "That's the Strangelove women."

I nudged myself so close to Hamlet, it was a surprise I didn't knock him over.

Barbara pointed. "There. That's Letitia, Wilma, and Dora."

I saw it again, the resemblance between Hamlet and his mother. It was distinct, and I could immediately tell they were related. A heavy sense of foreboding did land in my gut, though. The woman in the picture didn't resemble the one in the sketch I'd acquired. I was pretty sure they weren't the same woman. I felt doubts creep in, but I didn't want to give them a voice. Hamlet had his heart set on solving a mystery. I couldn't just drop that bomb on him. Turned out, I didn't need to.

"Oh," Hamlet said, the word sinking.

"What?" I asked, but knowing what he was concluding.

He looked up at me with a sort of panic in his eyes. "This isn't the woman Neil knew as Dora. I have no doubt that this isn't her. I've never seen this woman before, even an older version."

"Are you sure?" I looked at it again. "She would have aged a lot since this picture was taken, Hamlet. It was probably . . . well, before you were born." But I knew too.

"No, that's not it. There's no way this is the same person. Clearly, this woman is small-framed. The performer isn't. I mean, she's thin, but has wide shoulders. And, here, I get a sense of Dora's height—I've met Letitia, and she's petite. So is Dora in this picture. The street performer is tall."

"But she said her name is Dora, right?"

"Aye." Hamlet shrugged, trying hard to hide his disappointment. "That's what she said."

"If not Dora Strangelove, who is she, then?" I said.

Hamlet shrugged. "I have no idea."

I looked at Barbara and Ethan, who also shrugged.

The manuscript suddenly didn't matter at all. This new information seemed much more important. Was someone impersonating Dora Strangelove? And why?

We thanked the couple, promising once again to let them know if we learned anything new, and then left the library with the copy of the picture.

"Do you mind if we go talk to Letitia?" I asked Hamlet.

For a moment, I thought he might tell me he didn't want to, and I couldn't have blamed him. Letitia was his great-grandmother. Things had shifted in the universe since the last time he'd visited, and maybe she would recognize him now, or he might tell her who he was. Something other than a friendly visit could occur. I'd go by myself if he wasn't ready.

"Sure." Hamlet nodded. "Aye. Let's go."

THIRTY-TWO

Letitia was working.

The last time I was there, the door had been unlocked. This time, it was not only locked, but a sign hung from the knob that said FORTUNE UNFOLDING INSIDE. COME BACK IN AN HOUR.

"Now what?" I said.

"I don't know, Delaney." Hamlet looked at the picture of the Strangelove women again. "I can't believe this is my mother. I can't believe I thought the other woman was. I'm trying to catch up to everything."

The door opened suddenly, the force sending Hamlet and me back a step or two.

A young woman exited. She wasn't upset, but she didn't return my quick smile. She was surprised to see us and started, then took off before we could say anything.

"Everything okay?" I asked Letitia, who'd come to the door as well.

Letitia frowned but didn't answer. I saw recognition in her eyes when she looked at me and then even more when she looked at Hamlet.

"I thought you'd be by soon enough," she said as she turned

to make her way back to her side of the table. "Come in and close the door."

I lowered my voice and said to Hamlet, "I bet that's what all the fortune-tellers say."

The small joke was enough to relax us both, at least a little, as we made our way inside, shutting the door and sitting across from the old woman.

"Did you find Dora?" she asked me.

"I don't think so. I mean, we thought we did, but it turns out it's likely not her."

"But you thought you had? Tell me," Letitia said.

I'd thought about how to approach this. There were a few different angles, but it seemed all of them except one contained too many lies to keep track of.

I sighed. "Letitia, I think you know more about what happened to Dora than you've shared, but that's your right, of course. I wish you'd tell us more now, though."

She lifted her chin in slight defiance, but I suspected it was just for show.

"It's time," I said. I nodded at Hamlet. "You know who he is, don't you?"

Her defiance melted, and, as if she'd turned on a faucet, tears flowed from her eyes. Whatever façade she'd been maintaining, it crumbled.

"I didn't. Not at first."

Hamlet and I waited as she dabbed her eyes with a tissue and then stuck it up the sleeve of her fortune-teller robe. It was an endearing gesture.

She sighed even heavier than I had. "I came to the conclusion that this young man . . . was Dora's son after he left here recently, but, still, I was afraid to hope. I didn't know you two knew each other, and I don't understand what is going on to have brought you both to me, but in doing so you stirred up the past. I don't like to look back there very often because I've been disappointed so many times, but you've forced me to."

If she wanted an apology, it seemed that neither I nor Hamlet were willing to offer it.

After a long moment, I said, "What do you know about what happened to Dora?"

Letitia's eyes took in Hamlet. Years might have folded over in her thoughts. "Your mother loved you very much."

It was Hamlet's turn to tear up. I put my hand on his arm as Letitia handed him the box of tissues. He took a tissue and nodded. "Please, tell us whatever you can."

"Of course," Letitia said. "The time for secrets is gone, I suppose. It's not a pretty story; you need to know that before I begin."

I looked at Hamlet and really hoped he didn't mind hearing an ugly story, because my curiosity wasn't to be denied. He took a long moment to consider her warning, but he eventually nodded. I tried not to show my relief.

"Dora was gifted," Letitia began. "I know that most people doubt our skills, but if what we have is indeed a gift of some sort, Dora was exceptional. Her mother, Wilma, couldn't hold a candle to her. Neither could I, frankly. Wilma was . . . probably defined as wild. I was too, you must know that. We never did live by conventional rules, dear boy, and men weren't as important to us as they are to some women. We never felt the need to keep them around, but . . . that's only because we knew what we were born to do, and men seemed to get in the way." Letitia smiled. "Until you came along. We were all quite smitten with you."

My heart tumbled. Letitia was telling the story of the beginning of Hamlet's life, and I knew bad stuff was to come. He was an adult, but I hoped he could handle it. I hoped I could.

Letitia frowned but then smiled again. "Unfortunately, Dora wasn't made to take care of a baby. Neither was Wilma—in fact, Wilma was so ill equipped that I raised Dora more than she did. I tried, Eddie—that's what we called you.

"I go by Hamlet now."

Letitia nodded slowly. "Hamlet. I tried to take you away from Dora, but I was too old and considered far too strange to get much help from the authorities. Nevertheless, I did . . . well, I even snuck into places where Dora was living and took you while she was sleeping, brought you to my home. But she always came for you the next day, knowing it was me who was caring for you. She never said a word, just walked in and took you back. I had no right to stop her."

"Was she in a single room back then, near a bookshop that burned?" I asked.

"Aye." Letitia seemed impressed and then turned her attention back to Hamlet. "It wasn't the best place, but I made sure the rent got paid every month. She tried, and she loved you so much, but she just couldn't quite do what she needed to do. I would have allowed you both to live with me. I would have paid her rent forever, but she didn't want my help. She wanted to get away from me and her mother. It was rough. I believe Dora was what we now know as bipolar. It was described as manic-depressive or something like that back then. She would never allow herself to be properly diagnosed, and she'd never take medicine because it would dilute her ability to understand her visions.

"I had plans. Though I couldn't manage to steal you away

from her while she slept, I was preparing for her next low. She would be most vulnerable, and I would take advantage of that. I know that sounds horrible, but that's exactly how I thought—get her while she's down. I finally found someone to help me, who listened to my story and took me before a judge. If I could get Dora to sign you over to me, you'd be mine legally. I could have cared for you.

"I had the paperwork at the ready and I was just waiting. Dora's ups and downs weren't exactly predictable, but the cycle was never-ending, that much we knew. And then it happened. I knew she was on a downswing, so I went to her flat to meet with her."

Letitia's face fell.

"Go on," I said.

Letitia shook her head out of her thoughts. "I made it into the flat, but she wasn't alone. There was another woman there. I didn't know her. I'd never seen her before. I was confused by her behavior. She seemed to be taking the boy, taking you. I didn't understand, and neither did Dora, really. She was so very down in a dark place, but she wasn't agreeing to give you to this woman. There was a fight." Letitia fell silent a moment.

Oh no, I thought, but I bit my tongue, hoping she'd continue.

"The woman was younger than me and much stronger than Dora. There was only one of her, but she almost managed to get the best of us. We got her out of there, though. I gave chase, but she got away."

"Why didn't you call the police?" I asked.

Letitia nodded. "When I got back to the flat, Dora and the boy were gone. A man who lived there in the building told me they'd left, off to take care of something. I waited and waited and did call the police eventually. When they came, I told them everything. But Dora and Ed—Hamlet were gone. I searched for years. I've always searched in one way or another." She looked at Hamlet again. "When you came in recently, I saw her in your features, but I was afraid to admit that to myself. And when you left, I just hoped you"—she looked at me—"or someone would also find Dora."

"Did you ever figure out who the woman was?" I asked.

"No, but I described her to the police."

Oh no, I thought. I turned to Hamlet. "Ham, I'm going to show Letitia a picture of the sketch."

He nodded as I pulled it up on my phone again and held it out for her. "Could this be the woman you saw?"

"I just can't be sure," Letitia said. "This woman is older, but it's a sketch. I just don't know."

"But maybe? Could it be the woman who tried to take Hamlet?" I asked.

Letitia sighed. "I suppose. Maybe."

"Who is she?" Hamlet asked.

Of course, no one knew, but even though I had no idea how any of this had anything to do with Neil's murder, I knew it was time to call Inspector Winters again. Maybe the police could put the pieces together.

Hopefully, someone could.

THIRTY-THREE

Sometimes it seemed that things just needed to go full circle. Getting from A to B was rarely a straight line.

We left a message for Inspector Winters—it was just a re-counting of the story we'd heard from Letitia, and it seemed strange and probably unimportant to share it, but we did anyway.

However, it was that sense that I was still missing an important connection that took me to my next exploration. By myself. I felt safe enough. I also felt like there was a good chance I was way off track even if my quiet but insistent intuition wouldn't be denied. As Letitia had told us her story, something had stuck in my mind. I'd been listening too hard to stop her, ask her the question that occurred to me after I'd digested her words. Back at the bookshop, though, I did try to call her, but there was no answer.

I didn't take the time to stop by her shop before heading on to the place I thought might contain the person who really did have all the answers. The person who'd probably had them from the very beginning.

I entered Clarinda's law offices with a determination that

no receptionist would be able to thwart; I was prepared for a fight if one presented itself.

"Clarinda Creston, please," I said.

"Do you have an appointment? What's your name?" the girl asked.

"My name is Delaney Nichols," I said. "And if Clarinda won't take the time to see me, I'll go straight to the police with accusations of forgery. I doubt she'll want that."

The girl wasn't quite sure what to do, but the expression on my face must have been enough for her to pick up the phone and ring Clarinda. She said exactly what I'd threatened.

"Aye? I'll let her know." She hung up the phone. "She'll be right out to gather you."

"Thank you."

Surprising me, Clarinda was there to gather me before I could even take a seat.

"Delaney? What's going on?" she asked as she walked into the lobby. "Never mind. Come back to my office and tell me."

I followed her quick steps back to her luxurious office. She wasn't dressed in the court garb, but her suit was clearly expensive. She'd made a lot of money—as a defense attorney.

"Have a seat and tell me what's on your mind."

"Thanks for your time, Clarinda," I began. "I just have a few questions. First of all, have you always been a criminal defense attorney?"

She laughed once. "No, in fact, I haven't. At one time, I was a family attorney."

"I think I know what that means, but would you mind explaining it to me?"

"I handled all sorts of things, really. Divorce, prenuptials agreements, adoptions. Family things."

"Why did you become a defense attorney?"

She smiled so cordially, too cordially. She knew I was on to something but was honored I was asking her, and not willing enough to think about how strange it was that I, a Grassmarket bookseller, cared.

Her answer wasn't much of a surprise.

"Money, for one. That's the main thing." She leaned forward and placed her arms on her desk. "I'm very good in the courtroom, Delaney." She shrugged. "I had a talent that was going to waste. I was becoming frustrated by not allowing it to blossom."

"I get that," I said, and I did, no matter the ego that went along with it. She was unfulfilled and saw a way to remedy that. It would have been impressive if it weren't for everything else. I grabbed the manuscript from my bag again and slid it over the table. "You wrote this, didn't you?"

She examined it only a moment before her eyes widened. She looked at me. "I did not write this."

"But you gave it to Malcolm, right?"

She didn't want to answer, didn't have to, really, but she did. "Aye."

"You told him it was from his ex-wife Maria."

She nodded.

"Was that the truth?"

"It was."

"Did she write it?"

"I can't answer that, Delaney."

"Can't or won't?"

Nothing. No reaction at all, just a hard stare back at me.

Her stoicism only fueled the idea that I was on the right track—and then something else entirely occurred to me. I almost

gasped but managed to hold it back. I needed to research something else—it would only take a quick search on my phone, but
I was going to have to do it later. For now, I switched gears.

"Could I ask you about a specific adoption?"

"Oh." She sat back in her chair again. "I can't answer question about such things. Adoption records are usually kept sealed,
and I would never jeopardize the privacy of any of my clients."

"Of course, but this might not have been on the up-and-up,
so maybe it's okay," I said, my insides squeezing together at my
accusatory tone. I wasn't one to do such a thing, at least not usually. It wasn't comfortable, but I really wanted answers, and
it was beyond time to worry about getting them in a delicate
manner.

Clarinda frowned. "What do you mean?"

It was my turn to shrug. "I guess I mean that I'm curious
about what involvement you had with Dora Strangelove and
her baby about twenty-two years ago. The Strangelove women
are well known around town, so I bet you remember."

She was good at keeping a neutral or at least unfazed expression. That probably came with the job. But I was watching
her closely and something I'd said almost widened her eyes.
Almost.

"I'm afraid I don't recall any dealings whatsoever with any
of the Strangelove women."

I nodded. "Okay, so I guess *technically* your dealings might
have been with the woman who wanted to adopt Dora's child
and not Dora."

"Delaney, I can't talk about adoptions. I'm sorry, but I just
can't."

"This child wasn't adopted. He and Dora did disappear,
though."

"What?" she said. "And why would you think I had anything at all to do with any of that?"

I sat forward in my chair. I thought I knew. I was so certain, though I had no right to be. I had no right to accuse anyone of anything, but the truth seemed so big now, so obvious. I wanted to search for the date of Malcolm's bookshop fire on my phone. If I could also discern the date that Dora and Hamlet disappeared, I would know they hadn't happened close to the same time, as Clyde had said, probably on the exact same day, maybe on consecutive days, but very close. I wished I had pinpointed it better with Clyde, but I hadn't.

"It was Maria who wanted to adopt Hamlet. She came to you, didn't she?"

"What?" She seemed either genuinely confused or scared now.

"But when Maria attacked Dora, you had to distance yourself."

"Delaney, you're delusional."

"The thing I can't quite figure is why did you burn down Malcolm's bookshop and the Burns House? You had to kill Neil because he found out . . . something. What did he find out? Why was it so important that he die?"

"I did not kill Neil. I did not burn down anything, Delaney," she said firmly. "How dare you make such accusations."

"But I bet you know who did," I said. "Or at least you suspect someone."

I saw anger building in her eyes and the set of her jaw. She was probably about to throw me out of her office. My phone started buzzing in my pocket. The noise put a crimp in the contentious meeting, and she waited for me to gather my mobile as I tried to ignore it.

But it wouldn't stop buzzing. I was getting both calls and texts. Finally, I pulled the phone out of my pocket. It was ringing, but I saw the text from Rosie first. It said one word.

Fire!!!

I exploded from the chair and hurried out of the office. I doubted anyone else had ever sprinted as fast through these fine offices. Nothing and no one was going to stop me.

I ran the whole way.

THIRTY-FOUR

I darted and dodged and even bumped into a few people, but I just didn't care. As I turned the corner, I didn't even look inside the pub as my anxious eyes went to the far end of Grassmarket and my beloved bookshop. Fire trucks and police vehicles blocked my view, but I didn't see any smoke or flames. Was it over? Had it burned to the ground? Had the smoke dissipated up into the still-cloudless sky?

A crowd of people had gathered, and I knew I needed to slow down before I knocked anyone over, but it was a difficult maneuver, and I started to tumble.

Fortunately, I was caught by the handsomest man in Edinburgh before I went all the way down.

"Delaney," Tom said as he righted me. "It's okay. Everyone is okay."

"What? Rosie? Fire? Books?" I said in panic.

Tom nodded. "There was a small fire. It's been put out. No big damage. No one got hurt."

My knees buckled, and he caught me again, pulling me close as tears rolled down my cheeks. The relief was unlike anything I'd ever felt before.

A few moments later, I was able to stand on my own again and blow my nose into the tissue he handed me.

"I got a text from Rosie that said only *Fire!*" I said.

"I'm not surprised. I was trying to call you to let you know everything was okay in case you heard anything. The text might not have been the best idea, but she saved the day, Delaney. Come on, let's go talk to everyone."

Tom took my hand and led me through the crowd of people. I tried very hard to stop crying, but the tears kept coming and I kept wiping them away.

Inspector Winters was among the official people. He spotted us and hurried in our direction.

"I tried to call," he said to me. "Everyone's okay. The shop is fine. It was contained to a small part of the kitchen. Come on in."

As if this were just another normal day, Hector hurried to greet me as we entered. I picked him up and cried a little harder. He was fine. As I held him close to my face, I realized he didn't even smell like smoke. Rosie, Edwin, Hamlet, and Wyatt were all okay too. Not a scratch on them.

"I heard something," Rosie began. "Over there." She nodded toward the dark side.

"Superpower ears," Wyatt said. "It was just Hamlet, Rosie, and me. She's the only one who heard what she thought was breaking glass."

"I listen tae my gut, aye?" Rosie said.

I nodded.

"I went over, and the kitchen was on fire. Well, the containers on the counter were burning, the counter was burning, and the wee curtains around the window had gone almost all the way to ashes. I just grabbed the closest thing, the stroupie, and turned on the water, dousing the flames as they came. Oh, lass, it wasnae a big fire, but it was terrifying."

I knew "stroupie" was Scots for "teapot," and I wanted to ask how in the world she'd managed to put out a fire with a teapot, but it just didn't matter. I pulled her into a tight hug, and we both cried for a moment. "I'm so glad you're okay."

Inspector Winters's phone buzzed. He stepped away and answered it, returning to us just as Rosie and I mostly disengaged.

"We've got the video," he said. He looked at Edwin. "Nice work putting the camera in the close."

I'd forgotten all about it. There'd been some trouble over there a year earlier, and Edwin had said he was going to install a security camera, but I'd never noticed when he had or where the feed went. I looked at him.

He nodded. "Aye, some sort of security system, video going up to the clouds or something. I don't understand it, but it was the best and most hidden camera money could buy."

"Smart," Wyatt said.

Another officer came into the bookshop, bringing a tablet. He handed it to Inspector Winters, who turned it for us all to see.

The camera had been placed somewhere at the end of the close, aimed toward the opening to Grassmarket. It captured a hunched-over figure making their way toward the window to the bookshop's kitchenette, carrying a large restaurant-type five-gallon bucket. The figure's head and body were hidden in a winter coat. At first, it wasn't easy to see if it was a man or a woman.

The officer said, "Give it a minute."

We watched as the figure placed the bucket on the ground upside down, stood on it, and broke out the window with a rock. They pulled a rag and a lighter from a pocket of the coat, lit the rag, and threw it through the window. They hopped off the bucket and hurried to run away but stopped and turned again to retrieve the bucket. As they did, they looked up, and the camera caught a clear shot—of a woman's face.

"That's her," Hamlet said. "That's Dora—no, not Dora. That's the performance artist who we thought was Dora."

"Inspector Winters," Edwin interjected, a breathy catch to his voice. "I believe I recognize her. I think that's Maria Campbell. She was at one time married to Malcolm Campbell. His bookshop burned down years ago, and his new one almost did a few nights ago. She might have been the one to burn down the Burns House, maybe killed Neil, though I couldn't tell you any motives."

"How sure are you that this is her?" Inspector Winters asked.

Edwin looked at the tablet again. Inspector Winters had stopped the video, freezing it at the spot that best showed the woman's face.

"I'm ninety-five percent sure," he said a long moment later.

"I'm one hundred percent sure," I said. "I think she's been behind everything. I think she's the arsonist, the killer." I swallowed hard. "I even think she did something to Dora, but I don't understand what or how."

Everyone looked at me.

"Look up the date of the first fire. I know it was about the same time Dora and Hamlet disappeared from their small room, which was across the close from Malcolm's shop. I don't know what happened, but somehow Maria wanted to adopt Hamlet. I don't even know if Malcolm knew about it, but . . . I don't know, something happened. We need to find her."

Inspector Winters turned to another officer. "We need an all-points bulletin on this woman. Immediately. Maria Campbell or maybe going by the name Dora Strangelove."

The officer nodded and hurried away, leaving the tablet with Inspector Winters, who looked at me and Hamlet. "What else can you tell me?"

We all had plenty to say, but much of it was repetition. We told Inspector Winters where we'd searched for Dora. I told him about my visit with Clarinda Creston and how I suspected she was somehow in on Maria's activities. I even went so far as to say that Clarinda switched from family law to criminal law because of what had happened regarding Maria.

He took it all in, made more notes. When he was done, he headed toward the front door. I hadn't noticed, but the crowd had mostly dispersed, and the emergency vehicles were all gone but for his car.

He turned. "I'll find her."

As he left, we all hoped he would—and quickly.

THIRTY-FIVE

I wished so much that I could have gone with Inspector Winters, but since that hadn't happened, and the idea was probably unreasonable anyway, I did the next best thing. I organized a stakeout with my husband and brother. And we were having a good time.

We were inside Tom's car, across the street from Malcolm's new bookshop. We'd been drinking hot chocolate as we watched for Maria. She hadn't shown up yet, and might not, but something told me that she'd be there to try to finish the job, a job she and Clarinda must have started a long time ago. I ached for the piece that would finish the puzzle, give us the answers, but I also knew we'd never have that piece without Maria.

I'd called Inspector Winters to tell him I thought she might show up at Malcolm's. Even with everything else going on, he'd listened and said he'd have someone watching the bookshop.

But I couldn't stop wondering myself, so I asked Tom and Wyatt if they would be up for a trip over there ourselves. Tom would have gone just to make sure I didn't get in trouble. Wyatt was just as curious as the rest of us.

I told them I was leaving it to the police, but I was too curious, too sure and uncertain at the same time, not to see if there was any way she could be caught in another bad act.

What I still hadn't mentioned to anyone was that I suspected Maria Campbell had not only killed Neil Watterton, but also Dora Strangelove. Everyone was probably thinking the same thing, but it was as if we were all afraid to say it out loud. Murder was always awful, but there was still suspicion being aimed Hamlet's way, and I think we were afraid to jinx the idea that we were close to having the proof we needed that someone else had committed all these heinous crimes.

Nothing seemed to be going on at Malcolm's bookshop. It was dark inside, and Malcolm wasn't there. He was probably told to stay away. I didn't know if there were officers inside or maybe in the alley behind. I couldn't spot them in a vehicle anywhere nearby, and there were no panel vans in sight. There were plenty of cars moving up and down the street still and a few parked along it. If the police were there, they were doing a great job at hiding.

By midnight, I was close to asking Tom to drive us home. As much fun as we'd had talking, sharing stories with Wyatt, Tom and I did have work the next day. Just as I was going to suggest we give it up, though, Wyatt sat up in the back seat.

"Did you see that?" he asked.

"No," I said.

"What?" Tom said.

"There, in the shop a few doors from the bookshop. I thought I saw a flash, or, I don't know. Something."

My eyes moved down three doors, landing on a bagel bakery I'd thought about stopping by before. The bakery was housed in the same building as Malcolm's bookshop, part of the row of businesses that took up the bottom floor. For a breathless few moments, the bakery's window was shrouded in the same darkness as Malcolm's bookshop and the two other businesses in between them.

But then I saw it too: a flash of yellow light. "That could be a fire!" I pulled on the door handle and propelled myself out of the car. Tom caught up with me quickly.

"Call 999," Tom said over his shoulder to Wyatt as he and I crossed the street, hurrying toward the bakery.

"Oh no!" I said as we looked through the window.

There were flames burning one of the wooden chairs that had been set around a small café table toward the back of the bakery, right next to the back door, which was now wide open.

"We've got to put that fire out," I said.

Tom was already on it. He'd tried to open the door, but of course it was locked tight.

"Back draft. Move away, Delaney," he said as he crooked his elbow to slam it into the glass.

"Tom!" I said. "No."

"No choice. It's not a bad fire yet. Get back!"

I didn't get back, but it was okay. He broke the glass with his elbow—and, since it wasn't a terrible fire yet and the back door was open, there wasn't much back draft, but there was some. A huff of hot air hit us both, but flames didn't reach us. I hoped his sleeve-covered arm was fine as he reached through the opening and unlocked the door.

We were in a moment later. Fortunately, there was a woven throw rug along the floor in front of the front window. Tom grabbed it as I hurried behind the counter to the small sink. Water wasn't needed. Tom got the fire out quickly with the rug.

It hadn't been too big—yet. Maybe thirty more seconds,

though, and we wouldn't have been able to do anything to stop it.

"Do you suppose there are other fires in the building?" I asked him.

"I hope not."

The peal of sirens reached us. We both hurried outside to greet them and look around for other flames in other places, for someone who might have come through the open back door of the bakery and set the fire. We didn't spot either.

"Where are the police?" I asked Tom.

He knew what I meant—not the police now coming to the scene, but the ones who were supposed to be watching Malcolm's bookshop.

"Maybe they're in the shop?" Tom said just as its front door opened and two officers hurried out to see what the commotion was all about.

I didn't recognize them.

Confusion reigned for a few minutes as everyone tried to understand what was going on. Tom and I were equally heralded and scolded for what we'd done. We didn't care either way. We just wanted all the official people to make sure there were no other fires anywhere and find the person, presumably Maria, who'd set the one in the bakery.

At one point, I handed my phone to Wyatt and asked him to call Inspector Winters.

There was definitely no sign of any other fires. The police didn't find the person who'd set this one, but they were going to man the location even better now, not just with two officers in the bookshop.

I suspected there would be no more fires tonight, at least in this building. Edwin had hired a private security firm to watch the Cracked Spine, so I wasn't too worried about it either.

I stepped away from the crowd and joined my brother as he leaned against Tom's car.

"Inspector Winters is on his way," Wyatt said.

"Thank you."

"You guys probably saved that whole building."

"Tom did. I don't know if I would have broken out the glass to put out the fire."

"You would have. It wasn't a big fire yet, and you would have been worried about people inside the building."

"Maybe."

Wyatt nodded. "This is crazy, Sis. Dangerous in ways I would never have guessed."

I nodded. "I don't disagree. Maria needs to be caught." I cleared my throat. "Whoever did this needs to be caught."

"Well, if she was here, she must be long gone by now."

"Yeah."

"Where would she go?"

"That's the question, I suppose."

Inspector Winters pulled his car to a stop next to Tom and the crowd of officials. Tom hadn't been hurt at all. No cuts, no burns. The glass had broken easily, and he didn't seem any worse for the wear. I was grateful.

From across the street, Wyatt and I watched Inspector Winters digest what had happened and then talk to Tom. They came over to us together.

"You okay?" Inspector Winters asked me.

"Fine. Worried."

"I understand." He looked back toward the building and

the now-dispersing crowd and rubbed his chin. "Delaney, any idea at all where Maria might be?"

"I can only tell you where I know she's been. I told you about the shelter and the abandoned building. She performed near the statue of Robert Burns. That's all I know about her."

A voice came to me in my head. It wasn't a bookish voice. It was Hamlet, telling me about all the Robert Burns statues in the world. There were so many—in so many places. Someone had also told me that the performance artist, the woman we'd thought was Dora but was actually Maria, also spent time at the Burns Monument on Regent Road, which was very different from the statue outside the coffee shop. Who had told me that? The barista! The one from the coffee shop near the statue.

"I've been meaning to check out the official Burns monument. I haven't yet. Someone told me she spent time there to. That's the most important Burns monument in the world, right?"

"I suppose we Scots think of it that way," Inspector Winters said.

"I think . . . she could be there. It makes sense."

Inspector Winters sighed. "It's late, but it's worth a look."

He turned to go back to his car.

"Can we come with you or follow?" I said.

"I'd rather you all just go home."

"I can't. Not yet," I said.

Inspector Winters nodded. "You know, I don't really think Hamlet could hurt anyone."

"But until you find Maria, he's still under suspicion, right?"

"By others, aye."

"Are you okay if we follow you?" Tom put his hand on my arm. "We're going to, but I'd like you to be okay with it."

"Be careful." Inspector Winters turned and hurried to his car.

Though Edinburgh had traffic at all hours, it was cold out tonight, and most people were saving their sightseeing for the daytime. As we approached the monument, it seemed quiet and unpopulated.

Robert Burns was beloved throughout the world, but from what I knew, there was perhaps no monument more stunning than the one on Regent Road. Situated up on a grassy berm and looking out toward Arthur's Seat, the famous and main peak of a group of hills that form Holyrood Park, and the hill about which so many Scottish writers had written. The monument, made of stone, has a Grecian cupola encircled by pillars copied from an Athens temple. Three large griffins adorn the roof. There used to be a life-sized marble statue inside the chamber, but that was moved to a museum at some point. Tonight, the monument wasn't lit, but it was never closed.

The four of us stood on the pathway at the bottom of the berm and looked up as Inspector Winters shone his flashlight at the structure.

"There could be someone inside," I offered.

"That's why I'm going up alone to take a look," he said.

But just as he took one step onto the berm toward the low wrought-iron fence around the property, Maria herself stepped out of the enclosure above and to the edge of the monument, her figure spotlighted by the flashlight.

We all froze as we watched her, not sure for a moment if this was real or we were all imagining her. No, there she was. She seemed to enjoy the light, seemed to think it was for her and her performance.

She wasn't within reaching distance. She could jump off the

berm at any moment and attempt to run in the other direction, but one of us would probably catch her. However, none of us, Inspector Winters included, made a move to get closer. He held the light steady. We remained still as we watched.

Maria looked down toward us, but the light probably blinded her. She seemed tired, like she'd had a rough couple of days, and maybe like she'd just had enough of all of it. I hoped as much. I hoped running or chasing wasn't going to be involved. It was dark and cold outside.

She took a breath, letting out a cloudy fog, and seemed to somehow transform. I didn't know if she was taking on a character or if the change was her way of giving a nod to the words she next spoke:

"The best laid schemes o' mice and men. Gang aft a-gley. And leave us naught but grief and pain. For promised joy."

She transformed again, seemingly back to her regular self.

"It just didn't go as planned, and I've had enough," she said. "I was angry, felt betrayed. Everyone betrayed me, but I've had enough."

"Who's everyone?" I asked, sensing a bristled irritation from Inspector Winters, but he still made no move.

"Everyone."

"How did they betray you?" I asked.

A long beat later, she answered. "All I wanted was a child, but my body wouldn't allow it. I should have been a mother."

"I'm sorry," I said. I took a step up onto the berm. I felt Tom's hold on my arm, but I wasn't going to go far, just close enough to her so she could maybe see me off to the side of the light. "That had to be hard."

"I tried to adopt, but even that went awry." She shook her head. "They wouldn't let me."

"I'm sorry," I said again.

"Why? Why wouldn't they let you?" Inspector Winters asked.

"She said I wasn't stable enough. Clarinda. Some friend she turned out to be." Maria snorted a laugh and then wiped her hand over her chin. "I was stable! It was her betrayal that ruined me."

"Were you going to adopt Dora Strangelove's baby?" I asked.

"Of course not, but then . . . when they all told me no, I knew what I had to do."

"What happened?" I asked, trying to sound sympathetic.

"I went to take the boy. Sweet Eddie, but he introduced himself to me as Hamlet. He's all grown up, but I think I would have known him anywhere. He'd have been better off with me. But she and her grandmother fought. They fought hard." Maria slumped down and sat on the edge of the monument, leaning over it.

As smoothly as possible, Inspector Winters handed the flashlight to Wyatt, who held it steady in the same spot as the inspector snuck off and made his way around the monument grounds, probably hoping to take Maria by surprise from behind.

Maria reached into her pocket and took out a book of matches. She lit one match and let it go. It landed safely extinguished by the time it hit the cold ground.

"I watched them, you know," she said. "I could see them through our windows, across the close. Dora was a horrible mother."

I cringed. "How was she horrible?"

"She would just ignore the boy. She couldn't . . . cope. Sometimes, she was fine, sometimes she seemed to care to love him, but I could see her the other times, the times when the wee boy fended for himself. She ignored him! It was so wrong."

"I heard she read to him in the bookshop. Malcolm let them," I said.

Maria made a gurgled harrumph. "Malcolm! He could have helped me, but he refused to see how the boy would be better with us."

"But you didn't take him," I said.

"No, but I tried. God help me, I tried."

"What happened?"

"His mother. That . . . that awful Strangelove woman. She could barely feed the boy."

I understood Maria's anger over what she'd apparently witnessed. If what she was saying was true, Dora was unfit, but from this point, all these years later, how could we trust anything Maria was saying, and all indications were that she might not have been better than Dora?

"You fought Dora in her room?" I asked.

"Yes, her and that old lady. It was ridiculous. I ran off."

"Then what?"

"Dora marched herself and that boy over to the bookshop. She was going to talk to Malcolm about me." Maria smiled as she looked absently up to the dark sky. "But he wasn't there. I didn't live there anymore. I'd only run into the close to hide when I left Dora's room. No one else was down there, but I huddled low and covered myself with a blanket. I was waiting for her, surprised she came out so quickly. But she was bound to leave her room at some point. I was going to try again. I was going to take that boy."

"What happened?" I prompted, to keep her going.

"When she saw the door to the bookshop was locked, she

turned to leave. I . . . I grabbed her and pulled her into the close. There was no one around, no one to stop me."

"What did you do?" I asked.

She took another deep breath. "The boy ran off. I scared him so much he ran off. You know, I didn't even know where he'd gone." She smiled wistfully. "But I saw him just last week. He thought I was her. Dora! I took on her name, hoping to find him. I did. It took a long, long time, but I finally found him. It's too late now, though."

"What did you do to Dora?" I asked.

Maria lit another match and let it fly. "I got rid of her."

"You killed her?" I asked, trying to keep my voice as steady as possible.

"Well, she fought me again, in the close. I had to fight back. Her head hit the side of the bookshop building so hard. That thunk. I'll never forget it."

"Then what did you do?"

"Covered her with the blanket, and went to search for the boy, and just couldn't find him. When I went back to the close, other people were there, but no one noticed the body, just thought she was another one of them, sleeping under the blanket I'd used to hide. That night, I used a wheelbarrow—got her loaded in it and out of there before anyone even noticed. Or, if they did, they just didn't care."

"Where did you take her?"

Maria looked down toward me. "Right here, of course. It was the middle of the night, and no one stopped me. I brought her here."

"To the monument?" I clarified.

"Aye. Put her over there." She nodded back toward Arthur's Seat.

Arthur's Seat was less than a half mile away from the monument. In between the two of them was some green space, along with a variety of buildings, mostly businesses, I thought. I was pretty sure there were no homes over there unless they were inside apartment buildings.

"You hid her body over there?" I said.

Maria shook her head. "I burned it. Inside a wee house."

I looked that way, again thinking there were no houses over there, but maybe there were enough official records for the police to put that together into something coherent. Since I had her talking, I wanted to keep it going.

"Why did you burn your husband's bookshop?" I asked.

"To hide the blood on the side of the building and in the close, of course."

I wondered if the blood had disappeared or just gotten overlooked because of the fire. Hopefully, the police would be able to figure that out too, but it had been a long time.

I wanted to yell at her, scream, tell her that what had happened to Hamlet was all her fault, but I didn't want her to run. I needed to keep her there until Inspector Winters got to her.

"Why did you try to burn the Cracked Spine?"

She shrugged. "It seemed like the thing to do. Hamlet is all grown now." She looked out toward me. "I could have raised him just fine, but he's all grown and working there with Edwin. Edwin betrayed me too."

"How?"

"He was Malcolm's friend first. He bought the book from me but then told Malcolm what he'd done. I asked him not to tell."

Malcolm had come into the bookshop and found the book

on Rosie's desk. It had been . . . what had Rosie said, something about the secret not meant to be kept?

"I'm sorry." I paused. "But, Maria, why did you kill Neil?"

She frowned. "He was going to tell Hamlet that I was the one who'd killed his mother."

Oh, I thought, realizing we'd finally come upon the motive, the reason behind Neil's death. It seemed so big, even as I asked the question that sounded so small in the cold, dark night: "How did he figure it out?"

"I told him. He betrayed me worst of all. He acted like he was my friend. He would come listen to me. He was good to me, but when I told him what happened all those years ago, he was going to tell Hamlet. He was going to tell everyone, the police. I had to stop him. Hamlet was with him earlier that night. I saw them both in that place. I was afraid I was too late that night. But I wasn't."

She lit another match and let it drop. They were just gestures. They wouldn't burn anything here, not on this cold night. She was caught up by fire. Burning. Burns. Burns's words. Had it been the fact that she'd brought Dora's body to a place near the monument that had made her love Burns so much, or had she brought the body here because she'd already loved the bard? She'd sold the Burns book to Edwin and then allegedly claimed to him that she was leaving Scotland, but it was difficult to understand what came first.

My heart went out to her a little bit, but not much. She'd done some terrible things, and my Hamlet might have continued to be blamed for them, which was completely unacceptable. Had Malcolm known about her wanting a child? Had that contributed to the end of their marriage?

Just to keep her there, I said, "I'm so sorry, Maria. So very sorry."

She didn't seem to hear me. And Inspector Winters had her in his grasp and then cuffed about ten seconds later.

Tom and Wyatt hurried up the berm to help them both down. No one fought. No one ran. Nothing more burned. Hopefully, all of that was over now, I thought as I made my way back to Tom's car and sat, exhausted and relieved. And sad.

It seemed Mr. Burns had one more thing to say to me. Clearly in my head, with that voice my mind had given him, he spoke.

Even tho who mourn'st the Daisy's fate, that fate is thine.

Fate. We were all headed toward the same end, but, boy oh boy, our paths were so different and could be redirected at almost any turn.

As I watched Inspector Winters get Maria in his car, and Tom and Wyatt made their way toward me again, I felt so tired. I was working to understand Maria's motives and how they'd managed to change so many people's paths, caused so much destruction. How could one person have done so much so wrong to so many others? It was difficult to digest.

Nevertheless, and as I thought about fortune-tellers and how crazy all these events had been, I couldn't ignore that I was so grateful that my fates had been pretty good to me.

THIRTY-SIX

It was just Hamlet and me. Wyatt had gone back to the States; I missed him horribly. Maria had been arrested, charged with murder and multiple arsons. Dora's remains had been discovered—maybe. True to Maria's story, a small house tucked away near some government offices with a body inside it had burned all those years ago, but the body had never been identified. There was nothing left, no DNA, so we'd all just have to assume that Maria had told the truth about Dora's fate.

Though nothing had been done to rebuild or reinforce Malcolm's original bookshop, there was no sign of Dora's blood on the outside bricks in the close anymore. It had been too long.

Come to find out, and much to my embarrassment, Clarinda hadn't had anything to do with anything—other than passing the manuscript on to Malcolm. But, at the time, she had truly thought that Maria had simply mailed it to her, asking her to give it to Malcolm. Maria had admitted to writing it, which left us all bothered, as well as impressed. Unfortunately, Clarinda's involvement had made Malcolm give the manuscript more credibility than it deserved, thus his irritation at Neil and possible irritation at Artair. But that had passed a long time ago too.

No one knew how a copy made it into the Cracked Spine. Maybe we'd figure it out someday.

Clarinda might be in some trouble for not letting the authorities know about her past involvement with Maria Campbell. She claimed she didn't know she needed to tell anyone. She wasn't going to allow Maria to adopt a baby. But she'd never told Maria that she wasn't mentally stable enough. Instead, she'd told Maria that her life needed more stability before she could be considered for single parent adoption. And then Clarinda had quit family law and became a really good criminal attorney. I asked her why she didn't tell me that Neil had owned the Burns House. She told me she hadn't owed me any explanation, that she'd told the police and that was all she was required to do. She was right.

Charles, Malcolm, and Clarinda were still distraught about Neil, but everyone was trying to help everyone else through the grief. Edwin and Malcolm were even talking.

I'd taken Hamlet over to meet Clyde, which had made the man cry the happiest tears I'd ever seen.

Just yesterday, I'd spotted an article in the *Scotsman* about the reformation of Donald Rigalee. He was doing well, apparently, minding his own fishing business, keeping his nose clean, etc. I wondered if he was still enjoying the book we'd shared a moment over. I hoped so.

Hamlet had seen him around the archery club but hadn't put together that he'd been the same man Clarinda had defended with such success. Rigalee had also shopped in the Cracked Spine. None of us recognized him until he stopped by a couple of days after Maria had been arrested. He came in to apologize in case he'd scared me at the restaurant and said that he'd recognized me from somewhere but couldn't immediately place the bookshop. I hadn't told him I hadn't recognized him, but I hadn't. It had been a strange, awkward interaction, but then afterward he and Rosie searched the shelves for a new book for his reading pleasure.

It appeared that we were going to get to know him better. We hoped he was a good guy.

Hamlet had been spending time with Letitia, learning some about his very unusual biological family. No one, including Hamlet, knew where he had run to the day Maria killed Dora. He'd been two years old, and the only memories from his childhood didn't begin until a couple years after that. I told him that he and I might investigate it all a little closer someday. I didn't know if he wanted to or not. I'd wait and see.

It was a miracle that he'd survived, and I was grateful for that miracle.

Though I'd told Tom about my bookish voices, and the rest of my Scottish family had seen me behave as if I was distracted or in my own world, I hadn't shared with anyone how responsible I felt for everything that had transpired. If I hadn't heard the bookish voice of Shakespeare's Hamlet speak to me his most famous lines, I might have invited Wyatt to attend the dinner with me instead of my Hamlet. If he hadn't gone that night, everything that happened afterward, including Neil's murder, might not have occurred.

I knew no one could have predicted the turn of events, even Letitia, but I hoped my intuition would key in only on things with positive outcomes from here on. Unfortunately, that wasn't the way of intuition, though, or the way of life.

Rosie hadn't told Hamlet yet about his biological grandfather, but I thought she would soon. There was a more important link she thought he needed to explore first, though. There was still someone alive and well who might deserve to know the truth first.

Matthew Edison, the tartan shop owner, was most definitely Hamlet's biological father. Chances were fairly good that he didn't even know he'd fathered a child, but we weren't sure—he had stopped by the Cadies and Witchery shop, inquiring about Dora. Hamlet was very torn about telling him.

We stood outside the tartan shop and looked in the window as Matthew waited on a customer, an older woman wearing a cap with a feather sticking up from it. Even through the glass, we could see a kind, gentle man. Watch someone when they don't know you're observing, and you can pick up so many things. Even when Matthew turned away from the woman to gather something else, the expression on his face didn't change; he didn't frown or seem impatient.

You could just tell he was probably a pretty good guy.

"Do you think I should do this?" Hamlet asked.

"It's up to you." I paused and then turned to my friend. "Hamlet, anyone would be proud to say they are related to you. You don't need to do this if you don't want to, but if you do, I'm right here."

He bit his bottom lip as he continued to look through the window. A moment later, the woman with the feathered cap exited the store, sending us a friendly smile as she passed by.

Matthew made his way back behind the counter and seemed to be looking at some paperwork in front of him. I waited as Hamlet considered his options.

A long few beats later, he turned to me. "Let's go in."

I held the door for him.

ADDRESS TO A HAGGIS

Fair fa' your honest, sonsie face,
Great chieftain o the puddin'-race!
Aboon them a' ye tak your place,
Painch, tripe, or thairm:
Weel are ye wordy o' a grace
As lang's my arm.

The groaning trencher there ye fill,
Your hurdies like a distant hill,
Your pin wad help to mend a mill
In time o need,
While thro your pores the dews distil
Like amber bead.

His knife see rustic Labour dight,
An cut you up wi ready slight,
Trenching your gushing entrails bright,
Like onie ditch;
And then, O what a glorious sight,
Warm-reekin, rich!

Then, horn for horn, they stretch an strive:
Deil tak the hindmost, on they drive,
Till a' their weel-swall'd kytes belyve
Are bent like drums;
The auld Guidman, maist like to rive,
"Bethankit" hums.

Is there that owre his French ragout,
Or olio that wad staw a sow,
Or fricassee wad mak her spew
Wi perfect sconner,
Looks down wi sneering, scornfu view
On sic a dinner?

Poor devil! see him owre his trash,
As feckless as a wither'd rash,
His spindle shank a guid whip-lash,
His nieve a nit;
Thro bloody flood or field to dash,
O how unfit!

But mark the Rustic, haggis-fed,
The trembling earth resounds his tread,
Clap in his walie nieve a blade,
He'll make it whissle;
An legs an arms, an heads will sned,
Like taps o thrissle.

Ye Pow'rs, wha mak mankind your care,
And dish them out their bill o fare,
Auld Scotland wants nae skinking ware
That jaups in luggies:
But, if ye wish her gratefu prayer,
Gie her a Haggis!

ADDRESS TO A HAGGIS (TRANSLATION)

Good luck to you and your honest, plump face,
Great chieftain of the sausage race!
Above them all you take your place,
Stomach, tripe, or intestines:
Well are you worthy of a grace
As long as my arm.

The groaning trencher there you fill,
Your buttocks like a distant hill,
Your pin would help to mend a mill
In time of need,
While through your pores the dews distill
Like amber bead.

His knife see rustic Labour wipe,
And cut you up with ready slight,
Trenching your gushing entrails bright,
Like any ditch;
And then, O what a glorious sight,
Warm steaming, rich!

Then spoon for spoon, the stretch and strive:
Devil take the hindmost, on they drive,
Till all their well swollen bellies by-and-by
Are bent like drums;
Then old head of the table, most like to burst,
"The grace!" hums.

Is there that over his French ragout,
Or olio that would sicken a sow,
Or fricassee would make her vomit
With perfect disgust,
Looks down with sneering, scornful view
On such a dinner?

Poor devil! see him over his trash,
As feeble as a withered rush,
His thin legs a good whip-lash,
His fist a nut;
Through bloody flood or field to dash,
O how unfit.

But mark the Rustic, haggis-fed,
The trembling earth resounds his tread,
Clap in his ample fist a blade,
He'll make it whistle;
And legs, and arms, and heads will cut off
Like the heads of thistles.

You powers, who make mankind your care,
And dish them out their bill of fare,
Old Scotland wants no watery stuff,
That splashes in small wooden dishes;
But if you wish her grateful prayer,
Give her [Scotland] a Haggis!